"Don't touch me! I'm not one of your whores."

She fought the tears welling in her eyes. What a little fool she was! Why should she care with whom he lay?

Oh, but she did care.

And then he laughed. A hearty laugh the likes of which she'd never heard from him. She whirled on him, her face blazing. He shook his head and his laughter died. "*My* whores? Think ye I went, as well? To Inverness to rut with that chattel?"

"Didn't you?"

"Nay." His smile faded.

Her head pounded and her thoughts whirled in confusion. "But...I thought—"

"Nay, lass." He reached for her. She did not resist as he pulled her into his arms.

She looked up at him and his expression softened. Warmth radiated from his body. Her hands moved instinctively to his chest.

His voice was a whisper. "What I desire lies not in Inverness...!"

* * *

The Mackintosh Bride
Harlequin Historical #576—September 2001

THE MACKINTOSH BRIDE

DEBRA LEE BROWN

HARLEQUIN®

TORONTO • NEW YORK • LONDON
AMSTERDAM • PARIS • SYDNEY • HAMBURG
STOCKHOLM • ATHENS • TOKYO • MILAN • MADRID
PRAGUE • WARSAW • BUDAPEST • AUCKLAND

ISBN 0-373-29176-0

THE MACKINTOSH BRIDE

Copyright © 2001 by Debra Lee Brown

Visit us at www.eHarlequin.com

Printed in U.S.A.

Please address questions and book requests to:
Harlequin Reader Service
U.S.: 3010 Walden Ave., P.O. Box 1325, Buffalo, NY 14269
Canadian: P.O. Box 609, Fort Erie, Ont. L2A 5X3

To Sherri Browning,
Barbara Simmons and Michelle Collier-Johns

With love and heartfelt thanks

Prologue

The Highlands of Scotland, 1192

The girl tethered her pony in the forest and made her way on foot to the hidden copse. Shrouded in dawn's mist it seemed a sinister place, so changed from the afternoons she and Iain had lazed by the brook and basked in the sunlight streaming through the trees.

She moved cautiously over fallen branches and dried leaves, concealing her approach. A feeling of dread washed over her as she crouched low and parted the gorse bushes that stood like sentinels at the entrance to the thicket.

Jesu, he was here! He was safe!

Iain lay sprawled at the water's edge, bedraggled and still as death, his plaid wrapped carelessly around him. Infused with fear and relief, she crept forward and knelt beside him. His face, so gentle in sleep, was streaked with dirt and blood breached by small rivulets of still-damp tears.

The horrors of the night before came crashing in on her. Her heart went out to him and her own eyes welled. Fighting tears, she focused on the image engraved on his silver clan brooch: a cat reared up on hind legs, teeth and claws bared at the ready.

'Twas like him—fearless and brave—yet unlike him in its hard demeanor. Iain was different, tender, unlike any boy she'd known. On impulse she grazed a hand across his brow.

"Mackintosh! To arms!" He sprang into a crouch, nearly knocking her over. When his wild eyes found hers, he relaxed.

"A-are you hurt?" She reached for his bloodstained plaid.

"Nay!" He pulled away. "Ye shouldna be here, girl." His reprimand stung, more so as he wouldn't meet her gaze. He slumped back to the ground like one of her rag dolls.

She longed to comfort him, but knew not how. "I came as soon as I heard."

He stared into the mist, his face twisted with pain. "My father is dead—murdered—by the Grants. I couldna save him. I—I wanted to, but I couldna." His tears ran fresh and he fisted his hands at his sides, his knuckles white with tension.

Risking another rebuke, she placed her small hand on his large one. Surprisingly, he allowed it. He opened his palm to hers and at last met her gaze. She reveled in this show of trust, this small acceptance of her love, though she thought her heart would break from the torment she read in his eyes.

"Iain," she said, measuring her next words. "Your father slew Grant's son, Henry. Many witnessed the deed."

"Nay!" He shot to his knees and pulled her toward him. "'Tis a lie. 'Tis some foul treachery. John Grant was my da's friend. He would never harm his son. Never!" For a moment he gripped her shoulders so tightly she feared he would crush her.

She breathed at last and worked to quell her emotions. Time was short. The light grew white and flat around them. Soon she'd be missed from the stable. 'Twas dangerous, her being here with him. If someone should find them together—

Iain fidgeted and something winked a brilliant green from under the plaid bunched at his waist. Fascination overpowered her anxiety. ''What is that?'' She pointed at the object.

He fumbled in the folds of his plaid and, to her astonishment, withdrew from his belt a magnificent jeweled dagger.

''Jesu,'' she breathed, marveling at the weapon's hilt. 'Twas crafted of silver and gold, a dozen precious gems embedded in its intricate design. The hairs on her nape prickled as she recognized dried blood crusting on the wicked-looking blade. ''Where on earth did you get it?''

Iain laid the dagger at her feet. ''Ye must hide it for me until I can return.''

''Return? But, where are you going?''

''I dinna know. Away. We must leave Findhorn Castle. 'Twill no' be safe to stay. There are too few of us left to defend it.''

''Nay—you cannot!'' She grasped the front of his mud-streaked shirt. ''What of your clan, the alliance?''

Why just yesterday he'd told her of his father's dream of peace, to align four Highland clans: his own—Mackintosh, his mother's people—Davidson, and Macgillivray and MacBain. Clan Chattan, he'd called it. Clan of the Cats.

Her clan was not among them. 'Twould never be. Not now.

''There will be no alliance. Clan Chattan is no more.'' He took her hands in his, projecting a quiet strength that was almost frightening. The arrogant boy she'd known was gone. "I am The Mackintosh now. I must protect my mother and my brothers."

"Who would dare harm them?"

"Grant." He all but spat the word.

"Nay, he would not! The laird is a kind man. He—" Iain's eyes narrowed and she swallowed her words.

"Aye, well… Perhaps not him, but others in his household."

She knew of whom he spoke and shuddered at the thought. Last night in the stable yard she'd seen the bloodstained weapons and ruined livery, the frothing mounts, their eyes wild in the aftermath of some hideous carnage.

Without warning, a chill wind blasted through the copse. Hundreds of crisped leaves rained down on them in a shower of gold and cinnabar from the larch limbs above their heads. Absently, Iain plucked one from her tangled hair.

The mist was lifting. She pulled the edges of her cloak together and looked skyward, gauging the time by the rapidly growing whiteness of the morning sky. "When shall you leave?"

"Soon." He looked away and he, too, seemed to measure what time they had left. "Today."

"Nay!"

For months they'd met, once each sennight, here at their secret place. No one knew of their trysts, neither his clan nor hers. Why, her father would tan her hide did he know how far she rode from home. And yet, more than once she'd had the strangest feeling they weren't alone here. Even now.

"When shall I see you again?"

"I dinna know," he said quietly.

She remembered the dagger that lay among the dead leaves between them. 'Twas heavy and seemed almost a sword next to her delicate child's frame. Iain watched her with interest as she feathered a tress of hair from her head. She drew the blade of the dagger across it and the lock fell away in her hand. He tensed as she plucked a chestnut hank from his thick mane and freed it with the blade.

Working quickly she fashioned a circlet of their hair, chestnut and gold, braided with a strip of Mackintosh tartan she cut from the end of his plaid. She placed the circlet into Iain's hand and he studied it, rubbing the newly forged braid between his fingers.

"What is it?"

"A lovers' knot." Her cheeks warmed from the blush she knew he could see. "My mother made one for my father to keep with him whenever they were apart. She's French, you know."

Nay, he didn't know. In fact, he knew nothing about her family. She'd never told him anything about herself, not even her true name. 'Twas a game they played—one that had vexed him terribly. On each occasion they met, she'd pretend to be someone different. Her gaze strayed to the blood on his plaid, and she knew the time for games was long past.

His hand closed over the circlet. He gripped it for a moment before tucking it carefully into his sporran. Then he grasped the jeweled dagger and thrust it into the loamy earth between them. "It willna be long," he said. "I will return. For you and for this." He nodded at the dagger.

For her. He'd return for her! "Do you swear?" She searched his face, willing him to answer.

"Aye, I swear." He stood abruptly and looked down at her, blue eyes dark as midnight. "The Grants will pay. I willna rest until my father is avenged. Until every last one of them is dead."

"All of them?"

Before he could answer, the sound of hoofbeats broke the stillness of the forest. A tree branch snapped not far from where they stood.

"Listen—horses!" She scrambled to her feet.

Iain spun and narrowed his eyes toward the sound, straining to see through the mist. Voices carried over the gurgling of the brook. "They're coming."

Jesu, she must not be found here! "I must go." She backed away from the sound of the approaching riders, then turned to run.

"Wait!" Iain yanked the dagger from the ground, hacked a piece of plaid from off his shoulder and wrapped the jeweled weapon inside it. "Here. Take it. Hide it. I will return."

She clutched the bundle tight to her chest as if it would stop the pounding of her heart. She stood for a moment looking up at him, memorizing his face, his eyes, the gentle strength of his countenance.

And then she was gone.

"Girl! Your true name!" Iain called after her. "I dinna know it." But 'twas too late. The mist enfolded her like a cold, white shroud.

He turned to meet the approaching riders.

Chapter One

Eleven years later

Reynold Grant studied the parchment that held the key to his future....

> I, Beatrix d'Angoulême, firstborn of Comte Renaud d'Angoulême, emissary of Philip II of France, do on my deathbed acknowledge my natural daughter, Alena, as sole heir of my fortune and estates, in accordance with the laws of this realm.

'Twas dated May 1184, signed and witnessed, the gold-and-purple seal of Angoulême affixed at the bottom.

A smile bloomed on Reynold's face. He tucked the parchment back into its hiding place amongst his dead uncle's things and paced the rush-strewn floor. Aye, 'twas a brilliant idea. Position and power for the taking. And who better to seize it than himself?

His cousin Henry was eleven years dead, and his uncle, John Grant, fresh in the ground. Who was there left to stop him?

The grim, wide-eyed face of a boy flashed briefly in his

mind. That boy would be a man now, and Reynold knew he'd come for vengeance, for what once had been his.

A knock sounded at the door. Reynold snapped to attention as his kinsman, Perkins, entered the chamber.

"You sent for me, Laird?"

Laird. Aye, the title suited him, as he always knew it would. He moved to the writing table by the window. "I wish ye to deliver a message."

Leaning over the desk, he hastily penned a note. He signed the missive with a flourish, folded the parchment in half, and handed it to the waiting Perkins.

"To whom shall I deliver it?"

He studied Perkins's dark, wiry form. The man was weak and greedy. He liked that about him. "Alena Todd," he said. "The stablemaster's daughter."

"Ah..." Perkins's dark eyes shone. "Pretty." He tucked the parchment into the folds of his plaid. "But surely you wish the note delivered into the hands of her father."

"That cripple? Nay, I do not." He shot Perkins a pointed look. "The message is for her. See to it at once."

"But... She reads?"

"Aye, she does. One of my uncle's insane notions."

Perkins frowned. "I see. 'Twill be delivered right away, Laird." He moved toward the door, then stopped. "Oh, I nearly forgot. The sentries report Mackintosh warriors in the forest, a day's ride from here."

"How many?"

"Three. Four perhaps."

"Hmph. Did they recognize any of them?"

"Nay, they did not."

Reynold waved a hand, dismissing him. "All right, off with you. I want that note delivered now."

Perkins nodded and slipped from the chamber.

"Mackintosh, eh?" Reynold strode to the window and

looked out on what was now his demesne. "'Tis time I finished that business.''

He couldn't keep his mind on the hunt.

Iain Mackintosh leaned against the rotted stump and unstrung his longbow. The morning mist had disappeared, divided by shafts of sunlight. He unfurled his plaid, still damp from a night in the heather, and pulled it 'round his shoulders against the chill air.

For the second time that day he caught himself absently fingering the circlet of hair he carried with him always. The strip of plaid securing the braid was frayed and worn, but his memory of the girl was not.

When he'd been old enough, he'd returned to their secret copse. 'Twas dangerous as hell. The Grants held the lands for a half day's ride on all sides of it. Covertly he'd searched village after village, stared into the faces of countless lasses, but he never found her. Christ, 'twas impossible! He didn't even know her name, let alone her clan.

A whistle pierced the silence of the forest, jarring him from his thoughts. He vaulted onto his waiting horse and guided the roan stallion toward the sound. A few minutes later he caught sight of his kinsmen leisurely making their way toward him. Neither rider had game to show for the morning's effort.

"Hamish, ye missed the shot then?" he called out.

"Aye, dammit all to hell. 'Twas a beauty, too.''

The last Iain had seen of them that morning, Hamish and Will had been hot on the trail of a red stag.

"Two days out from Braedûn Lodge and we've nothing to show for it,'' Will said.

"Ye'd best go back with something, Will.'' Iain shot his friend a mischievous look. "Ye wouldna wish to disappoint a certain lass.''

Hamish spurred his mount forward, even with Iain's roan. "Lass? What lass?"

Will blushed scarlet, the tips of his ears pink as a bairn's. Iain grinned. "A particular lady's maid."

"Edwina?" Hamish boomed. "She's as old as the Craigh Mur standing stones. Will, I didna know—"

"Not Edwina, ye fool!" Will's voice cracked. "'Tis…'tis Hetty," he said, as if he'd just realized it himself.

"Ah…Hetty." Hamish's eyes lit up. He winked at Iain and continued his taunting. "She's a bonny one."

Will jerked his mount to a halt. "Aye, she is, but I dinna want ye noticing."

Iain and Hamish dissolved into laughter. After a moment Will's frown melted into a grin, and the three of them continued south through the larch wood forest.

"And what about you, Iain?" Hamish said. "What of all the lovely lassies your uncle Alistair's paraded past ye?"

Iain had never told Hamish about the girl. About his promise. He'd never told anyone. "I've no time for such foolery."

"Aye, perhaps not. But ye've been a bear of late. 'Tis time we made another trip to Inverness."

Iain recalled their last visit, made some months ago. Drinking and wenching, and then more drinking. His most vivid memory of the trip was the two-day headache that plagued him afterward. 'Twas the last thing he needed. Nay, his restlessness was driven by something far deeper than the lack of a woman in his bed.

'Twas time.

His mother had passed, God rest her soul, and his younger brothers were old enough to make their own way should he fall in battle. Aye, 'twas time to reclaim what was his and to bring the cur responsible for his father's murder, his clan's ruin, to justice under his sword.

The memory of that night burned fresh in his mind. All evidence had pointed to his father's guilt, but Iain would never believe it. Never.

He had to have that dagger! Strangely enough, 'twas not the jeweled weapon that haunted his dreams, but the vision of a dirty-faced sprite in leather breeches, a few stray leaves clinging to her wild tumble of hair.

The roan stallion jerked and Iain snapped to attention. Pushing the dark memories from his mind, he glanced quickly about him, instinctively checking the position of his weapons. All was well. He soothed the beast with a few gentle words, then looked back at his kinsmen.

"Hamish, what d'ye hear from Findhorn?" It had been years since Iain had looked upon his ancestral home. Few were left there now, living in the crofts outside the curtain wall. The keep, he'd heard, had fallen into disrepair, the lands overgrown and wild.

Hamish's brows shot up. "No' much is changed. Grant soldiers patrol the woods there still."

"But the clansmen who remain have no' been idle." Will nudged his mount forward, even with the roan.

"Aye." Hamish nodded. "They are loyal to The Mackintosh and stand ready to support ye."

Iain shrugged. "They are brave men and true to my father's memory."

"*You* are laird now," Hamish said. "They are loyal to *ye*."

"Aye, I'm laird." *And ye all know why.* His father was dead—murdered—and he'd done naught to stop it. Iain clenched his teeth, his mouth dry and bitter. He snatched the kidskin bladder hanging from his saddle, tilted his head back, and took a long draught.

"What will ye do?" Will asked.

"I'll claim what's mine, and strike down those who stole it from me. I should have done it long ago."

He'd burned to do it, in fact. For years that's all he'd thought about. But his mother's clan was small, and Alistair Davidson a prudent man. He'd barely let Iain out of his sight whilst he was growing up. And once he'd grown, Iain realized he bore the weight of not only a man's responsibilities, but a laird's. Nay, he could not have risked so many lives on a fool's mission.

"How do ye plan to take them?" Hamish asked. "Grant commands a sizable army."

Iain had spent years considering that very point, obsessed with the strategies and tactics of war, honing his battle skills and those of his remaining clansmen to a sharp-edged perfection.

At any time John Grant could have hunted him down and murdered what remained of his people. But he hadn't. That fact, coupled with Grant's sheer numbers, had been enough to quell Iain's bloodlust—for a time.

But things were different now. John Grant was dead, murdered some say, though no one knew who did it. His nephew, Reynold, was laird now. Iain spat. Aye, everything was different.

"We canna do it alone," he said. "That much I know."

"All the Mackintosh would follow ye into battle." Will's face shone with a loyalty that tore at Iain's gut.

He smiled bitterly. "So they would. But I willna bring death and destruction to what's left of my clan." Few of his father's warriors had escaped Reynold Grant's retribution for his cousin Henry's murder. The best of them had been slain, and their blood lay heavy on Iain's own hands. "Nay," he said, "we will come at him with ten score or none."

Hamish looked hard at him, blue eyes fixed in question.

"Aye." Iain nodded, holding his friend's gaze. "I mean to raise the Chattan."

"Clan Chattan—the alliance!" Will's eyes widened.

"Davidson is for us." Hamish absently twisted the hairs of his beard between thick fingers, weighing their options, Iain suspected. "Your uncle is laird. They will follow him."

"Aye, if he agrees."

"But what of Macgillivray and MacBain?" Will asked.

"Leave them to me."

Iain grew weary of their conversation. The morning's white sky dissolved into the pale blue of afternoon. He stretched and repositioned his longbow over his shoulder.

"'Tis a fine day for hunting."

She was master now, and squeezed her thighs together gently across his back to make the point. The gelding responded at once, trotting forward, graceful and compliant. Alena Todd was pleased. Of the new Arabians, the chestnut had been the most headstrong. Now he was hers.

The Clan Grant stable produced the finest horses in Scotland, swift and powerful, with unparalleled endurance. Her father would be pleased with this one. Would that he could have broken the mount himself.

The accident seemed a lifetime ago. Alena was twelve when Robert Todd was thrown from a stallion, permanently injuring his spine. He could still walk, but would never again sit a horse without great pain. Afterward, she'd moved easily into the roles her father could no longer perform: breaking new mounts to saddle, transforming them from wild, headstrong creatures into warhorses fit to bear the clan's warriors.

She urged the chestnut around the stable yard, leaning

slightly forward to maintain her balance. She, herself, never used a saddle, preferring the subtle communication achieved bareback between rider and mount.

"Alena!" The stable lad's voice startled her. She slowed the gelding as Martin jogged across the enclosure waving a folded note. "Perkins said 'tis for you."

"For me?" She wiped her hands on her worn leather breeches, and Martin handed her the parchment. "What ever could it—" She opened it, and the question died on her lips.

A half hour later, after enough fanfare to last her a lifetime, Alena urged the gelding up the hill toward Glenmore Castle's keep.

The training stable was built away from the keep, a half league down the wooded hillside where there was more space and better grazing. She was glad for the distance. It afforded her more freedom than if she'd lived among the rest of her clan. Stable lads ferried mounts between the Todds' stable and the small castle stable that housed the laird's steeds.

The *laird*.

Alena shuddered. She'd seen Reynold Grant at the old laird's burial just days ago, though his uncle's untimely death seemed not to grieve him overmuch.

Reynold was his nephew by marriage, so the story went. When Reynold's father died, his mother abandoned him to marry again for the wealth she'd always craved. Her English husband had no use for her unwanted son, so John Grant took Reynold in and raised him as his own. Though 'twas common knowledge Reynold and Henry never got along.

Without warning she felt the darkness again, like a black veil shrouding her heart. The night of the murders burned bright in her memory, even now, so many years later.

Aye, she remembered it all... John Grant returning to the keep, the body of his son, Henry, tied like baggage across his mount. Later that night, Reynold—he was but twenty then—had thundered into the stable yard with forty warriors demanding fresh horses. They'd reeked with the stench of blood, and a cold fear had seized her. A fear she still bore.

Mostly, though, she remembered him—the boy, Iain Mackintosh—his face, his promise, vivid still in her memory.

I will return.

She'd ridden often to their secret copse those first years after the slaughter, but had seen no sign of Iain nor any of his clan. He'd broken his vow.

After a while she'd just stopped going, and as she grew into a woman her father had tried everything to make her a suitable match. She'd have none of it, of course. Any one of the men he'd selected would have made her a fine husband, yet...

Oh, 'twas ridiculous! He was never coming back. The years she'd spent dreaming of Iain Mackintosh were years wasted. They'd been children, for pity's sake. Still, she was not yet ready to wed. Her parents needed her, her father especially. He could never run the stable on his own. Perhaps in another year, or two, or—

Oh, hang it all! Now was not the time for such thoughts. She must keep her mind on the task at hand. She urged the gelding faster.

This summons to the castle was puzzling, indeed. Why had Reynold asked for *her?* Surely he would speak with her father should the matter concern the stable. Robert Todd had wanted to accompany her, but the note said she should come alone.

'Twas safe enough. She knew the wood better than any

clansman, and had traveled unescorted since she was old enough to ride. A mischievous smile bloomed on her lips as she recalled the afternoons she'd spent with Iain at the copse.

'Twas warm for so early in the summer. The scent of heather and pine permeated her senses. Her mother had insisted she wear a special gown, an heirloom, really: a pale yellow silk that Madeleine Todd had brought with her from France years ago, when she was just Alena's age.

She'd wanted to wear her riding boots, but her mother wouldn't hear of it. Instead she'd donned a pair of soft kidskin slippers that complemented the gown. At her waist, as always, she wore the small dirk her father had given her.

The castle was in sight. Time to switch to…what had her father called it? *A position befitting a lady.* She maneuvered around and smoothed her skirts, covering her bare legs. "Sidesaddle, indeed." What a ridiculous way to sit a horse. Invented for women by men, no doubt.

She made her way into the bailey and guided her mount toward the keep, exchanging greetings with her kinsmen. Near the steps she dismounted and handed the chestnut's reins to a waiting lad.

Perkins greeted her inside. She didn't know him well and he made her nervous. 'Twas said Reynold met him during his travels last year. His dark brows rose as he raked his eyes over her body, appraising her as she would a new horse. "The laird is expecting you. This way." He indicated the stone steps leading to the castle's upper levels.

A few minutes later Perkins left her alone in what appeared to be the laird's private rooms. The chamber was rich with tapestries and ornate furniture. Rushes, woven into an intricate pattern, covered the stone floor. The day was warm, but a fire blazed in the hearth nonetheless.

A sound caught her attention. A door stood ajar at the

end of the room and without a second thought she moved closer to listen. She recognized men's voices. One of them was the laird's, though she could not make out his words. 'Twas an argument, it seemed. Reynold's voice grew louder, and she jumped as something—a fist, mayhap— slammed on a table. Then he roared a name that made her heart stop.

Iain Mackintosh.

He'd be a man now, a warrior. Oh, but he was always that. The half smile slid from her lips as she wondered if he'd taken some elegant lady to wife. *A lady of fortune and property.* His childhood boasts still burned in her ears. She pushed the thought from her mind. Whatever he was now, 'twas apparent Iain Mackintosh had angered her new laird.

She inclined her head toward the door and strained to hear more. Sharp footsteps moved rapidly across the flagstones. In the nick of time she jumped back. The door crashed open.

Reynold Grant stood before her, cool blue eyes drinking her in. She had never been so close to him before, and that closeness sparked her fear. He was about thirty, she guessed, tall and well-muscled, with fair skin and white-blond hair tied back in a leather thong. He was an imposing figure in the Clan Grant plaid—all warrior, and chieftain. The burnished metal of the sword and dirk belted at his waist caught the light.

She didn't like the way he openly leered at her, and avoided returning his gaze. "Laird. You sent for me."

"Alena," he said slowly, pronouncing each syllable as if her name were some newly minted word. He lifted her hand to his lips and kissed it, his eyes drawing her in. "How lovely ye are. Such beauty shouldna be hidden away in the stable." He loomed in close, and she fought the urge to step back.

"I have a matter to discuss with ye." To her relief he dropped her hand and walked toward the window. He cast a brief look outside. "What think ye of this place?"

The question took her by surprise. "'Tis…very fine. Surely one of the greatest stone castles in Scotland."

"Aye, 'tis true." He approached her, and she tensed as he again took her hand. "How would ye like to live here?"

His question confused her, and she knew it showed on her face. "I do live here, Laird, in my parents' cottage, at the training stable not a half league away."

He chuckled softly, as if in response to some private joke. "Nay, lass. How would ye like to live *here,* at the keep…with me?"

"I'm sorry, I don't understand." An awful premonition welled inside her. She tried to draw her hand away, but he held it fast.

"How old are you, Alena?" Reynold pulled her close.

"Ten and nine, sir. Almost twenty." Why on earth would her age interest him? Why had he sent for her?

"Ten and nine. Far past marriageable age, and yet ye are not wed." He arched his brows and smiled down at her. "Why?"

So that was it.

Her cheeks flushed hot. She yanked her hand away and looked him in the eyes. "I do not desire marriage, Laird. I wish to remain at the stable. There is much work to—"

"Not desire marriage? Surely your father doesna support this view."

Her suspicions were confirmed. Her father had put him up to this. "Nay, Laird, he does not."

"Nor do I. In truth, I've summoned ye here to tell ye that ye will be wed, and soon."

She did back away then, incredulous. "Wed? To whom?"

A smile broke across his ghost-white face. "To me. On Midsummer's Day."

Iain guided his mount down a steep, wooded ravine. He wasn't familiar with this part of the forest and moved cautiously, scanning the trees for any sign of movement.

Hamish and Will had continued south when Iain veered east tracking a red stag, the biggest he'd ever seen. He'd strayed onto Grant land at some point, but no matter. He'd soon have his game and be gone.

His kinsmen would wait for him at Loch Drurie, hours away from where he was now. He studied the afternoon sky, judging the light. There was time enough, but where was his prey?

The ravine was choked with gorse and whortleberry, making the footing difficult for his horse. Stands of larch and laurel rose up to touch the sky. It reminded him much of the copse, their secret place. His and the girl's. Sunlight pierced the emerald canopy, transforming the wood into a fairy forest of shadow and light.

He moved silently, directing the roan toward a stream near the bottom of the slope. Breathing in the cool, earthy scent of the forest, he scanned the surrounding foliage.

There! He saw it!

The red stag, drenched in sunlight and frozen against a backdrop of green. Fifty yards upwind, at most seventy-five. Few archers could make such a shot, but in his mind's eye Iain could already feel the weight of the stag on his back as he lifted it onto his horse. Aye, this one was his.

The stallion, trained to the hunt, stood motionless as Iain strung his longbow. He dipped into the grease pot that hung at his waist and ran his fingers lightly along the bowstring, his eyes never leaving his prey.

The stag stepped forward and dropped its head, raking

the ground with a hoof, then shook its great body sending a spray of water droplets flying from its coat.

'Twas now or never. Crossing himself, Iain offered up a wordless prayer to his patron saint. With a practiced hand he drew an arrow into the bow and sighted down the shaft to his prey.

This was the moment above all others that thrilled him. The years of training, preparation, the foregone pleasures— all proved worthwhile in that brief moment before he loosed the arrow toward its mark. A Mackintosh never missed.

Then it happened.

The stag's head shot up, ears pricked. A second before he heard the commotion, Iain sensed what the stag already knew— Riders!

"Saint Sebastian to bluidy hell!"

The stag bounded into the cover of the forest. Iain forced his mount sideways into the shadow of a larch, checked the placement of his other weapons, and leveled his bow at the sound.

A chestnut gelding crashed through the trees on the opposite side of the ravine, its rider a blur of yellow and gold driving the horse toward the stream at the bottom. At the last possible second the chestnut vaulted itself over the churning waters. The horse landed badly, flinging its rider to the ground.

Iain scanned the ridge line in all directions but saw no others. He guided his steed cautiously down the slope, arrow still nocked in his bow. The roar of the stream was deafening.

The chestnut writhed on the ground in pain. Its rider lay sprawled, facedown, a few yards in front of the horse. Good God, 'twas a woman! As Iain approached, she pushed herself to her knees and looked up, stunned from the fall.

His breath caught.

Her hair was a tumble of light—wheat and flaxen and gold—framing a round face with a slightly pointed chin. Her gown was ripped across the shoulder and the fabric gaped, exposing the swell of one creamy breast. Iain let his gaze linger there for a moment. She was spattered with mud, and a trail of bloody fingerprints snaked over her from neck to waist.

As she emerged from her daze she stiffened at the sight of him towering above her on the roan. Their eyes locked. She snatched a bloodied dirk from her belt and brandished it before her.

Iain had never seen a more beautiful woman in his life.

The thunder of hoofbeats wrenched him from his stupor. Horsemen were descending the ravine, sunlight glinting off their livery. Clan Grant livery.

The woman glanced back at them. He saw recognition, then fear, grow on her face. She scrambled to her feet and backed toward her horse, a white-knuckled grip on the dirk.

The warriors saw them and slowed their descent. Iain counted ten, maybe twelve. Too many. His decision made, he slung his longbow over his shoulder and offered the woman his hand. "Come on, lass, they're nearly upon us."

She studied him for a moment, glanced back at the riders, then sheathed her dirk and started toward him. Three quick steps and she stopped. "My horse!" she cried and turned back toward the injured beast. "I must help him."

Christ! He quickly restrung his bow, nocked an arrow, and loosed it into the gelding's breast. The horse shuddered once, then lay still.

The woman whirled on him. "You killed—"

In one swift motion he leaned from his mount and swept her into his lap. He spurred the roan up the hill, away from the approaching riders, and wondered what in bloody hell he'd gotten himself into.

Chapter Two

So much for hunting.

Iain reined his lathered stallion to a walk. They'd outridden the warriors, but on his life he knew not how. The terrain had been rugged and steep, and his steed already spent when the chase had begun.

The woman had swooned—from shock and exhaustion, no doubt—but not before she'd driven the roan to breakneck speed. Iain had never seen anything like it. As they'd topped the ridge above the ravine she'd leaned far forward in the saddle, her hands resting lightly on the stallion's neck. 'Twas almost as if she'd whispered something to the beast. The steed had responded immediately, had flown past larch and laurel, dodging stumps and boulders, leaving the Grants far behind.

Securing one arm 'round her waist, he draped the woman's legs over his thigh. Her head lolled back, spilling flaxen tresses across his plaid. Wisps of the fine hair grazed his bare leg like a thousand silken fingers. Her full lips were parted. "Holy God," he breathed, and fought the overwhelming urge to kiss her.

Feelings stirred inside him that he couldn't explain:

fierce protectiveness, awe, desire. He pushed them from his mind. Who had time for such foolishness?

He guided the roan toward a small creek and dismounted carefully, the woman in his arms. He laid her gently down onto a bed of wild grasses near the water's edge. They would be safe here, for a while at least.

God's truth, she was lovely. He hadn't spent much time with women. He'd been far too busy working toward the day he'd clear his father's name. That day was coming, and soon.

With a strip of cloth cut from his plaid, he washed the blood and caked mud from her face and neck, hesitating a moment before moving to her shoulders. He swallowed hard as he watched the rise and fall of her breasts with each slow, steady intake of breath.

A few stray leaves clung to her hair. As he plucked them from their golden nest he had the strangest feeling he knew her. Nay, 'twas impossible. He was certain he'd never seen her before. Hers was not a face a man would soon forget.

Examining the fine silk of her gown, he wondered about her family, to which clan she belonged. She was a lady, surely. Her mount had lacked distinctive markings or livery. In fact, the gelding had neither saddle nor stirrups. She'd ridden bareback and outrun the Grant. Now that was impressive.

On impulse he clasped one of her hands in his and ran his thumb lightly over her palm. 'Twas rough and callused, surprisingly so. A lady, surely, but with the hands of a servant? No matter. He'd solve the mystery soon enough.

"Wake up, lass," he whispered, and rubbed her cool hands between his.

She felt like ice.

Aye, except for her hands. They were warm. Oh, what

a terrible dream. She drew a breath and opened her eyes. ''Jesu!''

A huge warrior knelt above her, a dark shape against the setting sun. ''Nay!'' She wrenched her hands free of his grip and thrashed at him with her fists.

''Easy, lass, easy.'' The warrior grabbed her wrists to still her struggle. ''You're safe, you're safe now. No harm will come to ye.''

She stiffened in his grasp, then relaxed, letting her head fall back onto the soft pillow of heather. Oh, God, 'twas all true then!

The warrior held her hands in his, stroking the backs of them with his thumbs. Against all reason, she was not afraid of him. In truth, she felt strangely comforted by his presence. She felt...

Safe.

With a start, she remembered her pursuers. She bolted upright and scanned their surroundings for signs of the riders. ''Where are they? What—''

''Shh... Dinna fash.'' The warrior coaxed her into lying back down. ''We're well away from the soldiers and they willna follow us here.''

He revealed a square of damp cloth, hesitated for a moment as if to gauge her response, then pressed it to her brow. She lay still and let him do it.

His face intrigued her. 'Twas thoughtful yet strong, with finely chiseled features, and framed by a mane of deep brown hair. One thin braid strayed from his temple, and he absently pushed it back from his face. His expression was intent, and his eyes—those eyes—from where did she know them?

Jesu! He was sponging the rise of her breasts with the cloth. She sat up and batted his hand away.

''You're hurt,'' he said. ''The blood. Let me—''

"Nay!" She pulled the edges of her tattered gown together, covering her half-exposed breast. A flash of heat rose in her face, and she knew her cheeks blazed crimson. "'Tis...not my blood."

With revulsion she recalled Reynold Grant's hands on her. Their brief meeting had gone from bad to worse once his intentions were made clear. Why in God's name did he wish to wed her? 'Twas unfathomable. She was nothing, no one. He was laird and could have any woman he wanted.

He wanted *her*.

And used her parents' vulnerability to ensure her compliance. Did she not wed him on Midsummer's Day, he'd turn them out. Without the clan's protection, with no way to make a living, they'd perish.

Jesu, what had she done?

When she'd refused Reynold, he came at her and she'd panicked. In her struggle to get away she'd done something stupid. She'd cut him. On the face. Her dirk was in her hand before she'd even known what she was doing. 'Twas raw instinct, self-defense. Any maid would have done the same to preserve her virtue. She'd fled the keep and bolted into the forest on the waiting gelding. She didn't think, she just rode, faster and faster until—

The warrior's intense gaze pulled her back to the moment. He sat back on his heels, allowing her some space. "Have they...did they...harm ye, lass?"

His eyes beamed concern, and her heart fluttered. "Nay, I'm well. Truly." She pulled the gown tighter across her breasts, crossing her arms in front of her.

He leaned forward and offered her the damp cloth. "There's no need to fear me. I willna harm ye."

She accepted the square of plaid and wiped it across the curve of her neck, remembering with a shudder the soldiers who'd pursued her.

The warrior retrieved a leather bladder from the saddle of his horse and offered it to her. "Here, drink this. 'Twill calm ye."

Eager to slake her thirst, she took a long draught from the waterskin and nearly choked. "Wha—what is it?" she sputtered, and started to cough.

The warrior laughed. "A wee libation my brother concocted."

"'Tis terrible." She tried to catch her breath as the drink burned a path of liquid fire down her throat.

"Aye, 'tis." He chuckled. "But it's kept me warm on many a night in the rough."

She cleared her throat and felt a pleasant heat spread throughout her chest. She relaxed a little and handed the skin back to him.

He sat beside her, cross-legged, and she noticed for the first time his powerful physique: broad shoulders and long, muscular legs. Her mind drifted. She imagined the well-muscled chest and arms that lay hidden beneath his plaid and rough woolen shirt. He caught her staring, and her cheeks flushed hot. Quickly she looked away.

"So," he said. "What did ye do to incite a dozen Grants to run ye to ground like a rabbit?"

Her gaze flew to his, and she caught his half smile. "I did nothing! And I was *not* run to ground like a rabbit. I was doing just…fine."

"Aye, and I'm the king o' Scotland." His blue eyes flashed amusement. "Another moment and The Grant would ha' been on ye."

"If my horse hadn't faltered, I'd have outridden them easily."

The warrior put a hand to his chin and stroked a two-day growth of stubble. "*Your* horse? Ye are a Grant, then."

"Nay! I am not." The question unnerved her and instinct

compelled her to shield the truth from him. For now, at least. "Were I Grant, think you I'd flee my own kinsmen?"

"Oh, so ye *were* running away."

"Aye—nay!" He was twisting her words. She felt herself panicking. "I didn't say that."

The warrior leaned closer, his face inches from hers. 'Twas as if he stared right into her soul. "So, what were ye doing, then?"

"I was—I was— Wait! Who are *you?*"

The moment the words left her lips she knew.

He wore a common hunting plaid of muted browns and greens. As the last rays of the sun glinted off his clan brooch she recognized the emblem: a wild cat, reared up on hind legs, teeth and claws bared at the ready.

The warrior did not give his name. No matter. His face, those eyes— She would know him anywhere. He was Iain Mackintosh, her childhood love.

Chapter Three

Nothing in her girlish dreams had prepared her for this chance reunion.

She scrambled to her feet, shrugging off his attempt to help her. Her heart fluttered and she felt strangely light-headed. She told herself 'twas the drink and not the reappearance of Iain Mackintosh that caused her head to spin.

She took a step toward the roàn stallion, her thoughts racing. Perhaps if she was quick—

Iain's hand gripped her elbow, and she froze. "What's your name, lass?"

"'Tis, um…" She knew she was a poor liar. Perhaps part of the truth would suffice. "A-Alena. My name is Alena."

"Alena? 'Tis no a Scots name. Ye have the speech of a Scot, though 'tis strange." She could see his mind working. "There's something else about ye seems familiar."

Her heart skipped a beat. She turned away and absently stroked the stallion's neck. "Nay, I know you not." She could feel his eyes on her, and a chill of excitement shivered up her spine.

"Your surname—to which clan do ye belong?"

Clan? Oh no! She needed time to think. About Reynold,

her parents, about *him*. 'Twas by sheer luck Iain had found her in the wood. She must not forget that. 'Twas not as if he'd come looking for her. Why, he might kill her, or ransom her, if he knew she was a Grant. Nay, she must think of a plan. She turned and put on her boldest face. "I—I am Alena. That is enough for you to know."

He stood stock-still, a carefully controlled anger simmering in his eyes. 'Twas apparent no one dared speak to him so, or hadn't for long years. She recalled their childhood sparring.

His voice was deadly calm. "When I question ye, woman, ye will answer me. With the truth." He seemed to grow larger before her eyes. "Now, tell me your surname."

"I will not." She *must* not. She pursed her lips and riveted her gaze to his, the challenge set.

For a moment she thought he might strike her. Instead he loomed, motionless, fists clenched at his sides, and glared at her. She held her ground and glared back.

"Suit yourself, then. I'll leave ye as I found ye." He brushed past her and vaulted onto his horse.

In eleven years he hadn't changed a bit. He was still the most arrogant, maddening boy—well, man—she'd ever known. He nudged the roan toward the forest road. Jesu, did he truly mean to leave her?

She glanced skyward. The sun had set and the first stars peeked out at her from a flawless cerulean sky. 'Twould be deathly cold in no time. No mount, no weapons save her dirk, and her clothing reduced to rags. She looked a beggar and, she had to admit, she'd behaved badly. She regretted her impertinence. After all, he was only trying to help her.

As if he'd read her mind, he turned the steed. By the set of his jaw and the steely look in his eyes she knew his intention.

"Oh, n-nay, w-wait—"

Ignoring her protest, he leaned from his mount and swept her off her feet into his lap. One muscled forearm closed like a steel trap around her waist. His breath teased her hair.

Surrender seemed her only choice. For now. She sank back into the warmth of his chest and wondered what on earth she was going to do.

They rode in silence for what seemed hours. Alena tried several times, without success, to position herself astride the horse. Each time Iain held her fast across his lap.

At last he slowed the stallion to a walk and stopped in a clearing on the far side of a wooded ridge. The moon was little more than a sliver. Below them in its eerie light she spied the milk-white surface of a long loch.

Never had she been so far afield.

Iain guided the roan toward the water. The smell of wood smoke grew sharp as they approached the shore. They snaked along the bank until they reached an enormous standing stone positioned at the water's edge. 'Twas a marker of some kind. Here he turned his mount back into the wood. A campfire flickered in a clearing just ahead.

What was this place?

Two warriors stood just inside the firelight, their features outlined in its warm glow. One of them called out as they approached the clearing. "The hunter returns at la— Saint Columba, will ye look at that!"

The men approached them, mouths agape, their gazes riveted to her. The bigger one—Jesu, they were both huge!—recovered his tongue first. "A bonny prize, man, but she doesna look much like a red stag."

Iain shifted beneath her in the saddle. "She weighs as much as one. Here, take her."

Before she could dismount, Iain lifted her off his lap and

dumped her into the waiting arms of the huge warrior. As he set her down she felt her knees buckle. Hours of side-saddle riding pinned across Iain's thighs had lulled her limbs to sleep.

The second warrior rushed to support her, his puppyish face brimming concern. Alena smiled at him, and he beamed. She regained her balance and shot Iain a look of pure murder.

Iain scowled down at her, his eyes flashing blue-gray steel in the firelight. "Hmph." He dismounted, tangled a foot in the stirrup and nearly crashed to the ground. A litany of curses rattled under his breath.

The big warrior's bushy red brows shot up and he exploded into laughter. "Well, 'tis plain whose arrow struck whom." Iain's glare silenced him, but mirth still danced in his eyes.

"I found her in the forest." Iain tethered his steed and turned toward his kinsmen. "Her mount was lame."

"You killed him!" she said.

"It had to be done. There was—"

"He was a valuable gelding. I could have sav—"

"Silence!"

A chill shot through her. Iain Mackintosh was not a boy anymore. She'd do well to remember that. Her situation here was precarious at best.

Ignoring her, Iain turned toward his burly, red-haired kinsman. "Grant soldiers, a dozen or so. Chasin' her."

Surprise registered on the faces of both warriors. They exchanged glances, then studied her with renewed interest, their eyes drawn to her torn and bloodied gown. Her cheeks flamed. She pulled the ragged edges of her bodice together, but did not look away.

"Are ye hurt, lady?" the gentle one asked her.

"Nay," she replied, "just...cold."

The two men stepped toward her, each fumbling to unwrap his plaid. With a sharp look Iain stayed their hands. The one with the gentle eyes and puppyish face shrugged, then coaxed her to the fire. Iain watched them, but did not follow.

She held her hands out to the crackling blaze and fought off the chill of the night. Her mind raced, but one thing was clear—Iain was a Mackintosh, and she was a Grant.

"Enemies," she breathed.

"Eh?" The young warrior eyed her, his brows furrowed in question.

"Oh, 'tis nothing. I was just…"

A leg of venison lay spitted across the fire. Her mouth watered at the delicious smell of the roasting meat. Her stomach growled again, loud enough for the warrior who sat beside her to hear. He cut a portion from off the spit and divided it between them. She thanked him for his kindness and set upon the juicy slab as if it were her first meal in months.

They ate in silence and, once finished, she turned her attention to him. She was amused by his blush and tentative return of her glance. He was as tall as Iain, but slighter, with thoughtful brown eyes and a calm demeanor.

She smiled. "My name is Alena."

"'Tis an honor, Lady Alena. I'm called Will."

The name suited him. She was about to tell him she was not a lady, only a stablemaster's daughter, but thought better of revealing any more about herself than necessary.

She gestured toward the burly warrior standing with Iain at the edge of the firelight. "And your friend?"

"That's Hamish."

"Hamish." His most striking feature, other than his enormous size, was his wild mass of fire-bright hair. He had a thick red beard and hands the size of small hams.

She remembered the mirth in his clear blue eyes and his bellowing laugh when Iain nearly tumbled from his horse. She liked him, this giant of a man.

"And the other?" She nodded at Iain.

"Oh. Iain, ye mean?"

She was right! She would have bet her life on it. She had, in fact. A tiny smile bloomed on her lips.

"He didna tell you his name?"

"Nay." She arched a brow in question. "Iain…?"

"Mackintosh. *The* Mackintosh. Our laird."

"Laird?" This did not surprise her. "You speak so… frankly to him. He allows it?"

"Oh, aye. The three of us ha' been friends since boyhood, since the old laird, Iain's da, ever since he was—"

"Will!"

Both of them froze. She looked up to see Iain scowling at them from the opposite side of the fire. Her mind had been on Will's explanation and she hadn't heard Iain approach.

"We'll rest here tonight." Iain's eyes drifted to the spit over the fire and his expression softened. "What's for supper? Venison?"

"Aye," Hamish replied as he came up behind him. He rested one huge paw on his laird's shoulder. "Some of us were no' as lucky in the hunt as others." The warrior winked at her, and she suppressed a smile.

Iain grumbled something under his breath and shrugged off his kinsman's hand. They both sat down to eat. Iain seemed at ease here at the loch, much more so than when they'd been riding.

She realized they must be miles from Clan Grant land. They'd ridden steadily upward through the larch wood, farther into the Highlands, and away from Glenmore Castle.

How would she ever get back? Her parents would be worried sick.

Midsummer's Day.

Reynold's words throbbed in her head like a drumbeat. Nay, she would not think on it. Not now. Not yet.

Suddenly chilled, she stretched her arms toward the fire. Her shredded bodice gaped, and she moved quickly to cover herself. Across the campfire Iain watched her as he feasted on what remained of the venison leg.

"Lady Alena," Will whispered. "I've a sewing needle and a bit o' thread. Comes in handy all too often in the rough. Would ye like to borrow it? For your gown, I mean?"

"Aye." She smiled at him. "My thanks."

Will dipped into his sporran and pulled out a square of cloth pierced by a needle trailing a goodly amount of thread. "This should do." He handed it to her.

To her surprise, Iain stood and unpinned the clan brooch that held his plaid in place over his shoulder. He unfurled a long length of the hunting tartan and cut it away with his dirk, then tucked the rest into his belt. "Here, lass," he said, and tossed it over the campfire into her lap. "Ye can wear this whilst ye do your sewing."

The gesture touched her. She was reminded of him as a boy, how one minute he seemed not to care about her and the next, well...

She held his gaze for a moment, then thanked him and rose, turning toward the cover of the forest. Before she could take a step, he said, "No' that way. Go down by the loch. 'Tis...safer."

She read something in his eyes, a stoic sort of honor she remembered well. She knew then that he meant to protect her, even though he knew not who she was.

At the water's edge she dropped Iain's plaid and wrestled

with the laces of her gown. The garment was bloodstained, mud-caked, and ripped in a dozen places. But 'twas her mother's gift to her, and she would salvage it somehow.

She worked the laces free and pulled the fine silk over her head. Draping the gown carefully over the standing stone marking the clearing twenty yards away, she turned toward the water and drew a heady breath of night air.

A stiff breeze penetrated the thin fabric of her shift. Feelings of relief and freedom washed over her. She was safe here, with Iain, as long as he didn't discover her identity. She must think of a plan, but not tonight.

Exhaustion consumed her and she wavered slightly on her feet. Best get this over with quickly. She tore a strip of cloth from the hem of her shift and dipped it into the frigid water. 'Twas the briefest, coldest sponge bath of her life. She grabbed Iain's plaid and wrapped it around her. 'Twas warm from his body and held the strong male scent of him.

She felt herself drifting and succumbed to the dreamy exhaustion. Sinking to the ground, she drew her knees up close to her chest and rested her back against the ancient standing stone marking the path back to their camp. She pulled Iain's plaid tight and nestled her cheek against its warm folds. Just for a moment she would rest her eyes.

Visions flashed bright against the midnight backdrop of her eyelids: white-blond hair against a bloodred field, ice-blue eyes cold as death. She shuddered at the brink of sleep, then let go the awareness of her surroundings and drifted deeper.

In her mind's eye she saw the boy, his wild hair and tear-streaked face, the jeweled dagger clutched to his heart. The image faded, and in its place crouched a silver cat, sleek and muscular. And finally the man, the warrior, his indigo eyes burning into the very depths of her soul.

She sighed as a gentle hand cupped her cheek. She was

lifted free of her burdens and carried home, warm and safe in his arms.

Through slitted eyes Alena perceived the gray dawn. Heat radiated from behind her, and she backed against the solid warmth. A comforting weight, hot as a firebrand, moved over the curve of her waist and came to rest just below her breast.

She felt...wonderful.

Her eyes flew open. The campfire directly in front of her was reduced to smoldering ash, and the bundled forms of two sleepers lay flanking it. A shock of red hair poked out from one of the plaids. Of course! Hamish and Will.

And Iain!

Alena lifted the plaid and saw Iain's bare arm draped over her. She felt the heat of his body at her back, the thin fabric of her shift the only barrier between her skin and his. He snored lightly, his hot breath ruffling her hair. Taking care not to wake him, she wriggled out from beneath his heavy arm and scrambled to her feet.

On a nearby rock she spied her gown, folded neatly and covered with a square of plaid to protect it from the morning dew. She shook out the pale yellow silk and saw it had been mended with dozens of small, straight stitches, and had been carefully cleaned of the mud and blood that had covered it the night before. She glanced at the sleeping pile of plaid that was Will and smiled.

Wasting no time, she pulled the gown over her head and laced it as best she could. Her hair was a tangle of curls in the mist. She leaned forward, letting her thick mane hang nearly to the ground, and combed it through with her fingers.

A minute later she gasped as two large boots came into view through the honey-wheat curtain. She whipped her head back and found herself face-to-face with Iain. Her eyes widened.

He stood before her with hands on hips, studying her, it seemed, with no small amount of curiosity. She tipped her chin and met his gaze, determined to not let him intimidate her.

"They're green," he said plainly. "I hadna thought so last night."

"What are green?"

"Your eyes." He stared at her for a moment then turned back toward the fire ring.

Gooseflesh rose on her skin, but not from fear.

She excused herself and returned to the loch to gain some privacy for her morning ablutions. The sun rose over the treetops in the east and cast thin fingers of light across the mist blanketing the water.

Alena gazed at the ancient standing stone and tried to recall exactly when and how she'd ended up half naked, rolled in a plaid with Iain Mackintosh.

The foursome burst out of the larch wood into the open terrain: a rugged and rocky carpet of green sprayed with clumps of late spring wildflowers. The air was fresh and full of the scent of the Highland heather blanketing the hillsides in amethyst waves. 'Twas lovely, and reminded her of the days she and Iain had spent together when he was twelve and she eight.

So very long ago, she reminded herself.

They rested awhile by a small brook, taking a meal of oakcakes and cheese. Their horses grazed nearby, contented, nibbling at the sweet, wild grasses.

Alena walked over and studied the roan, running her hands down each leg and along the stallion's well-muscled flanks. He was a fine warhorse, and well cared for. English

Shire bred with native Clydesdale, she suspected. She examined the other two mounts and found them to be the same. Not as powerful, perhaps, as Iain's steed, but excellent warhorses all the same. Whoever had bred and cared for them knew what they were doing.

Standing back, she looked them over again, hands on hips, and nodded her approval. Iain's eyes bored into her back. She straightened her spine and faced him.

"If our mounts meet with your approval, Lady, we'll be on our way." He mounted and offered her his hand.

Waking that morning in his arms had unnerved her. The way their bodies fit together, the way she'd felt in his embrace… Nay, they weren't children anymore.

She ignored Iain's proffered hand and moved toward Will who was strapping a cloth bag of provisions onto his black gelding. "May I ride with you this afternoon, Will?"

"O'—o' course, Lady. I'd be most—" The words died in his throat as Iain urged the roan toward them and scooped Alena into his lap.

Jesu, not again! She kicked and struggled, but he held her fast. "Must you do that?"

He spurred the stallion up the hill as she wrestled to position herself astride the horse. Her gown was twisted and rucked to her knees, exposing her ankles and calves to his view. She quickly smoothed the thin silk to cover herself.

Each time she tried to lean forward, away from him, Iain roughly pulled her back against his chest. By God, she refused to be held in his lap like a bairn! "I am perfectly capable of sitting a horse without assistance, thank you."

"Ye might fall off," he replied evenly.

She bristled at his comment. "I'm the best rider, man or woman, of my clan."

"Oh, aye? And what clan is that?"

"That's not your business." She pulled forward again, out of his grip.

His thick forearm closed around her, just under her breasts, and jerked her firmly back against his chest. "Oh, but it is my business, lass. And dinna fool yourself. I'll find out who ye are." His voice was chillingly calm. The skin on her nape prickled.

"Where are you taking me?"

"Home. And there I intend to keep ye until I know what your connection is to Grant."

Her heart fluttered and her mouth went dry. Jesu, what was she going to do? And where, exactly, was *home?*

A while later they topped a bald ridge, and she marveled at the view. The larch forest lay far below them. Beyond it was a great glen. In the distance a thin line snaked silver down the valley: the river Spey, its meandering path leading north toward Glenmore Castle—and Reynold Grant.

At least now she knew where she was.

Her eyes glassed as she remembered the events of the previous day. It seemed a lifetime ago she had fled. Her parents would be frantic by now. Somehow she must get word to them she was safe. Now that she'd had time to think about it, she realized her father would have never sought a match for her with their new laird. Nay, this was Reynold's doing alone. But why?

She wiped at her eyes, pushed the thoughts from her mind, and focused instead on the beauty of the Highlands and the man who held her close to his beating heart. There would be time to sort it all out. Midsummer's Day was weeks away.

Iain released his grip on her and struggled with something behind her. The stallion fidgeted beneath them as a whoosh of oatmeal cloth cut across her peripheral vision. She turned in the saddle to see Iain, bare-chested, jamming his woolen shirt into a leather bag that hung from the horse's livery.

"It's bluidy hot," he said, and pulled her back against him, spurring the roan upward and south along the ridge line.

It dawned on her that he was leading them farther away from both Mackintosh and Grant land. Where on earth were they going?

Will and Hamish lagged behind after stopping to transfer a good-size stag—Will's prize from yesterday's hunt— from Hamish's horse to Will's.

The afternoon grew warm, and she lifted her face to the sun. Already her skin was bronzed from weeks working outdoors with her father's new mounts. A light spray of freckles barely noticeable in the winter months appeared across her nose each summer, much to her mother's vexation. She smiled at the thought.

Growing up a lady's maid at the French court, Madeleine Todd had definite ideas of how a lady should dress and how she should behave. Alena had shunned most of her mother's well-meaning attempts to transform her into such a creature, preferring instead the freedom of loose clothing and a simple coiffure for her work at the stable.

Reaching behind to her nape, she gathered her mass of thick hair and pulled it free. She'd been sitting on it. Iain pulled her back against his chest and their bare skin connected. Immediately she realized her mistake. She'd forgotten the dipping neckline at the back of her gown.

He was pure heat and the chestnut curls of his chest hair were slightly damp, sending a wave of sensation through her like nothing she'd ever experienced. She was conscious of his muscular thighs pressed up against her buttocks, gently undulating with the motion of the stallion beneath them. The thin cloth of her garments and the light wool of his plaid did little to shield her from the inferno of his body.

There was something she must know, and now seemed as good a time as any to ask him. "Iain?"

He grunted in response.

"Last night, at the loch. I—I don't remember…"

"Oh," he said, seeming to know what she meant. "I found ye asleep by the water and carried ye back to the fire."

She recalled her dream, and a pleasant shiver coursed through her. "But…when I woke up, I was—you were…"

"Aye, well, ye didna expect I'd take the chance of ye stealin' off in the night, did you?"

Nay, she did not. 'Twas clear he wasn't about to let her go anywhere. For now, at least.

A few hours later they passed into another small forest, less densely wooded than the lands to the northeast. The stallion fell into a well-worn path and increased his speed. Of his own accord he broke into a gallop. Iain did nothing to slow his pace. They flew past pine and laurel and up over a broad, green hillside, the steed pushing harder as they gained the top.

"Jesu!" She sucked in a breath.

A great lodge of timber and stone loomed before them, its chimneys billowing a smoky welcome to the weary travelers. 'Twas big as a castle, twenty rooms at least, positioned at the top of a hill and surrounded by a thick rock wall. She could see the tops of cottages and other buildings peeking out above the stones.

"What is this place?"

"Braedûn Lodge," Iain said. "Home of my uncle, Alistair Davidson, and my aunt Margaret."

Of course! Iain had often spoken of his mother when they were children. Ellen. Yes, that was her name. Ellen

Davidson Mackintosh. She must have fled here with her
sons when Iain's father was killed and the Grants laid claim
to Findhorn Castle.

Iain directed the stallion into the great courtyard. Kinsmen shouted words of welcome to the three warriors as
they approached. She noticed the bronze clan badges they
wore in their bonnets, and the Davidson plaid, different
from the Mackintosh colors Iain and his kinsmen sported.

Their smiles and greetings turned to wide-mouthed looks
of surprise as they noticed her perched atop the roan, Iain's
arm wrapped possessively 'round her waist.

The spectators made way for the stallion who seemed to
know exactly where he was going. She spotted a large stable and training yard ahead, set just off from the lodge.
Iain's steed made for the gate.

As the riders passed the main entrance to the lodge, she
spied a young woman standing on the steps leading up to
the great door. Dressed simply and clutching a basket of
wildflowers to her breast, she was a tiny thing with delicate
features and dark hair. Alena guessed her to be sixteen or
so, the plumpness of childhood still noticeable in her
peaches-and-cream face.

Will guided his mount to the steps and stopped. The girl
beamed a smile at him, radiant as summer sunshine. His
face flushed scarlet as he returned her gaze. With a nod of
his head he indicated the red stag strapped to the back of
his horse. Its broad rack of antlers was impressive, even to
Alena. The girl voiced her approval, and Will puffed up in
the saddle, nearly bursting with pride.

Hamish and Iain were still chuckling when their mounts
halted just inside the stable yard. Two lads sprang forward
and the warriors dropped their reins.

An older man with silver hair, dressed in a Mackintosh
plaid and leather riding boots, stood waiting for them to

dismount. His bright eyes were riveted to hers. Strange. She almost felt she knew him. 'Twas silly. She'd never seen him or this place before.

Iain began to lift her from the saddle. Sweet Jesu, not again! She struggled out of his grip. "Will you please unhand me! I've dismounted hundreds of horses under my own power."

He threw up his hands in surrender. "All right, all right! As ye wish, vixen."

She caught that last word, mumbled under his breath, and shot him a look that could freeze water.

He threw a leg over the back of the roan and dropped to the ground. He glared up at her for a moment with those stormy eyes, then turned to the silver-haired man and softened his expression. "Duncan."

"Laird." The man smiled warmly. "Welcome home."

Iain clapped his kinsman on the back and strode toward the horse trough butted up against the stable where Hamish was already washing the road dust from his burly arms.

Alena was still mounted. The old man, Duncan, approached her, offering a strong, leathery arm. He had a kind face that was weathered with years of work in the sun. She smiled and leaned against him for support as she slid from the stallion's back.

Their gazes locked. He grinned, and a strange premonition washed over her.

"So, Alena Todd, what brings ye to Braedûn Lodge?"

Chapter Four

There was no reasoning with the man.

Alena paced the wooden floor of the richly furnished bed chamber and fought to control her anger. Before she'd had a chance to recover from Duncan's startling recognition of her, she'd been whisked off to the main house and installed in a room abovestairs.

She'd protested the choice of accommodation, but Iain would have none of it. It made much more sense for her to sleep in the stable, she'd argued. He'd laughed and told her he wanted her where he could keep an eye on her.

What was she, a prisoner?

The room *was* beautiful. She ran a hand over the brightly colored stitches of a hanging tapestry. A fire blazed in the hearth and a large wooden tub sat before it, presumably for her bath. 'Twas a luxury afforded to few, and she had to admit 'twas preferable to a frigid dunk in the stable yard water trough. Even now, Hetty, the young woman she'd seen on the steps talking to Will, was in the kitchen seeing to the hot water.

A large window looked out over the stable yard where Duncan inspected the hooves of the mounts they had just ridden in on. Two stable lads, and another man who looked a younger version of Duncan, wiped down the lathered coats of the three horses. Duncan stood back and barked instructions. 'Twas as she'd suspected. Duncan was the stablemaster.

How on earth did he know her name?

The door to her chamber opened, forcing her thoughts to the task at hand. Hetty directed two men with steaming buckets toward the tub. Behind them marched an old woman, a Mackintosh plaid draped over her hunched shoulders. She stood with hands on hips, eyeing the men as they poured the water into the vessel, making sure, it seemed, they didn't spill a drop.

When they'd finished, the men left the chamber and Hetty unrolled the heavy deerskin window covering to keep out the breeze and ensure their privacy.

She supposed she should be friendly, though the old woman did not seem overly warm. She risked a smile. "My name is Alena."

"Aye, Lady, so I've been told. I'm Edwina. Now strip off and get into this tub before the water goes cold." She opened a leather pouch and emptied it into the steaming water. A burst of fragrance filled the air.

Hetty slipped behind her and, with expert fingers, released her laces. "'Tis a lovely gown, Lady."

All this formality made her uncomfortable. "Please, won't you both call me Alena."

Edwina arched a brow. Hetty pulled the bedraggled gown over Alena's head. The old woman inspected it with more than casual interest. "It's a wreck," she decreed. "What were ye doin' in it, sloppin' pigs?"

She recalled with revulsion Reynold Grant's hands splayed across the fine yellow silk. "Something like that."

"Weel, ye'll need some new clothes. This is past savin'." Edwina tossed the gown to the floor.

"Oh, nay!" she cried as she struggled out of her shift. "It's very dear to me."

Hetty retrieved it from the floor. "I'll make it right for ye, Lady."

"My thanks, Hetty."

Edwina led her to the steaming tub. Alena stepped into it and was instantly bathed in its aromatic warmth. She sank into the deliciously hot water and closed her eyes.

Oh, 'twas heavenly. Two days hard travel and a night in the rough had taken its toll on her. Edwina stooped and began to lather her hair with soap. The scent of heather and rosemary permeated her senses. She succumbed to the old woman's practiced ministrations and let her head go heavy in her hands.

But relaxation did not come. A score of unanswered questions whirled in her mind, and she knew she could not rest until some of them were answered. She decided to start with something innocuous. "What position have you in the household, Edwina?"

"I am—I *was*—maid and kinswoman to Lady Ellen Mackintosh."

"Iain's mother."

"Aye."

"You said *was*. Do you no longer serve her?"

"Nay. She's dead. Now dunk." Edwina pushed firmly on her head.

Alena held her breath and slipped below the surface to rinse the soap from her hair. She came up sputtering. Edwina scooted around to the side of the tub and began to scrub her arms.

"I'm sorry. When did it happen?"

"At Beltane."

Barely a month ago. No wonder Iain seemed so irritable. She would remember to treat him more kindly.

She was curious about what had happened after the Mackintoshes fled their own lands. "Lady Mackintosh—she lived here with Iain?"

"Aye, and the other two lads, as well. We came to Braedûn Lodge right after the—" Edwina met her questioning gaze with a hard look. "Lady Ellen was born here," she said flatly.

"Oh, I see."

Edwina scooted to end of the tub and started on her legs.

She decided to be bold. "And what of Findhorn Castle?"

"Held by the Grants these eleven years. Not a one lives there, but Grant soldiers surround the demesne, foulin' the lands and waters with their filth. May they be damned to hell."

Edwina was scrubbing the skin off her! Alena tucked her legs under her. "Och, sorry, my lady," Edwina said, and continued with a more gentle hand. "I forgot myself, thinkin' on those vermin."

Vermin. So this is how it was. She'd been right to conceal her identity, after all.

"And how stands Iain?" She knew the answer, but voiced her question all the same. "Grant is his enemy?"

"That's puttin' it mildly. Reynold Grant killed his father. 'Twas a nasty piece o' work, that."

She had shared Iain's anguish that chill, gray morning so very long ago. "Aye, it was," she whispered.

"Eh?"

"Oh, I—" She'd best change the subject. "I understand this is the home of Iain's uncle. Alistair, I think he said his name was."

"Aye, Alistair Davidson is laird here. And a finer man ye'll ne'er meet." Edwina held out a large towel.

Alena stepped from the tub and into it. "I didn't see him when we arrived."

"Nay. He and Lady Margaret are away on business. They're no' expected back for a fortnight."

Edwina completed her vigorous rubbing, and Alena stepped from the towel, her skin pink and glowing in the firelight. Hetty held out a clean shift and helped it over her head.

The girl indicated a small stool by the hearth. "Come sit by the fire, Lady, and I'll comb out your hair."

Edwina hurried toward the door. "Supper's in an hour. I'll send up a gown for ye to wear."

"My thanks, Edwina." Alena turned to smile at her, but the old woman had already gone.

Hetty seemed intent on staying, despite Alena's protests that she needed no help with her hair. Finally she relented, and sat on the stool as instructed. Hetty's gentle strokes coupled with the warmth of the fire made her sleepy.

She was exhausted, if truth be told, and a menagerie of random thoughts jumbled their way through her mind. She fought the weariness and sat tall, willing her eyes stay open.

Hetty began to hum an old lullaby. For some reason Alena was reminded of Will, the gentle warrior whom Iain Mackintosh called friend. "Hetty," she said. The comb stopped in midstroke. "Do you have a sweetheart?" The comb pulled, and Alena cried out.

"Och, sorry." Hetty resumed the long, gentle strokes. "Not a sweetheart, exactly. But there is a lad I fancy."

"It's Will, isn't it?"

The comb pulled again. "How did ye know, Lady?"

"I saw the way he looked at you on the steps when we arrived." She felt Hetty's fingers tremble as the girl drew the comb through her hair.

"Really? D'ye think he took much notice of me?"

"Oh, I'd say he did. Will's a fine man."

Hetty stared into the fire with huge, liquid eyes, oblivious to all else. "He's a Mackintosh warrior—one of the laird's closest kinsmen." She sighed and turned her eyes on Alena. "D'ye think there's any hope for me, Lady?"

Alena smiled to herself, the image of a besotted Will fresh in her memory. "Oh, I think there's more than hope."

Hetty placed the brush on a chest near the bed. "I'll leave ye, now, to get some rest before supper."

As soon as the door closed, Alena dragged herself to the bed and collapsed into the soft pile of furs. She was exhausted, but didn't think she could sleep.

Edwina's words troubled her. *Grant soldiers surround the demesne… May they be damned to hell.*

Alena hadn't known about the soldiers at Findhorn. Over the years she had questioned her father about the Mackintoshes, but Robert Todd had given her only vague answers that held little information.

It must be terrible for Iain—his home overrun by her kinsmen. To her knowledge he'd done nothing to reclaim it. Was it any wonder? Reynold's army numbered near a thousand men. From what she knew, few Mackintosh warriors remained. She'd seen only a handful of Iain's clan here at Braedûn Lodge. Perhaps there were others in the north.

It dawned on her that Iain would be signing his own death warrant should he challenge Reynold Grant. Her stomach tightened, and she buried her face in the soft furs.

There was no use denying it. She loved him still. The truth of it raced hot through her veins.

She recalled Iain's first words to her that morning. *They're green. Your eyes.* He had seen her, held her, in her shift. The memory of his arm around her waist and his breath, hot on the back of her neck, lit tiny sparks at her very core.

She should tell him the truth.

About her, about Grant's threat to her family, and the wedding he planned that she could see no way out of. Oh, she longed to tell him. But 'twould only force him into the thick of her troubles. What would he do, then? Perhaps nothing. Why would he?

He'd broken his vow. He'd never returned.

Her insides twisted tighter. She meant naught to him. A childhood playmate, no more. He might not even remember her. After all, she had never once given him her true name.

Oh, but how he'd looked at her yesterday when he sponged the dirt and blood from her skin, his eyes full of tenderness and concern.

What if he did care?

Nay, she would not tell him. She would not risk his life on her behalf. For truth, what could he do? She must deal with Reynold Grant on her own. Tomorrow she would think on it.

Her mind drifted, and she burrowed deeper into the warmth of the furs.

Music. Nay, birds. Larks. Alena's eyelids fluttered, and she squinted against the sunlight breaching the window.

Hetty tied off the rolled deerskin drape. "Did ye sleep well, Lady?"

Judging by the intensity of the daylight, Alena knew 'twas well past dawn. "What's the time?" she said, and pulled herself from the bed.

"Ye've missed breakfast, but I saved ye some ale and a bit of cheese." Hetty nodded her head in the direction of the hearth, where a small tray sat atop a table.

"My thanks."

"Ye were sleepin' so soundly last night, like a babe. Edwina said not to wake ye. Iain—the laird, I mean—kept askin' to see ye, but Edwina wouldna allow it."

"Did he?" The butterflies in her stomach gave way to knots when it occurred to her that Iain might have found her out—who she was, and why she was running.

"Aye, he did, and he wasna happy when Edwina stood and blocked the door and wouldna let him enter."

So, the old woman was kinder than first impressions would have led her to believe. "Please tell Edwina I thank her for preserving my...privacy."

Hetty smiled, then opened a trunk at the foot of the bed and retrieved a gown of pale green wool. She laid it on the bed and turned to help Alena into it.

This was really all too much. She was not used to having someone dress and undress her. "Hetty, I really don't need you to fawn over me. I can dress myself."

The girl looked as if she'd been wounded. "Ye are not pleased with me, Lady?" Her doe eyes glassed.

"Oh, Hetty." She clasped the girl's hands in hers. "I'm very pleased with you. It's just that...well, I'm not used to so much attention."

Hetty's face brightened. "Oh, 'tis no trouble. I like doin' for ye. Edwina says I must take good care of ye or Iain— I mean the *laird*—will be angry."

"Will he?" A smile tugged at her mouth.

"Oh, aye. Ye should have seen him last eve, worried about ye like a mam frettin' over a bairn."

She felt herself flush and pulled the gown over her head to hide the evidence from Hetty.

"'Tis lovely on you."

Alena shrugged off the compliment. She'd never thought much about such things. Most of her days were spent in breeks and leather boots. "Whose gown is it?"

"It belonged to Lady Ellen, when she was young."

"Iain's mother? Do you think I should be wearing her clothes? Wouldn't Iain be angry?"

Hetty snatched the hairbrush from the table and pulled it through Alena's hair. "Oh, nay. Edwina says the laird would find it charming."

Charming? A question that had burned in her mind since her arrival, could no longer go unasked. "Wouldn't it be better if Lady Ellen's clothes were given to Iain's wife?" She held her breath and waited for Hetty's answer.

"Oh, nay, he's not married. He doesna even keep a mistress."

Her heart skipped a beat.

"Now, that Gilchrist—he's another story, if ye take my meaning." Hetty shot her a knowing look.

"Who is Gilchrist?"

"Gilchrist Mackintosh, Iain's younger brother. And a handsomer lad ye've ne'er seen. Except for my Will, of course."

Both of them jumped as a crash of timber sounded from the stable yard. All at once men were shouting over the angry snorts and distressed cries of a horse. Alena moved quickly to the window and looked out.

A black stallion rampaged through the yard, rearing in anger against a training tether pulled tight around his neck. Duncan, and a man who looked a younger version of him, were trying, without success, to calm the distressed beast.

She was shocked to see a lad of fourteen or fifteen lurking dangerously close to the rearing steed. Duncan waved him off but the lad would not give ground.

"Who is that boy, Hetty?"

"Saints preserve us! That's Conall Mackintosh, the laird's youngest brother."

The stallion reared again, and the boy inched closer. Without another thought Alena shot from the room, barefoot, raced down the staircase and burst outside. The black reared again. The boy ducked under the steed's hooves and tried to grab the bridle.

"Conall!" The voice was Iain's, but he was nowhere in sight. "Move away, lad!"

The boy ignored his brother's command. The stallion bucked as Duncan jerked on the tether. A crowd gathered around them, frightening the beast into greater frenzy. Conall moved in and reached for the bridle.

She knew the steed would rear.

"Boy, you're too close!" She shot forward and grabbed him. Conall stumbled backward, and they both tripped to the ground. For one heart-stopping moment she thought she'd been too late. The stallion crashed to earth, his powerful hooves landing inches from the boy's head.

There was no time. She could see in the stallion's eyes that he would rear again. She scrambled to her feet, unsheathed her dirk and cut the training tether. He was free. In a smooth motion that was second nature to her, she grasped the steed's mane and pulled herself onto his bare back. A split second later he lurched ahead.

There was only the one thing she did well, and this was it.

Without benefit of tether or bridle, she guided the black in a wide circuit around the stable yard. The tensed muscles of his neck relaxed as she stroked his sweat-drenched coat and whispered words of comfort into his ear. In seconds he'd calmed to her voice and touch.

Duncan scooped Conall from the dirt and bore him safely out of the way. She glanced briefly at the old man and shrugged.

"Weel, I'll be damned," he said, and stroked his silvered beard.

This was not how she'd intended to start her day.

She slowed the stallion to a walk. 'Twas then she noticed

Iain standing alone at the stable yard gate, the crowd parted around him. She had the distinct impression he was not happy with her actions.

His face flamed red as an autumn apple. His eyes were live coals. Even at ten paces she could see the tendons tightening in his neck.

Jesu, what would he have had her do? Stand by helpless? She met his gaze, and what she read there unnerved her far more than had the incident with the stallion. She was barely aware of Duncan helping her down from the horse and leading him away.

In three steps Iain covered the distance between them and stood glaring down at her, hands fisted at his sides. She forced herself to not move. He was so close she could feel his breath on her face.

Before she could say anything, he turned abruptly toward his brother Conall who leaned casually against the fence. Iain grabbed him by the collar and near dragged him toward the house. "Hamish! Will! To me. Now!" he bellowed.

The small crowd that had gathered burst into a cacophony of laughter and general chatter. Words of praise—and chastisement—were shouted in her direction. Aye, she supposed it was stupid of her. Both she and the boy could have been hurt.

Duncan, along with the other man who had helped him with the stallion, appeared at her side and led her to a bench by the water trough. She was more shook up than she'd first realized. She collapsed on the wooden seat.

"There, there, lass. Ye did a fine job." Duncan rested a hand paternally on her shoulder.

"The boy," she said. "Is he all right?"

"Conall? Dinna worry yourself about him. More than likely he's wishin' he was back under the black's hooves."

She frowned, and the other man laughed. "Aye," he said. "Iain's givin' him a thrashin' he'll no' soon forget."

"He wouldn't hurt him?" She'd never seen Iain so angry, yet she suspected a goodly portion of his wrath was reserved for her.

"Weel," Duncan said, fingering his beard, "Conall may no' sit much for the next day or two. But nay, lass, he wouldna truly hurt him."

"Aye," the younger man said. "He loves that boy like a son."

"When their da was killed," Duncan said, "'twas Iain who raised the lad, and the other, as well."

"Gilchrist, you mean."

"Aye. They're both fine, braw laddies. Thanks to Iain." The younger man knelt beside her. "Are ye all right? Can I draw ye some water from the well?"

"My thanks, but nay." His concern touched her. She pressed her hand lightly on his arm. "I'm well."

"More afeared o' the laird than that stallion, I'll wager." Duncan's voice was primed with amusement.

"Aye, you have that right."

"Och, dinna worry, lass. He'll come 'round. He's a stubborn one, and as much as I love him he can be dumb as a stone sometimes." Duncan shot her a meaningful look, but she had no idea what he was trying to tell her.

More than anything, she wanted to ask him how it was he knew her surname, but she preferred to wait until they were alone. She turned to the younger man. "My name is Alena."

"Aye, so I've heard. I'm called Gavin."

"Gavin," she repeated.

"My son." Duncan beamed a smile and slapped the young man on the back.

Before she could comment on the resemblance, Hamish

appeared, towering over them, a huge grin on his face. "Lady," he said, "I'm to escort ye back to the house."

Iain's instructions, no doubt. No matter. She was starved and had had enough excitement for one morning. Her conversation with Duncan would have to wait. It seemed whatever he knew about her, he had kept it to himself.

Or had he?

She recalled Iain's bloodred face.

She rose and accepted the warrior's arm. "Lead the way, Hamish. I'm so famished I could devour a horse."

He grinned down at her, blue eyes flashing mirth. "I thought ye just had."

Alena spent the afternoon exploring the Davidson stronghold and meeting the clanfolk who lived there. The incident with the stallion had spread like wildfire, and those she met eyed her with no small amount of suspicion.

Hamish never left her side—not for one moment. Iain's orders. She hadn't seen him since that morning and caught herself more than once wondering where he was and what he was doing.

Beyond the stable lay the archery butts and a large training ground where the clan's warriors honed their battle skills. These were Iain's own additions to the Davidson demesne, Hamish told her. The place was a bustle of activity that afternoon, and Hamish barred her entrance from the area.

He was probably there.

Just as well. After witnessing Iain's rage that morning, Alena wasn't sure she was ready for a chance meeting just yet. Besides, she had no desire to cut short her afternoon excursion.

In every place they walked, from the kitchens at the main lodge to the farrier's to the brew house, she spied odd stashes of weapons: broadswords, longbows with sheaves of arrows, double-headed axes, and dirks of every variety. Braedûn Lodge looked more like an armory than an estate. When she questioned Hamish about the weapons he just shrugged and said "'twas Iain's doing."

She recalled the arms Iain bore while hunting—two swords, a longbow, two dirks that she could see, and probably others that lay hidden on his person.

What did it all mean?

She knew not, but had a bad feeling about it. After exhausting Hamish with a bevy of questions he didn't answer, and when the sun dipped low in the sky, she returned to her chamber to ready herself for supper.

Hetty's attempt to coax her into donning a more lavish gown failed. The borrowed pale green wool suited her fine. 'Twas simple and reasonably comfortable, though tight about the bodice. She resisted Hetty's bid to coif her hair, and wore it loose about her, as always, a wild tumble of honey-gold cascading to her hips.

Raucous chatter rose from the great hall as she descended the staircase to join her hosts. Or jailers. She wasn't sure which to call them. Alena stopped near the bottom step and searched the crowd for familiar faces.

There were eight or ten tables filled with people, many of whom she had met that afternoon. Most were attired in the Davidson plaid. What few Mackintosh clansmen there were stood out among the rest.

The table closest to the hearth was raised on a dais, so the men seated there were visible to everyone in the room. Iain sat at the head, flanked by Conall on his left and another young man dressed in Mackintosh colors on his right. Hamish and Will sat farther down with a number of other warriors who sported the Davidson tartan.

Hamish smiled broadly at her while Will bore his usual,

puppy-dog expression. Only Iain scowled, and when Alena met his gaze she lifted her chin in provocation. Perhaps 'twas the gown that irritated him.

The young warrior seated to Iain's right stood and extended his hand. "Lady Alena," he called out, "will ye join us?"

He was nearly as tall as Iain, but not as well-muscled. He had Iain's strong features and the same stormy eyes, but the resemblance ended there. Iain was dark, with wild chestnut hair, and a brooding sort of expression. This man was blond, like her, and wore a dazzling, almost dangerous smile. He looked as if he could charm a lass right out of her shift. She was mildly shocked at her own bold appraisal of him. He could only be one man—Iain's brother, Gilchrist.

She made her way to the dais, took the young warrior's proffered hand, and a moment later found herself seated between him and Iain. A half dozen men offered their drinking horns. Not sure how to respond, she looked to Iain. Their eyes locked, but a sour expression ruled his face. He snatched his own goblet from the table and placed it in front of her.

"Thank you," she said, and lifted the ale cup to her lips.

The blond warrior turned to her and said, "I am Gilchrist, second son of Colum Mackintosh."

So, she'd been right. Hetty's description of him was accurate. "I am happy to meet you, Gilchrist," she said.

Across the table young Conall sat, transfixed, staring openly at her. His boyish good looks reminded her of the young Iain. A rush of tenderness overwhelmed her. She smiled at the lad and he nearly fell off the bench. Iain shot him a disgusted smirk.

"What's the matter, Conall, laddie, have ye ne'er seen a lady before?" Gilchrist said.

"Never one so fair, truth be told."

Iain snorted and muttered something under his breath Alena could not make out.

Gilchrist slid closer along the bench. "Nor have I." To her astonishment, he covered her hand, which rested lightly on the table, with his own.

Aye, Hetty was doubly right. This one was a rogue.

"Enough!" Iain smashed his fist onto the table, causing trenchers and goblets to jump. Like lightning, Gilchrist removed his hand from hers.

Delight shivered up her spine at Iain's overwrought response to his brother's harmless flirtation. She fought to maintain a serious expression, but felt the corners of her mouth edge upward. She dared not look at Iain, and turned instead toward the other end of the table.

Hamish rubbed a beefy paw over his face, trying without success to squelch his laughter. The other warriors at the table, Mackintosh and Davidson alike, seemed vastly amused by the little scene.

'Twas time to break the ice.

She turned and caught Iain staring at her. He instantly dropped his eyes and feigned a healthy interest in the trencher of venison that rested before him.

"Iain, I—"

"All save a few call me *Laird*—but I shall allow ye to call me Iain, if ye wish." He speared a hunk of meat with his dirk and raised it to his mouth.

Good God, he was arrogant. Mayhap the insufferable boy she remembered lived still inside the man.

"And you may call me Alena," she shot back.

He halted his attack on the venison in midbite and looked at her with a kind of surprise. He started to speak but then changed his mind, his mouth opening and closing a few times—much like a trout.

Now was clearly not a good time to provoke him. They ate in silence for a while, then she thought to try again at conversation. "Your uncle is laird here?"

"Aye," Iain said. "He is The Davidson."

"Yet you sit at the head of his table."

"In his absence I am responsible for his clan and his lands."

This surprised her. "Has he no son—or daughter," she couldn't help adding, "to lead in his stead?"

Iain looked directly at her. "Nay. Alistair and Margaret have no issue. When Gilchrist is of age, he will be laird here."

"But he is a Mackintosh. Surely the Davidsons will protest."

Iain smiled—more to himself than to her, as if remembering something. "Gilchrist is a Davidson *and* a Mackintosh. He was raised here and is well loved by my mother's clan. Nay, they will accept him. They already do."

He nodded toward Gilchrist who was engaged in telling some bawdy joke to the Davidson clansmen at the other end of the table.

"I see what you mean. And what of you, Iain Mackintosh? Where lies your future?"

For the second time in as many days his eyes reached into her soul. "Elsewhere," he breathed.

Jesu, but the man had a power over her she could not explain. In truth, he always had. She wet her lips as he held her in a gaze so intense, so *personal,* she felt both the strength and the will to break away slip from her.

The sounds of the diners faded from her perception as he leaned in close. His face hovered inches from hers. She tilted her chin toward him, her lips parting of their own accord in some dreamlike expectation.

A deafening *hurrah* shattered her momentary enchantment and she turned to see half a dozen clansmen on their feet, horns and goblets raised. They were toasting her, she realized, and quickly collected herself.

Her heart was still thrumming in her chest when Iain stood and let go her hand. Why, she hadn't even realized he'd been holding it!

From the other end of the room, Duncan related in a loud and very drunken voice how she had tamed the wild stallion and saved Conall from certain death. The old stablemaster embellished the facts to the point Alena was embarrassed. But the warriors echoed Duncan's pleasure, and she accepted their praise with as much grace as she could muster.

She glanced at Conall, who was fair beaming, and then at Hamish and Will, who lifted their ale cups to her. The room settled back into its normal state of chaos and she turned her attention to Iain, who promptly took his seat.

He fidgeted in his chair and would not look at her. Finally he said, "I didna thank ye, Lady, for saving my brother today."

She felt a tightening in her chest. Never once when they were children had he thanked her for anything. "'Twas nothing, Laird, I assure you. I am well skilled with horses."

"So 'twould seem. But ye must promise me you'll ne'er take such a fool's chance again."

"Truly, Iain, there was no danger to me."

His eyes clouded and she watched him swallow hard. He grasped her hand and squeezed it tight. Her heart was in her throat and, had she willed it, she couldn't have spoken a word at that moment to save her life.

"Ye...ye could have been killed." He squeezed her hand tighter, and she thought surely she would swoon from the tenderness in his eyes.

He *did* care. He did!

The realization was a bolt of white heat that shook her to the mettle. Her expression, she feared, betrayed her raw emotion, her desire, her love. All that she felt for him.

"Iain, I..." She leaned closer, then felt his hand slip away.

He drew back abruptly. His eyes, which only a moment ago brimmed with tenderness, grew cold. He fisted his hands and pressed them, white-knuckled, into the table.

A well-practiced scowl, the one she was beginning to think he reserved solely for her, etched his face. "Ye will no' go near that stallion again, d'ye understand? 'Tis a valuable animal."

It took a full second for his words to sink in.

"D'ye hear me, woman?"

Her anger rose faster than the galloping chestnut who'd thrown her into Iain Mackintosh's cursed path. "A valuable animal? Is that all you care—"

"Enough! I'll hear no more on it."

The hall went deadly quiet. All eyes were on the laird. Iain stood, shoved back his chair hard enough to send it sprawling, and stormed from the hall.

She sat there wondering what on earth had just happened. His disposition was more changeable than the weather! One minute he was concerned for her safety, and the next...

Her head spinning, she turned to Gilchrist and shot him a questioning look.

A stupefying grin bloomed on the young warrior's face. "I'll be damned. He's in love."

Chapter Five

'Twas time to find out just how much he knew.

At dawn Alena splashed some water on her face, quickly dressed, and went to the stable in search of Duncan. She found him repairing a bridle in one of the connecting buildings that housed the Davidson livery.

"Good morrow, Duncan," she said brightly.

The old man looked up and smiled. "Ah, Alena, lass. Ye're about early. Did ye sleep well?"

"Aye, I did. And you?" she asked mischievously, recalling his drunken state the previous evening.

"Weel, it's no' the lack o' sleep, but the bluidy headache the next day that can do an old man in."

She laughed at that, then turned her thoughts to more serious matters. "You are stablemaster here, Duncan?"

"I am," he said, his eyes on his work.

He'd worn the Mackintosh plaid the day they'd arrived at Braedûn, but today he was dressed in leather breeches and a russet shirt. She studied the clan badge pinned to his bonnet: a cat reared up on hind legs. "But you are a Mackintosh."

Duncan looked up from his work. "Aye, that, too." He

stared at her for a few moments, then said, "I came here with Lady Ellen and the lads—after Iain's da was killed."

"So you've known Iain since he was a boy."

Duncan sheathed his dirk and tossed the bridle over a post. He gestured to a stool next to the one on which he was perched. "Sit here, lass."

She obeyed and Duncan settled in, resting his leathered forearms on his thighs. "Ye see, Colum Mackintosh and I grew up together. My own da was stablemaster to his da. And when Colum and Ellen had those boys, weel, they were like my own sons."

"I see."

"And after...the trouble, the Davidsons took us in. I've been stablemaster here since. And I watch over the laddies," he added, smiling.

'Twas now or never. She leaned forward and met his gaze. "Duncan, when we arrived, what made you call me by that name? Alena...*Todd?*"

He chuckled. "Are ye tellin' me, lass, that ye are no' Alena Todd, Rob and Maddy's daughter?"

She nearly fell off the stool.

"You know my father? And my—"

"Aye, that I do. Rob and I raised trouble together before ye were e'en a twinklin' in his eye." Duncan laughed. His bright blue eyes seemed focused on things far away.

He continued in a soothing voice, as if he were telling a bedtime story to a child too anxious to sleep. "Back before ye were born, when the old lairds, the Mackintosh and the Grant, were allies, yer da and I traveled together in search o' breedin' stock. Och, we was green as sticks, but what a time we had. England, Spain, France..."

"France was where he met my mother!"

"Aye, and a bonnier lass there ne'er was—until now." He looked her over with a sort of paternal approval.

"Oh," she said, and felt her cheeks warm. "I'm afraid I was not blessed with my mother's fair looks. She is small and delicate, and I'm...well, I'm—" She shrugged her shoulders.

"Ye are like a sorrel filly in high summer. A beauty, ye are, and many a man's took notice." A mischievous grin creased his wrinkled face. "Some more than others, I'd say."

She felt her blush deepen, then remembered why she'd come. "But, Duncan, how did you know it was me? We've never met."

"Och, I used to see ye in the forest playin' with the lad."

Her eyes widened. "It was you! I *knew* someone was watching us."

"Aye, I was there." He grinned, but then his expression sobered. "D'ye think The Mackintosh would ha' let his son run wild about the wood wi' nary a soul to protect him?"

"Nay, I expect he wouldn't have." She'd never really considered that.

"And you. Do ye think yer da ne'er missed the fact ye were gone long hours from the Grant stable?"

"I did wonder how it was he never found out. I always thought 'twas because I was so clever."

"Clever?" Duncan laughed.

"But how did you recognize me? I was but a child when last I met Iain at the copse."

"Och, lass, who else could ye ha' been? There was only the one lassie who could vex Iain so."

She opened her mouth in wonder at this admission.

"One look at the both o' ye perched atop that stallion like a pair o' snarlin' wildcats, and I knew ye. And that wild mop o' gold atop yer head was another clue." He took her hand in both of his and squeezed it. "Aye," he said, warmth and affection shining from his eyes. "I knew ye, girl."

Alena wiped at her eyes, then stood and looked out a small window at the rising sun, a fireball in the east. Somewhere under its roving eye Glenmore Castle slept, and in it the man who would mold her future to his will.

"You won't tell Iain—about who I am?"

"He doesna know?" Duncan sat up straight.

"Nay."

The old man stroked his white-silver beard and looked hard at her. "Ye would keep the truth from him?"

"I...I plan to tell him, but not just yet," she lied.

"All know of how he saved ye from the Grant. And he's mad as a hornet that ye willna make plain what ye were about."

Alena knew this all too well. She recalled Iain's barely controlled anger at her refusal to explain her circumstances.

"Can ye tell me, lass?"

She paced the straw-strewn floor and wouldn't meet the stablemaster's eyes. "Nay. Nay, I cannot."

They were silent for a moment and Alena heard the warbling of a lark and the comforting clatter of the waking estate.

"Weel," Duncan said, drawing out the word. "I willna press ye—but I willna lie to the laird, neither. If he asks me, I'll tell him what I know."

"Oh, please—let me tell him. In my own way."

"And what of yer parents? They canna know ye're here?"

"Nay, they do not." Guilt and fear knotted her stomach. "They must be worried sick." She knelt before Duncan. "I must get word to them. Can you help me?"

The old man stroked his beard again, his eyes far away. "Weel," he began, and Alena knew he'd hatched a plan.

"There's a travelin' priest makes the Highland circuit amongst all the old Chattan clans. He's no' due here for more than a fortnight yet, but he'll pass through Davidson land on the forest road—tomorrow, methinks—headed north past Glenmore to Inverness."

"Father Ambrose! I know him!"

"Aye, he's the one."

"Can he be trusted?" she asked.

"Och, lassie, he's a priest." Duncan stood abruptly and Alena heard his bones creak. She rose and followed him to the door. "I'll send Gavin out on the morrow to meet him. Ambrose will get word to yer da that ye're safe and here with us."

Relief washed over her. Each night she prayed that they were safe, as well. "Thank you, Duncan."

They walked out into the stable yard and were bathed in sunlight. Alena shook off a chill and raised her face to its warmth.

"And now, lassie, perhaps ye can do something for me?"

"Aye, anything."

"Ye've a talent with horses—'tis plain to see. Rob taught ye well. We've a new group of Percherons to break before high summer." Duncan indicated the enclosure that lay at the end of the stable yard farthest from the lodge.

A small herd of horses grazed in the wild grass that grew, untrammeled, at the edges of the corral.

"Gavin's a good lad—does the work o' two men, but we could use another pair o' skilled hands." The stablemaster looked at her, gauging her ability, it seemed. "Are ye game, lass?"

"Oh, aye. I'd be pleased to help." And relieved to have something to occupy her hands whilst she considered her next move.

"Weel, then, ye willna be much use to me in that." He nodded at her attire, the too tight woolen gown. He then pointed at the stable lads newly arrived from their beds to work, still rubbing the sleep out of their eyes. "See if young Jamie or Fergus has a pair o' breeches that will accommodate ye."

She nodded. If she were here at the stable Duncan would be able to keep an eye on her. She smiled to herself. He and her father were two of a kind.

Iain adjusted the bracer on the youth's forearm, checked his shooting glove and finger stalls, and slapped him on the back. "Have at it, lad." The boy grunted as he drew the longbow slowly back. "More," Iain said. "Aye, that's it. Now sight along the shaft."

He stepped back and appraised the boy's form. The target, a standard English archery butt, was positioned thirty yards away.

"Shoot!" he ordered.

The boy loosed his arrow and with a whoosh it found its mark, piercing the haystack just left of the bull's-eye.

"Good lad! Now, do it again, and this time imagine the center of the target as if it were your enemy's heart."

Iain stepped back and scanned the training grounds. A half dozen Davidson youths honed their archery skills using the four butts that were positioned anywhere from thirty to fifty yards away. Iain moved into line with the farthest target.

Hamish approached from the direction of the house just as Iain was stringing his bow. He stopped and smiled at his huge friend. "What brings ye to the butts, Hamish? Are ye ready to take up a real man's weapon?"

"Nay, not I. I prefer a well-forged sword." Hamish reached over his shoulder and patted the hilt of the weapon sheathed across his back. He nodded at the boys who practiced in the yard. "How goes it with the lads?"

"Well, methinks. Another year and most of them would best any English yeoman." Iain smiled at his charges, then squinted at the sun, judging it near midday. "After their meal, would ye spend some time with them at swords—and double-headed axes, as well?"

"Ye drive them hard, Iain."

"Aye, but 'tis for their own good. Every clansman should be well skilled—and in all weapons. A warrior doesna always know what enemies lie in wait, nor what weapons will be at hand at the time." He met Hamish's eyes and read in them an unsentimental understanding.

"Your father, again."

"Aye." Iain dipped two fingers, well-callused from years of pulling a bowstring, into the grease pot tied to his belt, then pulled an arrow from his quiver.

"It wasna your fault, man."

"I had no weapon. I could have saved his life, but I had no weapon." He sighted down the arrow's shaft and imagined Reynold Grant's face at the center of the target. The arrow sliced the air with a whistle, piercing the target dead center, fifty yards away. "I was a fool."

"Ye were a lad, a boy of twelve. No match for a skilled warrior. Had ye a weapon, ye would likely not ha' lived to use it."

"Perhaps not. But we'll never know, will we?" He shot Hamish a hard look, pushed away the guilt gnawing at his gut, and drew another arrow from the quiver.

Hamish let it go. "So." He cocked a brow at Iain. "I see ye've every Davidson arrowsmith, fletcher, smithie and tinker in the land makin' weapons. What are your plans, Laird?"

Iain eyed him. 'Twasn't often Hamish addressed him as

"Laird." "As soon as Alistair returns, we'll make ready. I intend to spend next winter at Findhorn Castle."

"D'ye think he's convinced the others to join us?"

"The Macgillivrays for certain." Iain nocked his arrow and let it fly. "Damn!" It pierced the target right of center. "The MacBains, I know not. We must wait and see what news my uncle brings."

"So be it." Hamish looked at him hard, his generally merry expression now sober. "And the girl?"

"Alena. Aye, I know what you're thinking. Is she a Grant? And if not, could she still be in league with him somehow?"

Hamish nodded. "'Tis possible. Ye said yourself those who followed her were clearly Grant soldiers."

"Aye, they were. But..." Iain rubbed a hand over the stubble on his chin. "Nay, she isna one of them. She was running and she was afeared." He recalled the wild look in her eyes when first he saw her sprawled on the ground in the wood.

"She could be a spy. It wouldna be the first time a neighboring chieftain used a woman so." He paused then said, "They can be verra clever, Iain, at...well...*coaxing* a man into believin' their story."

Iain threw down the bow, unstrapped the quiver of arrows from his back and tossed it along with the grease pot onto a pile of equipment on the ground behind him.

"Nay, she's no' a spy." He'd be damned if she was. Irked by the very idea of it, he started for the house, then looked back. "Will ye mind the lads?"

"Aye, Laird." Hamish whistled at the group of boys who were stowing their gear, preparing to head to the house for the midday meal.

Iain wasn't hungry. His stomach roiled, in fact. He walked around to the back of the stable yard and saw Jamie, one of the stable lads, leading the roan into a meadow to graze. The horse was unsaddled, but Iain didn't care. He needed some time alone, to think, away from the bustle of the Davidson estate. Moments later he was mounted and making his way into the wood at the back of the house.

As he guided the roan through the trees, he considered Hamish's words. What if she *were* a spy? Nay, she couldn't be. He pushed the thought from his mind. What Grant spy would save young Conall's life?

The image of Alena clinging to the back of that wild black stallion flashed before Iain's eyes. His throat went dry. What the hell had she been thinking? By God, she was the most annoying woman. The way she dared speak to him—so impudent, so fiery.

So beautiful.

When he'd found her asleep by the loch, the moonlight casting a silver halo around her face, he'd wanted to gather her up and crush her against him.

His loins stirred with the memory of her firm body, light as a feather, as he'd carried her back to the campfire and laid her upon his plaid. He'd battled every instinct urging him to kiss her, compelling him to take her right then and there. God's truth, he didn't know what had stopped him. Except, mayhap—

Nay, he didn't truly care about her. What was she to him?

He fought the emotions welling inside him. She seemed so damned familiar. So *comfortable,* the way their bodies fit together atop his horse or rolled in his plaid before the fire. As if she were meant for him.

A branch slapped him in the face and he jerked the stallion away from the offending tree. He'd been riding in a stupor, like some besotted pup! Well, he'd think no more on it. He had work to do, plans to make, a war to wage.

A promise to keep.

He slipped his hand into the badgerskin sporran that hung at his waist and fingered the circlet of hair within. A *lovers' knot,* the girl had called it.

Aye, and keep it he would.

Nothing would stop him. Least of all some headstrong, fire-tongued wench. Beauty or no', he'd have none of her. And mayhap Hamish was right. Mayhap she *was* a spy.

An hour later, back at Braedûn Lodge, Iain jerked the roan to a halt and stared openmouthed at the sight before him. Alena rode bareback astride the black devil who just yesterday nearly cost his brother Conall his life.

She directed the steed 'round the training ring in a slow canter, her easy grace and fresh, unspoiled beauty disarming Iain completely. 'Twas as if the hour he spent in the wood clearing his head had never happened.

The black seemed to respond to her voice and the subtle commands of her every movement. Iain could feel his own growing response to her movements, as well.

She was dressed in a pair of worn leather breeches that outlined the curve of her hips and small waist, and a loose woolen shirt that did little to control or conceal the movement of her breasts as the stallion picked up speed. Her hair flew out behind her, wild and free, a waterfall of light tinged with amber and wheat.

She reined the black abruptly to a halt, her back to him, and leaned forward to praise her charge. Iain's gaze was riveted to her shapely breech-clad bottom.

Out of the corner of his eye he saw movement at the end of the yard. It seemed he was not the only spectator admiring Alena's skill with the black. Not to mention her other attributes.

He urged his mount forward. Will and Gilchrist perched

on the gate to the training yard, engaged by Alena's every move. A handful of Davidson clansmen leaned against the fence, equally captivated.

"Sons of—" He spurred the roan forward, driving the stallion directly toward the group of clansmen. At the last moment they scattered and Iain forced the roan against the gate, knocking Gilchrist and Will to the ground.

"What are ye gapin' at?" He turned to the clansmen. "Get back to your duties!" In an instant they were gone, dispersed in the direction of the house and courtyard.

Alena trotted up on the black as Iain maneuvered his mount through the gate and into the yard. Will and Gilchrist righted themselves and brushed clods of mud from their plaids.

"Gilchrist, did no' I ask ye to oversee the weapons inventory?"

"Aye, ye did." His brother's blue eyes flashed mischief.

"Well, be gone with ye, then!"

"Aye, Laird." The corners of Gilchrist's mouth turned up as he skulked away.

By God, what was he running here, a circus? Gilchrist's casual attitude was enough to make his blood boil. He turned to Will, who looked up at him expectantly. "You, as well."

"But, Laird, ye told me to mind her." Will nodded toward Alena, who was still mounted on the black.

"Aye, and now I'm tellin' ye to mind your other duties. Be gone! I'll watch her myself the rest of this day." And every day, he thought, casting Alena a sideways glance. Her cat-green eyes were appraising him. Damn her!

Edwina appeared at the gate. Lord, now what? Her eyes blazed and she pointed a wrinkled finger at Will. "I'll have a word with ye, lad, about young Hetty."

Will's face colored and he took a step back as the old woman approached him.

"And dinna pretend ye dinna ken what I mean." She grabbed Will by his shirt and pulled him from the stable yard in the direction of the house.

Alena laughed. 'Twas like the music of clear, running water. Aye, and that's what his head needed. A good, cold soaking. He turned to her and scowled. "What are ye laughing at?"

"At Will. He's smitten with her."

"With whom?"

"Why, the girl, Hetty, of course."

Iain snorted and the stallion fidgeted underneath him. "He's not. Will's a warrior. His mind is on his duty to his clan. And to me."

"A warrior he may be," she said, "but any fool can see he's in love with her."

Her green eyes flashed, and Iain felt his defenses crumbling. "And fool he is, should it be so."

She squared her shoulders and tipped her chin. By God, she was impertinent. And lovely. She turned the black and spurred him toward the stable. Before she could reach the entrance Iain cut her off and grabbed the stallion's bridle. Both horses nearly reared. She looked at him, expectantly, as if he were a wayward bairn about to explain some bit of mischief.

He bristled and set his jaw. "I wish to speak with you. Now." He'd find out the truth about her if he had to wring it out of her. He nodded toward the forest behind the stable yard. "Ye shall ride with me."

She tipped her chin higher. "As you see, I'm engaged with this animal." She turned the black out of his path and nudged him forward.

"Engaged with—" He jerked the bridle and prevented

her escape. 'Twas then he noticed Duncan leaning casually against the door frame of the stable entrance, smiling like an idiot.

Iain snorted. "Saint Sebastian to bluidy hell. Have it your own way, lass." He urged the roan forward and swept Alena onto his lap. "Aye, go ahead, fight me."

She struggled uselessly—he rather enjoyed it—then managed to position herself astride the horse. He goaded the stallion out the gate and toward the woods behind the house. After a minute Alena settled back against his chest, surrendering to his will. Hmph. 'Twas about time.

She was still now, her head resting just below his chin. He breathed deep of the fragrance of her hair, redolent with spring and summer and fall, and seasons yet unknown— but that he was intent on exploring.

God help him, he wanted her. She was like no other woman he'd ever known.

She was perfect.

Chapter Six

She was a shrew.

Iain didn't know whether to kiss her or to kill her. During their ride Alena had tried how many times—he'd lost count—to slip from his mount's back? Finally he'd snaked his arm tight about her, and had no intention of letting her go.

The roan labored up a steep hill and charged out of the forest onto a stark, windswept ridge. Iain urged the steed toward the top where the stone walls of an ancient keep lay, black and daunting, in ruin.

He loosened his grip on her and was astonished she didn't bolt from his arms. The woman was completely unpredictable. She rested calmly against his chest. The wind blew up golden tendrils of her hair that tickled his face. Lord, he felt good.

From this height they could view his uncle's entire demesne. Davidson land stretched out for miles in all directions. Braedûn Lodge was a tiny speck below them, beyond the forest through which they'd come.

"'Tis beautiful," Alena said, surprising him yet again.

He studied her face, a mere hairbreadth from his own. Her eyes, pale green in the full light, fixed on the horizon.

For the first time he noticed her lashes: dark at the roots and turning to pure gold at their tips.

"Aye, lass. Beautiful." He ran both hands lightly up her arms, and she shivered at his touch. "Are ye cold?"

"Nay." She turned and looked up at him.

At that moment he would have bartered his soul to the devil to be lost in her eyes forever.

God's truth, she bewitched him. And he knew not why. He wasn't the same man when he was near her. Hell, he hadn't been the same man since he'd found her. The truth of it unsettled him.

He swung a leg over the horse's rump and dropped to the ground. He reached for her, but something made him stop short of circling her waist with his hands. He looked up at her, willing her to fall into his arms.

Alena hesitated, trying to make sense of her conflicting emotions. She shouldn't be here alone with him. She could think of a dozen reasons why she should kick the roan into a gallop and flee, but all of them escaped her when she gazed into Iain's eyes. Jesu, he was everything she wanted.

The only thing she wanted.

'Twas so easy to lean from the saddle and slip into his arms. He caught her 'round the waist and, without another thought, she wrapped her arms around him, her fingers tangling in the chestnut hair at the nape of his neck.

He drew her into his embrace, his big hands sliding down to cup her bottom. She shouldn't let him hold her this way but, heaven help her, she thrilled at the feel of his hands on her. Her breasts were crushed against his chest and she felt his heart pound fierce as a drumbeat. She marveled at the heat of his body and the strength of his embrace.

What was happening to her? Her cheeks flamed and a rush of heat consumed her. Her mouth went dry. She parted her lips and wet them with her tongue.

And then he kissed her.

Once, twice. Oh, 'twas heavenly. His eyes held a question and in answer she breathed his name. "Iain."

She'd been kissed before, but never like this. His lips nibbled at hers, gently at first, teasing and tasting. His eyes narrowed to slits, the image of a wildcat plundering its prey.

The stubble of his beard raked across her skin as his lips moved to her neck. A shiver shot up her spine. She closed her eyes again, succumbing to the dreamlike state that threatened to consume her: pure heat and desire, the likes of which she'd never known.

Iain growled at her response and claimed her mouth again. His tongue slid along her lips, forcing them apart. She felt feverish, light-headed, as his tongue mated with hers.

She realized he was shaking, and perceived a barely controlled urgency growing within him. She clung to him and dug her nails into the front of his shirt. Wanton desire, fear and confusion all raged within her as she felt the evidence of Iain's own desire pressed hard against her body.

Her eyes flew open.

She pushed him away, breaking the kiss, but Iain held her fast in his embrace. His eyes smoldered passion, deep blue heat. His heart pounded against the flat of her palm.

"Nay, I cannot," she breathed. She struggled free of him and stumbled toward the burned-out ruins of the ancient keep. His footfalls sounded behind her. She scrambled to the pinnacle of blackened rubble and stood for a moment, her back to him, trying to catch her breath and make sense of her feelings. His hands lit on her shoulders. She collected herself as best she could and turned to face him.

"What is it, lass?" His voice was ragged and his face flushed from their kissing.

"It's... I..." She had no idea what she wanted to say to him. An impulse to tell him everything washed over her, but she beat it back and stood silent, looking up at him.

His face looked stricken, suddenly, as if she'd said something unexpected and unwelcome. "Are ye married, then? Is that what you're tryin' to tell me?"

She choked back a half laugh. "Nay. Of course not."

The tension drained from his face, then he frowned as if something else occurred to him. "Betrothed, then, to some great laird, mayhap?"

Reynold Grant's face flashed huge and vile before her, a burning imprint on the backs of her eyelids. Anger erupted inside her. She pushed the image from her mind. "Nay, I am betrothed to no man."

She read triumph in his eyes, and for some reason that made her bristle. Her anger at Grant and her fear of her own unbridled response to Iain's desire compelled her to lash out. "And if I were, t'would be none of your concern."

Iain's expression hardened. He caught her arms in a steely grip. "Ah, but t'would be verra much my concern. Can ye no' guess why?"

She felt his warm breath on her face and was conscious of her racing heart. "Nay, I cannot imagine." But she could imagine, and the truth of it both thrilled and frightened her.

She stepped back, shaking, and Iain released her. Before she knew what she was doing, she scrambled to the base of the ruins and pulled herself onto the stallion's back. Iain stood rigid atop the pile of rubble, fists clenched at his sides, his gaze burning into her. Without a word she spurred his mount down the hill and into the forest.

Reynold Grant slammed a fist on the table. The impact of flesh on wood echoed off the stone walls of Glenmore

Castle's great hall. "Where is she? I want her found and brought to me! Is that clear?"

Perkins stood before him with a senior soldier and two others. They all disgusted him. Useless idiots. He could have retrieved the girl himself by now.

The senior soldier spoke. "'Twas a Mackintosh who carried her off, Laird."

Reynold drummed his fingers on the table. "You're certain?"

"Aye," Perkins said. "We followed them far to the southeast, to Davidson land."

Reynold considered the implications. "Alistair Davidson. Hmph." He pushed back his chair and rose from the table. "'Tis his uncle."

Perkins smiled, but the soldiers raised their brows and exchanged confused looks. "Whose uncle, Laird?" the senior soldier asked.

"*His* uncle, ye twit! Alistair Davidson is *Iain Mackintosh*'s uncle."

The name sparked immediate recognition among them. The senior soldier half grinned. "The Mackintosh laird would dare to travel alone across Grant land?"

Reynold glared at each of them in turn. His nails dug into his palms as his fists tightened around the imaginary neck of his enemy. "He was on my land, and I didna know it?" His barely controlled rage showed in the fearful expressions of the men who stood before him. "And where were all of you when this insult occurred?"

The soldiers fidgeted and would not meet his eyes. Perkins stood smirking and silent. Reynold fought the urge to smash his ugly little face into the table.

He strode to the massive hearth and leaned against the cool stones, staring into the fire as if it held the answers to his questions.

He'd get her back, but how? 'Twould be premature to raise his army and take her. Nay, he wanted it all: Findhorn Castle, the Mackintosh lands, and Alena of Angoulême.

He'd hoped to wed her first, before waging war against Mackintosh. The alliance with France would be useful. And the tie to England.

Nay, he'd wait. He wouldn't risk the possibility Mackintosh would raise the Chattan against him. He'd find a way to draw her out. In the meantime, he'd drive the wedge between the clans deeper. MacBain. Aye, he was the one to sway.

Reynold turned toward his men. "Perkins, I want ye to arrange a meeting—quietly—with the MacBains."

A thin smile creased Perkins's mustached lips. "Aye, Laird. Leave it to me."

"And the rest of you—" Reynold eyed the soldiers. "What news from our scouts?"

The senior soldier's face brightened. "The Davidson laird and his wife have crossed to Macgillivray land."

Now this was interesting news. "And their escort?"

"Only twenty of their own. But they ride under the protection of The Macgillivray."

Perkins interrupted. "Aye, but on his return Alistair Davidson must first travel east 'round the mountains bordering *our* land before riding north to Braedûn Lodge."

Reynold knew there was a reason he put up with Perkins's insolence. The man was clever. T'would be of great benefit to have the Davidson laird out of the picture.

Reynold waved a hand. "Leave me. I must think." He slumped into a chair by the hearth and stretched his legs toward the fire. Behind him he heard the retreating footsteps of his men.

He cleared his mind and recalled the lovely skin and wide green eyes of Alena Todd. Stablemaster's daughter indeed. "Ha!" The bitch was bred of nobles and kin to royalty. And soon she would be his.

His eyes clouded. 'Twas Mackintosh who had her now. A sour taste coated his mouth. The sooner Iain Mackintosh joined his father in hell, the better. Reynold ground his teeth and gripped the velvet-covered arms of the chair.

"Nay, Iain Mackintosh, ye won't be keeping her long."

The hare blinked, transfixed, from a thicket of whortle-berry and gorse.

Iain reached instinctively for his bow. It wasn't there. "Damn the woman!" He kicked up some stones in the direction of the hare and swore again under his breath.

He'd been walking an hour and guessed it to be another league or more to his uncle's estate. He quickened his pace, scanning the forest in all directions.

She'd had the audacity to commandeer his mount. And he let her do it! "Fool, idiot!"

He checked his weapons for the tenth time: broadsword, two dirks, and the small *sgian dhu* in his boot. 'Twas enough. The roan stallion had carried his longbow, another sword and a dirk. And where was his mount now?

Where was *she* now? On her way back to retrieve him, ready to offer sweet, apologetic kisses? His loins stirred at the memory of her lips, full and swollen—autumn apples ripe for the picking.

"Och!" He beat the image from his mind. More likely she was halfway back to Glenmore Castle bearing news of all she'd seen and heard. Hamish was probably right. Even now the vixen could be meeting with her Grant lover, reporting Iain's every move, tallies of his weapons, the status of his men.

He stopped and breathed a sigh, studying for a moment

the brilliant blue of the sky through the trees. "Nay, she's no' a spy." And there is no lover. Of that he was sure.

She was a maid. God's truth, her kisses were those of an innocent, but her passion... He sighed again. Her response to him had been immediate, wanton. And he'd been dangerously out of control. No matter who she was, he couldn't allow that to happen again.

Who *was* she?

He was so smitten with her he'd completely forgotten the purpose of seeking her out that day. He'd meant to question her again about her identity, her clan. Those intentions had vanished the moment he looked into her eyes.

Above all, he must stay focused. He had plans to make, promises to keep.

He leaned against a stout larch and let his gaze wander up the wrinkled bark. Pressing his face against its rough texture, he was reminded of another tree in another forest far from here, its surface riddled with scars from the hundreds of arrows he and the girl had shot into it during those long afternoons.

The girl.

He smiled to himself and dipped a hand into his sporran, drawing out the lovers' knot the wee lass had given him long years ago. He ran his fingers over the fine texture of the braid—chestnut and gold, the Mackintosh tartan still bright after years of abuse tumbling about in the badgerskin bag.

He'd vowed to return for her, and return he would.

A child's promise, but a promise nonetheless. And who was *she?* It occurred to him he didn't know *her* name, either. Iain laughed. God's blood, how many mystery women could one man abide? No matter. He'd find her. And the dagger.

A flurry of memory and emotion swept over him. He

thrust the token back into his sporran as the sound of crashing brush startled him to attention.

What now? He reached instinctively for the hilt of his sword, but stayed his hand when he recognized the three riders climbing through the wood. Hamish and two Davidson warriors.

One of them led a fourth mount—the roan stallion, its saddle empty.

Chapter Seven

Iain's heart skipped a beat. He charged down the slope and met the riders halfway, skidding to a halt in front of Hamish's great warhorse. He nodded at the roan's empty saddle.

"Where is she?"

Hamish grinned, to Iain's annoyance, then cocked a bushy red brow. "At the stable. Where else?"

He closed his eyes for a moment and exhaled. "Ye found her then, and brought her back."

"Nay. She came chargin' out o' the wood at a full gallop and drove your mount clear over the wall at the back o' the house, right into the stable yard."

"I'll be damned."

Hamish's eyes lit up. "Och, 'twas quite a sight, too— her wild hair flyin' and those bonny cheeks flushed red as ripe cherries."

A vision of Alena atop the roan throbbed in Iain's head. He stared vacantly into the wood.

The two Davidson warriors made lewd comments.

"Enough." Iain shot them a hard look, and their faces sobered.

He whistled and his mount trotted forward. Vaulting onto

the stallion's back, he turned toward home. "Let's away. The day's nearly gone."

Hamish followed and raised a brow in question. "Well, Iain, what think ye of her now?"

"God's truth, Hamish, I dinna know what to make of her."

"Nor I. But this is how I see it..." Hamish stroked his beard and leveled his gaze at him. "The lass had a fair chance to run, but she didna."

"Nay, she did not. But why?" A number of possibilities occurred to him. He gave the roan a light kick and the horse quickened his pace.

A burst of laughter broke his concentration. He turned to see Hamish grinning, exchanging knowing looks with the two warriors. He glared hard at the three of them.

"Hell, man," Hamish said, "why don't ye swive her and have done with it?"

Every muscle in Iain's body tensed. He bit back a retort, surprised by his own anger. Hamish read it in his eyes and immediately softened his expression. The two Davidson warriors sensed it, too, and moved on, leaving them alone.

Iain met Hamish's bright eyes. Eyes that had seen the years of Iain's struggle to rebuild their clan, eyes that had witnessed his pain and unrelenting guilt over his father's murder, eyes that held a wealth of understanding.

The tension drained from his body. He smiled weakly at his friend and shrugged.

"Aye, well," Hamish said quietly. "So that's how it is between ye."

He recalled the silken heat of Alena's skin against his mouth, her cat-green eyes clouded with desire—and something more.

For him there was also something more, something beyond a need of the flesh. Aye, he wanted her, and badly.

But the ache in his gut told him that one lusty romp 'neath the furs wouldn't quench the fire that burned within him, that burned for her.

"Aye," he breathed. "That's how it is."

He nudged his mount forward again, and this time Hamish didn't follow.

The mystery that was Alena continued to gnaw at him.

What more could there possibly be between them? Since his father's murder, he'd lived his whole life in preparation for the bloody vengeance he would wreak against the Grants—one Grant in particular. There wasn't room in his life for a woman. There never had been.

Oh, he'd had his share of youthful tumbles with willing wenches, but none had left any lasting impression on him, none had made him feel as she had. He shook off the muddle of emotions that threatened to consume him.

His clan had been scattered to high heaven, but he was still their laird. His people depended on him to regain their homeland, their honor. And he would, or go to his death trying.

Braedûn Lodge was in sight, and he spurred the roan homeward. 'Twas time to act.

Alena supped in her room that eve, ignoring Hetty's and Edwina's attempts to coax her belowstairs. She feigned exhaustion from the day's activity and bade the women offer her apologies to those assembled in the great hall.

Truth be told, she needed time alone.

Iain's kisses had left their burning imprint on her lips and in her heart. She was heady with the memory of his embrace, the clean, masculine scent of him, his powerful hands blazing a trail across her body as if she were some new uncharted land.

She whispered his name and ran her fingers lightly over

her lips, across the line of her jaw and downward, tracing the path his mouth had blazed across her virgin skin.

No man had ever roused such feelings in her.

She was not surprised at her response to him. From the moment she'd seen him looming over her in the forest, his penetrating eyes reaching right into her soul, Alena knew he was the one.

She slept poorly that night and woke just after dawn. The bed coverings were bunched at her feet, and her shift clung damp and twisted to her body.

She had dreamed of a wide green glen bursting with wildflowers. She was there, riding the black at a full gallop, the wind whipping her hair behind her. Iain appeared, long-bow in hand. She thrilled at the sight of him, but there was something in his expression that unnerved her. Fear. He looked past her, but at what she knew not.

She shrugged off the last vestiges of sleep and cast the unsettling remnants of the dream from her mind. She rose, dressed quickly in her work clothes, and made her way to the stable yard, eager to begin the training of the new Percherons.

Duncan met her at the gate. "Good morrow, lass. Are ye ready to begin?"

"Aye, 'tis a fine day for it." They paused for a moment and studied the cloudless sky.

She noticed Gavin leading a mare, heavy with foal, toward one of the small outbuildings, and nodded her head toward the pair. "How soon is her time?"

"A sennight—perhaps less. Come, I'd like ye to see her."

She followed the old stablemaster into the structure. 'Twas larger than it looked on the outside and had been set up as a foaling shed. The floor was covered in sweet-smelling straw. A small hayloft overlooked one corner.

Gavin tethered the mare. "What think ye, Alena, of our prize broodmare?"

She ran her hand over the animal's lustrous coat and down each flank. The mare nuzzled her hand and she smiled. "A Scottish Clydesdale. She's very fine."

"Aye," Gavin said. "One of our own."

"And who is the sire?"

"The black," Duncan said, and grinned as if he were the proud papa himself.

"The Arabian." Alena's interest grew. "'Twill be a beautiful foal."

"Aye, but I expect a difficult birth. This is her second issue and the first near killed her in the bearin'."

"Whose mount is she?"

"Young Conall's," Gavin said. "A gift from his mam."

Ellen Mackintosh had died recently. 'Twould be a tragedy for Iain's brother to lose the mare, too.

She studied the Clydesdale's swollen belly. "Then why did you breed her again?"

Gavin fought a smile. She lifted her brows in question.

"Weel, 'tis the black," Duncan said. "We couldna keep him from her. When her time came, he all but leveled the stable to get to her. I've ne'er seen the like of it—at least no' with horses." His eyes sparked mischief.

A blush warmed her cheeks. She snatched a handful straw from the ground to hide her embarrassment. "I can do this." Gavin stepped back as she went to work on the mare's coat. "I'm sure you have others to see to."

"Not today. Half the mounts are gone—with the laird."

"Iain is gone?" She tried to sound casual, but knew by Duncan's interested expression she hadn't succeeded.

"Oh, aye," Gavin said. "To Inverness with Hamish and some others."

Inverness was at least two days' ride from Braedûn

Lodge. A small ache settled in the pit of her stomach. "When shall they return?"

Duncan started to speak, but Gavin cut him off. "A sennight, mayhap. There's only so much drinkin' and wenchin' a man can take, aye?"

"Drinking and...?" The ache deepened.

Duncan frowned hard at his son. "Be off with ye, lad. Take young Jamie and Fergus and round up the new group. We'll follow directly."

Gavin shrugged, cast his father a sheepish look and left.

Purposefully, she turned her attention back to the mare and continued her grooming with increased rigor. Duncan reached out and stilled her hand, but she would not meet his eyes.

"Dinna fash about it, lass," he said gently. "Aye, he might have gone to Inverness with the others, but what Gavin said—about the wenchin' and the drinkin'—'tis not his way." She smiled weakly at the old man, and he squeezed her hand in his gnarled paw. "Come, we've got mounts to break."

She tossed the straw to the ground and followed Duncan from the shed. A sudden thought made her stop short. "Duncan? Did Gavin meet Father Ambrose? Was he able to get word to my parents?"

"Oh, aye. He met the priest near dark, yester eve, on the forest road. 'Tis done."

Relief and tenderness welled inside her. "Bless you."

From dawn until nightfall each day Alena worked in the stable and collapsed each evening, exhausted, on her bed. Between the three of them they'd made excellent progress with the new mounts.

Iain had left his brother Gilchrist in charge of the estate. Most of the other Mackintosh clansmen had ridden with

Iain, save his youngest brother, Conall, and Will, who kept a constant watch on her.

She had supped with the three young warriors twice now, and on both occasions they'd talked of nothing but Iain—his bravery and skill with a bow, both clans' respect and loyalty for him, and his fierce love of his people, Mackintosh and Davidson alike.

She'd pressed them to tell her more of Iain's relationships with the neighboring clans, but they always managed to steer the conversation away from that topic. Once she'd even mentioned the Grants by name, and Will and Gilchrist had both gone quiet. Only young Conall spoke, but was quickly silenced by a harsh look from his older brother.

Her days were filled with activity, but the nights seemed endless and offered her little distraction from her thoughts. Her parents' safety, her clan, her future—all weighed heavy on her. But foremost in her mind was Iain. She tossed and turned in the ornate bed, unable to clear his visage from her mind.

In whose bed was *he* now?

She rebuked herself for allowing the question to cross her mind. Why should she care? He obviously cared nothing for her. She was naught but an outlet for his lust. Had she not escaped him at the ruined keep—

Her heart fluttered at the thought of what might have occurred.

She rose from her bed and padded barefoot to the window. Pulling back the fur covering, she gazed out at the night sky. A thousand stars blinked back at her, cool and luminous against a field of midnight.

Where was Iain now?

Wenchin' and drinkin'.

Days later, Gavin's words still stung. She snatched the fur window cover and ripped it from the wall. Iain was merely a man, base and crude. The moment she'd refused him he'd gone in search of another woman. Or women. The thought sickened her and fed her anger, both at him and at herself for acting the smitten virgin.

Gooseflesh rose on her skin as a chill wind blasted through the window. She hurried back to bed and dove, shivering, beneath a pile of plaids and furs.

She would leave this place and return to her parents, her clan. They needed her, they loved her.

And then there was Reynold Grant.

Alena crouched in the stable yard, one of the black stallion's great hooves perched upon her knee. With an iron tool she cleaned and shaped his rough nail. The steed snorted, but allowed her ministrations.

Duncan encouraged her partnership with the horse. She was, in fact, the only person the stallion would permit to ride him. Alena dug inside the pocket of her breeches for the bit of raw cabbage she'd scrounged from the kitchen that morning, and fed it to her happy charge.

On their way into the stalls the black became suddenly agitated. She held fast to the bridle and whispered soothing words in his ear as the clatter of livery and the thud of hoofbeats drew her eyes toward the stable yard gate.

A group of Mackintosh warriors, grim-faced and spattered with mud, herded their mounts past the house and into the enclosure. Iain led the pack. Hamish followed with a number of others she recognized.

She stiffened her spine and tipped her chin as Iain rode past her. Prepared for some curt greeting, she was stunned when he rode on, silent, purposefully not looking at her, merely scowling in her direction.

"Hmph." She turned on her heel and headed for one of

the outbuildings, pulling the black in her wake. Hamish's soft chuckle sounded behind her. She bristled.

Once inside she watched Iain from the window. He dismounted, tossed his reins to Gavin, and headed for the watering trough. He turned briefly in her direction. She ducked out of sight.

A moment later she peeked over the window frame. Iain stood with his back to her, stripped of his shirt, his plaid bunched at his waist, and vigorously washed the mud and road dust from his body.

Her gaze fixed on the sinewy muscles of his back and shoulders working beneath his skin as he splashed water over his torso. ''Jesu,'' she breathed, and willed herself to look away.

She busied herself in the shed, rearranging brushes and tools, and by the time she stole another glance from the window he was gone.

He stayed clear of her the rest of that day and the next. In the great hall both evenings she was offered not her customary place to Iain's right, but a seat at the opposite end of the table, wedged in between two Davidson warriors.

'Twas fine with her, if that's the way he wished it. She had more important things to think about. Escaping the Davidson stronghold was the most pressing, and not easily accomplished. Midsummer's Day loomed close.

Hamish had been absent the previous evening, but tonight he appeared and boasted loudly from across the table of his kinsmen's exploits in Inverness. Alena caught herself listening for Iain's name in the recounting of these bawdy adventures, but 'twas never mentioned.

On several occasions she looked up from her trencher to find Iain appraising her coldly, his mouth rigid, his eyes blue steel.

Her sentiments exactly.

She excused herself early to check on the pregnant mare before retiring to her chamber. The Clydesdale's time was near, and she had promised Duncan she'd assist with the delivery.

After that, she'd find a way to leave Braedûn Lodge.

Late that night the door to her chamber crashed open.

Alena bolted upright, plaids and furs flying. She scrambled to the edge of the bed and reached for her dirk, which hung in its sheath from the bedpost.

A small, hunched figure holding a lit taper moved quickly toward the bed. Alena let her breath out as she recognized the old clanswoman, clothed in her shift, a Mackintosh plaid draped around her shoulders. "Edwina, what's amiss?"

The old woman's withered face shone in the candlelight. Her eyebrows peaked as a grin broke across her face. "'Tis time, lass. The foal is coming."

Chapter Eight

There was no time to dress.

Iain hefted his broadsword and charged out the door of his chamber, stark-naked, clutching his plaid. He'd heard the commotion and now saw the torchlight at the end of the hall. In three strides he was there, brandishing the sword before him.

The two figures froze. The taller whirled on him, and Iain saw a flash of steel as a small dirk whistled from its scabbard. He dropped the plaid and wielded his sword with both hands.

And then he recognized her.

Alena's eyes widened. She opened her mouth as if to speak but no words came forth. For a moment they stood there, unyielding, gazes locked, weapons at the ready.

He surveyed her garments: breeches, boots and a loose woolen shirt. Her hair was swept up, coiled close to her head. 'Twas small wonder he didn't recognize her.

Her face blazed scarlet, and he suddenly remembered he was unclothed. He snatched his plaid from the floor and wrapped it awkwardly around his waist.

A cackle of laughter burst from the second figure. The

hunched shape could be only one woman. Edwina. Iain scowled at her in the half light.

Alena sheathed her dirk and turned away.

"No' so fast." He stepped in front of her. "Where are ye off to, dressed like that, at this time o' night?"

Her cheeks were still flushed and a few tendrils of loose hair spilled over the collar of her shirt, glinting gold in the torchlight. God's truth, she was lovely.

Her eyes darted back and forth as if she didn't know where to look, then finally lit on his. She tipped her chin and pursed her lips in that defiant pose he found amusing. "Duncan needs me. The mare is foaling." She brushed past him.

He stood there for a moment and watched the light dance off the walls as the two women descended the staircase. Ten minutes later he was dressed and at her side in the foaling shed.

Duncan handed her a bundle of rags, and Alena set them on the straw-covered ground. The mare lay heaving on her side. Iain watched as she soothed the laboring beast with comforting words and gentle strokes. Oh, that he were the beneficiary of such consolation. He marveled at the mare's tranquil response to her calming touch.

Crouched beside the horse's great belly, she elbowed Iain out of the way as she moved toward the mare's head. He sat back on his heels and watched her, silent.

"You're not needed here," she said, not looking up from her work. "Duncan and I can manage."

How dare she speak to him so? He was laird and she was, well... He was more determined than ever to find out. He looked at Duncan who leaned against a post, arms crossed, one brow arched in amusement.

Not needed? Iain grabbed the bundle of rags and inched

closer to Alena. "'Tis no' a job for a lady." Surely she'd agree and defer to him.

To his astonishment her eyes flashed fire. "Ha!" She looked as if at any moment she'd spit venom. "'Tis the job you leave us. Men spawning like trout wherever they please, and women left to bear their wee-uns and clean up the mess after."

What had come over her? He shot Duncan a questioning look, but the stablemaster just shrugged in response.

She checked the mare's eyes and ran her fingers gently along the inside edge of the horse's mouth. "And besides, I've assisted dozens of births. Some of the finest warhorses in Scotland were issued from my stable."

Iain could well believe it. The woman had spirit, he'd grant her that. "Oh, aye," he said, "and what stable might that be?"

She shot him a nasty look and continued her evaluation of the mare.

He watched her, marveling at her quiet command of the situation. She moved with an economy of motion around the mare, poking and prodding, gently massaging, her small hands seeking and discovering clues to the horse's condition.

Duncan held back and allowed her to do what she would, appraising her skill as a master would an apprentice.

Iain studied her, as well, but for different reasons. He'd foresworn this mad attraction to her the afternoon at the ruins and had quit Braedûn Lodge that night to strengthen his resolve. But five days away from her and two more avoiding her did naught to cool his ardor.

Her face haunted him by day, and by night his dreams were rich with the feel of her firm body 'neath his hands, the scent of her hair, the taste of her warm skin.

He knew in his heart he couldn't give her up. "Damn."

She glanced up and caught him watching her.

Even now he felt the last of the thin barrier he'd tried to erect between them shatter and fall away. As he watched her movements—slow, deliberate, with a patience and single-mindedness that awed him—he felt his heart moving toward her in a way he couldn't explain.

And he knew she shared his affliction. Her passionate response when he'd kissed her had laid bare her desire. But he'd seen more in her eyes, felt more in her innocent kisses, than physical hunger.

They were connected, somehow, he and she.

He knew it. He felt it, and knew she did, as well.

She sat back on her heels and rolled up her sleeves. He drank in the beauty of her slender forearms, golden in the torchlight, finely muscled, tapering to slim wrists. He longed to take her hands in his and press his lips to the undersides of those wrists, to feel her pulse throb gently against his mouth.

She reached past him toward a bucket of water and inadvertently brushed his arm with hers. He tensed and felt her do the same.

"Lady," he said, placing his hand gently on her shoulder. She drew back, rigid, and flashed tentative eyes at him. "Let me." He picked up the bucket and set it down beside her.

"My thanks. I—"

The mare shuddered, and Alena quickly focused her attention on the panting beast whose breathing had become more labored. She sprang to her feet, skirted around him and knelt beside the mare's rear legs. In a move that surprised him, she placed one hand soothingly on the mare's rump and with the other gauged her condition.

'Twas fair strange how she didn't look at the mare, but stared unfocused at the wall and seemed to know by touch what was occurring. He looked to Duncan who stood smiling down at her as would a proud father regarding his child.

"'Tis time," she said.

Duncan knelt beside her. He examined the laboring horse and the opaque sac that pressed outward from the birth canal. "Aye."

The mare let out a shrill whicker and bucked her rear legs, toppling Alena to the ground. Iain rushed to help her but she fought against his grasp. The pins that held her hair tight against her head loosened, and her wild tresses tumbled free.

"Unhand me!" She scrambled to her knees and shot him a surly look.

What had he done, he wondered, to elicit such a response from her? He sat back on his heels and considered her nasty disposition. One moment she'd been panting in his arms, and now this unfathomable coldness.

He hadn't much experience with women, beyond the bedding of willing wenches when his need distracted him from his work. He'd put off taking a wife, though his uncle had paraded by him every eligible virgin from a half dozen clans. Any of them would have made a good political match, and most were lovely, but he'd always held back.

He'd vowed first to regain his life, his honor, his home. Aye, and he'd made another vow. One born in a wood by a stream in the mist, eleven years ago. He looked with longing at Alena and found himself questioning the price of that pledge.

The mare bucked again, and Alena caught his eye. "Place your hands here," she said, and put her hands on the horse's flank. "Try to keep her still."

He did as she bade him, and she examined the mare in earnest. Duncan lifted a torch from its sconce on the wall and knelt beside her, offering her more light.

Iain watched as she pushed her sleeves higher and assessed the situation. The mare shuddered again, and he tried to soothe her with steady hands.

Alena worked by touch. At last she met his eyes and, to his surprise, she didn't look away. He held her gaze and felt the corners of his mouth bloom in a smile. She smiled back and his heart beat faster.

The mare shuddered and Alena's expression sobered. The beast's breathing became labored, deep. "'Tis time."

Alena pulled gently at the saclike bubble, tearing it enough to reveal one slick, black hoof. Iain realized with a shock that what protruded was a rear foot.

"The foal—'tis the wrong way 'round!" Her eyes sought Duncan's and the stablemaster looked at her, grim-faced.

"'Tis what I'd feared," Duncan said. "'Twas the same with her last issue."

"Wh-what did you do?"

Duncan shrugged and looked way. "We didna have a choice. We had to save the mare." He rose stiffly, plucked a few tools from a nearby table and returned to Alena's side. Iain recognized the implements. Beside her Duncan laid two knives, one of them curved, and a small iron hook.

Her face blanched. "N-nay, you will not."

Duncan lowered his eyes.

"It must be done, lass," Iain whispered. "Duncan's right."

She stared blindly at the wall of the shed, then he saw a change come over her. She drew a breath and met his gaze. "Nay. The foal will turn. I will turn it." She shot Duncan a confident glance. "I've done it many times. 'Twill be all right."

Iain studied her face. Tiny beads of perspiration broke across her forehead. She clenched her teeth and with one hand swept the evil-looking tools aside.

Before either of them could respond, young Jamie came bursting through the door to the shed. "I saw the light. Is it come?"

"No' yet, lad," Duncan said.

Alena turned to the boy. "Jamie, I'll need a long leather strap. Go and cut one from a bridle. And some thin rope. Mayhap a bowstring would do."

Jamie looked at the stablemaster, and Duncan nodded his agreement. "Aye, Lady," the boy said, and turned to leave.

"Wait, lad." Iain rummaged in his sporran and drew out a long bowstring, one of two spares he kept at all times. "Here," he said, and offered it to Alena.

She smiled. "My thanks."

Iain watched her as she moved quickly, piling more fresh straw and assembling the things she would need. During the next hour she worked to turn the foal.

Her face, slicked with perspiration, shimmered in the torchlight. The loose shirt clung to her damp body, outlining the swell of her breasts and the curve of her small waist. Iain was more than distracted by her. He was aroused, and fought to focus his attention on the mare.

The Clydesdale's breathing grew rapid and shallow. Duncan moved quickly to examine her. "'Tis too late, lass—we're losin' her."

"Nay! We're not." One arm sheathed to her shoulder, Alena worked to turn the foal, grunting with the effort. Then she eased back and withdrew her arm from the mare's body.

For a moment all was still. Iain offered up a silent prayer.

To his astonishment, the mare suddenly convulsed and one slender foreleg shot from her body. Another followed. The mare pushed again, and Iain recognized a wet black nose. The foal's head emerged, and Duncan laughed in relief.

Alena crouched closer and positioned her arms under the awkward bundle. The mare strained. One final push and the new babe slid into the world.

''I'll be damned,'' Iain said.

Collapsing backward on the straw-covered floor, Alena cradled the slick black bundle in her lap. The air was thick with the smell of new life.

The foal thrashed and struggled, kicking its spindly legs in an effort to stand. As Alena opened her arms the foal sprang to its feet and wobbled, quivering, toward its mother.

Iain had witnessed many births in the stable, but never one that moved him as this one did. 'Twas *her* that moved him. Her strength, that iron will, and a quiet confidence she didn't realize she possessed.

The mare scrambled to her feet and emitted a low rumbling nicker, announcing to the world the birth of her son. She licked dry her babe's wet coat. The foal nudged his head against the mare's belly and soon after Iain heard the gentle suckling sounds of the newborn at his mother's teat.

Alena's trembling hand caught his forearm, and he sucked in a breath. She turned to look up at him. As he met her gaze a dazzling smile broke across her face. He drank her in and felt a tightening in his chest. Nothing in his experience prepared him for this one moment of clarity.

He loved her.

Saint Sebastian be damned! He loved her.

Her smile faded. She lowered her eyes and drew her hand from his arm. Mayhap she'd read his mind and did not return his feelings. He stood and offered her a hand up, but she turned away from him and scrambled to her feet. He could see now how shaky she was. She stumbled, and he instinctively reached out for her.

''No need,'' she said, and steadied herself.

Duncan grinned at her, nodding his approval. "Ye did a fine job, lass."

"'Tis a fine mare. She did all the work. And 'tis a bonny son she's born."

Jamie catapulted through the door of the shed and stared, wide-eyed, at the foal. "Why, he's the image o' the black!"

"Aye, lad, that he is," Iain said. "Now, go wake young Conall and tell him he's got two horses to care for."

Jamie backed toward the door, his eyes fixed on the foal. He laughed, then turned and sprinted into the night.

Iain watched as Alena drew an arm across her brow, pushing the damp locks of hair from off her forehead. Would that she would let him comfort her. She closed her eyes and leaned against the post.

He knew she was exhausted. Small beads of perspiration shone on her face and neck. Her clothes were ruined, soaked with sweat and the bloody fluids from the birth.

Duncan watched her, as well. "Go on, lass. Ye've done a good night's work. Jamie and I will finish up here."

"Aye, 'twill be dawn soon." Her voice was weak, thin. She opened her eyes and inspected her hands and clothes. "I'm a mess. I'd best clean up outside."

She brushed past Iain without so much as a glance. He knew she was not as composed as she pretended. Determined, he followed her out into the cold night.

The moon was nearly set and cast an eerie light on the stable yard. Alena walked unsteadily toward the water trough, fighting her exhaustion. She was conscious of Iain's footsteps behind her.

Jesu, that was close. She stopped for a moment and closed her eyes. Visions of the mare, the foal, Iain's grave expression and Duncan's calm, weathered face spun in her head.

Only a few more steps.

She opened her eyes and reached one hand toward the edge of the water trough. Too late. She stumbled.

And then he was there.

Iain gathered her in his arms and held her close against his body. She didn't want to give in to his aid, but could not help herself. She drew a breath and collapsed against him, surrendering her weight to his strength.

"It's all right, lass," he whispered into her hair. "I've got you."

She felt her strength returning as he rocked her in his arms, as if he'd restored it with his own energy. She placed her hands against his chest to steady herself, but he continued to hold her close.

"Ye were brave and braw this night. Duncan was proud."

He ran a gentle hand up her back, through the web of her tangled hair, and drew a finger across her jawline. She trembled at his touch.

His eyes shone black in the moonlight and seemed different somehow. Gone was the wild, animal desire that had consumed him the afternoon at the ruins. She sensed warmth, concern, and something else. 'Twas in his touch, as well. A gentle strength that buoyed her, renewed her spirit.

"*I* was proud," he whispered, and covered her mouth with his.

'Twas the gentlest of kisses, a dove's wings lighting softly against her lips. Oh, 'twas surely possible to die from the sweet pleasure of it. She opened her mouth in invitation and he ran his tongue, warm and slick, across her lips. She moaned softly, and he deepened the kiss, clutching her tightly to him. A low groan escaped his throat as his hands moved over the rise of her buttocks.

Nay, wait. This wasn't what she wanted.

She pushed against his chest, tearing her mouth free of the kiss. Her heart pounded wildly as she wrenched herself away from him. He reached for her, and she batted his hands away.

'Twas lust he felt for her, not love. Aye, he was naught but a rogue, hell-bent on ruining her. She wiped the back of her hand across her mouth to rid herself of the taste of him.

Again he reached for her, and this time she slapped him hard across the face. The blow stunned him. And her. Jesu, she was in for it now!

A slow anger brewed in his expression. His features turned cold and hard. She pursed her lips and took another step back, her eyes riveted to his. She bumped into the water trough and nearly jumped out of her skin.

In less than a second Iain closed the distance between them. He pushed her back against the cistern and claimed her mouth in a punishing kiss.

She beat at him with her fists, struggling to free herself. "Nay! Nay, I say! Think you I'm one of your Inverness strumpets?" She shot him the most venomous expression she could muster.

His grip went slack but he did not move away. He studied her for a long moment, confusion gracing his features. "What did ye say?"

"I said I'm not one of your whores to be used and discarded on a whim." She felt herself trembling, not from the sweet fusion of desire and fear his kisses wrought from her, but from anger.

"In truth, lass, I dinna know what ye mean. I have never thought ye—"

"Ha! Will you tell me now, when it suits your purpose, that your party did *not* go to Inverness?"

He opened his mouth to speak, then closed it. He seemed

truly surprised at her outburst. "Nay," he said, "I willna. They did go, most of them."

She turned away and grasped the edges of the water trough. He didn't touch her but she could hear his ragged breathing. The next words came hard for her. "You... They...went to..."

"To find a bit o' pleasure with the local wenches. Is that what ye mean?"

She felt suddenly sick. "Aye."

"They did, those unmarried. And would ye begrudge it them?"

She stared into the blackness of the cistern and forced herself to respond. "Nay, of course not. It does not concern me."

"Nay, it doesna," he said evenly.

She stiffened as he gripped her shoulders. "Don't touch me! I'm not one of your whores." She fought the tears welling in her eyes. What a little fool she was! Why should she care with whom he lay?

Oh, but she did care.

And then he laughed. A hearty laugh the likes of which she'd never heard from him. She whirled on him, her face blazing. He shook his head and his laughter died. "*My* whores? Think ye I went, as well? To Inverness to rut with that chattel?"

"Didn't you?"

"Nay." His smile faded.

Her head pounded and her thoughts whirled in confusion. "But...I thought—"

"Nay, lass." He reached for her, and she did not resist as he pulled her into his arms.

She looked up at him and his expression softened. Warmth radiated from his body. Her hands moved instinctively to his chest.

"What I desire lies not in Inverness." His voice was a whisper, his mouth a hairbreadth from hers.

All at once she felt light-headed. "It doesn't?"

"Nay, love," he murmured, and his mouth possessed hers.

His kiss was filled with tenderness, and she surrendered to the joy she felt. Then a thought occurred to her. She broke free of his lips. "Then, if not in Inverness, where were you?"

The question surprised him. He started to speak, then changed his mind. Finally he said, "Ye shouldna question me, lass. I am laird—it isna done."

"But—"

"Hush," he whispered, and brushed his lips across hers.

She let it go for the moment. Closing her eyes, she reveled in the gentle caress of his mouth on her skin. "Oh, I never thought to feel so—"

"Neither did I." He drew her hands into his and pressed each palm, in turn, to his lips.

"Do not—I'm filthy." She pulled away and rubbed her palms together, still sticky from the foal's birth.

"You're beautiful."

Quickly she turned toward the cistern and plunged her arms into the icy water. Splashing her face, she rinsed away the perspiration. Iain offered her the end of his plaid and she dried herself with the coarse woolen cloth.

"'Twas grim in there, but ye didna give up." He took her hands again in his and smiled.

"I—I couldn't. The mare…Conall…"

"Ye'd never done it before, had ye?" She knew what he meant. "Turning a foal like that, inside the mother's womb."

"Nay."

He grazed his lips across hers, then smiled. "I didna

think so.'' Standing silent, he looked at her for what seemed a long time. She willed him with her eyes, her very soul, to possess her lips again, but he did not.

''Iain.''

Abruptly he stepped back and raised his hand up as if he would stop her from following. ''Go to bed, lass. 'Tis nearly day.''

She glanced skyward. Only a few stars glimmered like tiny pinpoints against heavens that had bled from inky-black to a clear, midnight-blue. When she turned her gaze back to Iain, she saw that he'd already turned and was striding toward the house.

The whack of the stable yard gate intruded on the pre-dawn silence as Conall and Jamie burst into the enclosure. They darted past her, panting, into the foaling shed.

She drew a breath, closed her eyes and wondered what in heaven she'd do now.

Chapter Nine

She would leave him.

Alena stood at the window and looked out on the torrential rain that had turned the stable yard into a lake of brown mud. The sky was black with clouds, broken only by an occasional flash of lightning lending a sharp, metallic bouquet to the air.

Iain had left Braedûn Lodge that morning whilst she was still asleep. He hadn't even bothered to say goodbye. Who knew how long he'd be gone? It could be weeks—that's what Will had told her.

Thunder rumbled in the distance. Rain pummeled against the side of the house. She was glad Iain was out in it. He deserved to be miserable—as was she.

She'd been at Braedûn nearly a fortnight. Midsummer's Day was fast approaching and she could think of no viable alternative to wedding Reynold Grant.

What possible interest could she hold for him? He was laird of a great clan. He was expected to wed some titled woman, or at least the daughter of a potential ally. She could not fathom his motivation.

Her parents were old and would not survive outside the

protection of their clan. She'd thought of bringing them here, of enlisting Iain's help, but that could never happen.

Should Reynold find out where she was, who knew what he might do? She would not put Iain's clan at risk on her behalf. Grant's army numbered near a thousand—more than triple what she could count of the Davidsons and the Mackintoshes combined.

Nay, she must go back. 'Twas her only choice. Besides, Iain was gone. 'Twas too late, now, to share her burden with him even if she had wished to.

The memory of his kisses blazed fresh in her mind. She ached at the thought of never seeing him again. *Love,* he'd called her last night. Would it were so.

The door to her chamber whooshed open, interrupting her thoughts. Hetty marched into the room bearing a tray of food. ''Lady, come away from that window,'' she chirped. ''Ye'll catch yer death.''

She smiled at the girl and let the fur window covering drop back into place. The hearth fire burned bright. The smell of fresh-baked bread and roasted meat filled the air.

''Come, Lady, ye must eat something. Ye slept through the morning meal and didna come to table at midday. Ye have a tired look about ye. Ye must eat.''

''Nay, Hetty, but thank you. I've no appetite.''

''Och, come now. Ye dinna want to be skin and bones when next he sees ye.''

''What do you mean? Who do you mean, *he?*''

Hetty giggled and poured a cup of ale from the ewer on the tray. ''Lady, the whole clan knows of his affection for ye, and yer feelings for him.'' She handed her the ale cup.

''But, 'tis not—''

''Och, dinna fash about it. 'Tis a good match. Everyone says so, even Edwina.''

"Edwina?" Alena was incredulous. "What would she or anyone know of— There's naught to know!"

Hetty moved to the hearth and stoked the fire. "'Tis plain enough to see ye're a pair. Iain—I mean, the laird—denies it, as well. That's what my Will says."

Alena's cheeks warmed and she knew the crackling fire wasn't to blame. She drained the ale cup and slammed it down on the table. "Oh does he? We'll see about that."

She rose, strode to the chest by the bed and retrieved a heavy plaid from its depths. She whirled the garment around her shoulders and quit the room. Hetty's objections faded as she made her way down the corridor.

The great hall was a bustle of activity. The heavy rain had driven a number of clanfolk to work inside. Gilchrist sat at the main table conversing with Will and two Davidson warriors whom she recognized.

As she approached them Gilchrist stood and smiled. "Lady Alena, ye are a vision and look full recovered from last night's labor."

"'Twas the mare who labored, not I."

Gilchrist's brows shot up.

She hadn't meant to sound so curt. He was only being polite. She softened her voice. "Laird, I would speak with you."

The warrior's blue eyes danced. "Come, come, Lady. 'Tis my brother who's laird, and he's got the brooding temperament to prove it." Will and the others chuckled. "Won't you call me Gilchrist?"

He was all charm. A true rogue. But she liked him and smiled in return. "Gilchrist, then, I would speak with you."

"Please," he said, offering his chair to her. "Won't you sit?"

She had wanted to see him alone. Scanning the roomful

of people, she knew this wasn't a likely prospect given the weather. She accepted the seat Gilchrist offered.

"Now, then," he began. "What service might I offer ye?"

The four men fixed their eyes on her and waited politely for her response.

"I—I wish to leave and would ask that you loan me a mount."

They stared at her in silence. Will's eyes darted to Gilchrist, gauging his response, then back to her.

Perhaps they did not understand her. She was about to rephrase her question when a slow smile broke across Gilchrist's handsome face.

"Ye wish to leave?" he said.

"Aye, I do."

Gilchrist turned to Will and the others. "She wishes to leave."

They were all smiling now.

"So...might I borrow a mount?"

Silence.

"I'd return it straightaway—as soon as I reach my destination."

"Lady," Gilchrist said, "after the precious gifts ye've given us—not least of all my brother Conall's life and that of the mare and her bonny colt—any mount ye desire, be it Mackintosh or Davidson, 'tis yours."

She smiled. "Then, I—"

"But I canna let ye leave this place." Gilchrist's expression turned to stone, and her smile abruptly faded.

"Why not?"

All four of them grinned again. Will exchanged mischievous looks with the two Davidsons, but Gilchrist's eyes never left hers. "Because my brother would have my head should I no' keep ye safe until his return."

"Your brother? Iain asked you to—"

"He didna ask, Lady. 'Twas a direct order and not one I'd likely challenge."

"But…" She was panicking now. It might be weeks until Iain returned. 'Twould be too late! She must leave within a sennight, or… A dull ache throbbed at her temple.

Gilchrist covered her hand with his. "Dinna worry, lass. He'll be back in a day or two."

She looked to Will. "But you said—"

"I know him," Gilchrist said, "and I've ne'er seen him so… Mark me, he'll be back ere the moon is full."

'Twas but two days hence!

"Besides, Lady," Will said, "we plan a celebration, with music and a bit o' dancing on the night o' the full moon. To honor the birth of the colt. Ye must be there."

"Will is right," Gilchrist said. "Duncan—and others— would be mightily disappointed should ye no' attend."

They were all grinning again. She felt like slapping each one of them. "Hmph," was all she could manage.

Two more days, and then she would go home.

"Aye, well, I would not disappoint Duncan," she said, and rose to leave. And if there was a chance of seeing Iain one last time…

Gilchrist rose with her. "About the mount…which would ye choose?"

"The black."

"Are ye daft? Iain will—"

"The black." She quit the room and did not look back. The argument that erupted in her wake made her smile. Iain would have a fit.

She pulled her plaid up over her head, pushed open the great door of the house and stepped out into the storm. The rain had eased. The air was fresh, and she longed to be outdoors.

Will appeared out of nowhere on the doorstep behind her.

"'Tis your turn to watch me, then?"

"Aye," he said, and blushed.

This practice of assigning a warrior to dog her every step was becoming annoying. She pulled the plaid tightly around her and marched down the stone steps and out across the muddy courtyard. "Well, watch me, then."

She headed for the stable, Will right behind her.

"But—this weather is foul. Ye dinna want to be out in it."

"'Tis a fine Scottish day," she called over her shoulder, not breaking her stride.

The stable yard was a bog unfit for man or beast. She lifted her skirts and slogged through the mud to the stable entrance. She was glad she'd worn her riding boots under the gown and not those ridiculous slippers.

Will caught her up and held the door. "Ye canna be thinkin' of ridin'?"

The look of misery on his face was enough to melt her heart. "Nay, not today. But there's work to be done here and I'll not sit idle in the house while others labor."

"Nay, I didna think ye would." The voice was Duncan's. He stepped out of a nearby stall and tossed Will a sack of fresh straw. "Conall's mare could use a groomin', and I expect ye'd like to see the colt."

"Aye, I would." Alena smiled.

"Off with ye, then. I'll have other chores for ye later."

She turned to leave, then remembered something. "Duncan, I never properly thanked your son for conveying that message for me." Oh, would that her parents were here, safe.

Will narrowed his eyes, and she realized she'd made a blunder. Secrets were near impossible to keep in a place like this. She must be more careful.

"'Twas nothing," Duncan said nonchalantly, and returned to his work.

She and Will snaked their way to the foaling shed through the labyrinth of connected buildings. The mare stood feeding from a trough on the wall. The colt pressed in close, attached himself to one of her teats and began to nurse. Both mother and babe looked well.

Alena proceeded to wipe down the mare's coat with handfuls of straw whilst Will pulled up a stool and sat down to watch her.

"What did ye mean in there?" he said. "What message?"

For all his relaxed demeanor and unassuming expressions, Will didn't miss a thing. Iain had chosen his companions well.

"Oh, 'twas nothing." Jesu, she had better change the subject, and fast. "So, uh, where is your laird?"

"Away. On business."

"Aye, so everyone says. But where?"

"Dinna worry. Hamish is with him, and a score of clansmen. And knowin' Iain, he's carried half the Davidson arsenal along with him."

This was news, indeed. She leaned into her work, feigning indifference to their conversation. "And why would he need such weapons?"

"Och, like as he wouldna. The Grants are no match for the Mackintosh—fancy weapons or no."

"The Grants?" She froze in midstroke.

"Besides, their horses are slow and could never keep pace with our steeds."

She whirled on him. "What do you mean, slow? I myself—" Jesu, what was she saying!

Will rocked back on the stool, his arms crossed over his chest, and sucked on the long piece of straw he held between his teeth. He cocked a brow in question.

"I—I mean, when they pursued me I was hard-pressed to outrun them." She swore silently to herself for reacting to his obvious bait. She redoubled her efforts with the mare. "Their mounts seemed quite fast to me."

He didn't respond, so she pressed on. "But why would Iain—I mean, your laird—wish to meet up with the Grants?"

"Oh, he doesna especially want to meet them—well, not yet, at any rate. It's just that we'd heard they were in the wood, on the border of their land and ours—well, the Davidsons'."

Alena knew the huge demesne that belonged to Clan Grant stretched from near Inverness in the north, south to the Grampian Mountains, and bordered in turn the lands of each of the four Chattan clans: MacBain, Mackintosh, Davidson and Macgillivray. She also knew it wasn't often Reynold's warriors patrolled the wood this far south.

"What would bring Grant so far from home?"

Will leveled his gaze at her. "I thought, mayhap, ye'd tell me."

Her blood chilled in her veins. She looked away. "And what would I know of the Grants?"

"I dinna know," he said far too casually.

The sounds of scuffling and laughter echoed from the connecting buildings. The commotion grew louder and Will rose from the stool.

Conall and Jamie burst through the doorway of the foaling shed. They skidded to a stopped, eyes wide, as Will loomed before them, one hand on the hilt of his dirk.

He relaxed. "What are ye doin' runnin' about the place like a pack o' wild dogs?" His voice was stern, but Alena saw warmth in his soft brown eyes. "Jamie, have ye no' got work to do?"

The stable lad looked sheepish and fidgeted on his feet. "Aye," he said, and shuffled backward out of the shed.

"And you," Will said, and took a step toward Conall. "Look at ye." The warrior shook his head, eyeing the youth's appearance.

Conall's shirt was wet and rumpled and had come untucked from his plaid, which was twisted on his body and streaked with mud.

"But—"

"Och, lad, ye'll be a chieftain one day. Ye'd best start to act like one."

The youth's face crumpled. Will made a low, rumbling sound in his throat and slapped him affectionately on the shoulder. "All right, lad. See to your horses. Lady Alena shouldna be doin' your work for ye."

Conall's expression brightened. He peeked around Will's tall frame at the mare and her colt. His eyes finally lit on Alena, and she smiled. "Oh, good morrow," he said, and grinned at her. He skirted Will and knelt beside the colt who was busily nursing.

Alena handed him the bag of straw, and Will relaxed against a post.

"I never did thank ye, proper," Conall said. "For saving my mare. And the colt." His green eyes sparkled as he drank in the sight of the gangly black colt secured to its mother's teat.

She studied him and was surprised to find he favored Iain more than she'd first thought. His hair was a wild, red-gold mass, much lighter than Iain's, but with the same tiny braids at each temple that the Mackintosh warriors seemed to favor.

Conall was much taller than her already. Alena guessed he'd equal Iain in stature before too long. His eyes were intense, and had the same fathomless quality about them as did Iain's. But it was his face that most reminded her of his eldest brother: strong, angular, with prominent cheekbones and a long, straight nose. He was a handsome youth and would grow into a striking man.

She suddenly remembered Will's words. Iain had gone in search of the Grants. Jesu, what was he thinking?

She reminded herself he was a skilled warrior who'd spent years preparing to face his enemy. He was not a man who made hasty decisions. Whatever he did was well thought out, every move carefully considered. She must trust his judgment, but could she trust him with the truth about herself?

Nay, she could not.

And soon it wouldn't matter. She would return to her clan the morning after the celebration. Her future was already determined, and she could foresee nothing that would alter that bitter destiny.

Iain glared across the ravine at the riders, not believing his eyes. Three score Grant warriors, thrice the number of his own party and sporting battle regalia, peppered the ridge opposite them.

It had rained for two days straight. Iain and his men were soaked to the skin, their plaids hanging on them like wet rags. The smell of sweat, wet wool and lathered horse nearly choked him. He shook off a chill and glanced skyward. Patches of blue snaked haphazardly among the angry clouds. 'Twas clearing.

He returned his attention to the riders. Not since the days

following his father's murder had he seen so many Grants this close to his uncle's land. The ravine between them ran roughly north-south for half a league, and divided Grant land from Davidson along the southeastern edge of his uncle's demesne.

Something foul was afoot, but he knew not what. He slid a hand across his body in silent inventory, brushing the hilts of both dirks, the longbow slung across his shoulder and the leather strap belting his broadsword to his back. He flexed his muscles and the sword's leather sheath pressed reassuringly against him.

Hamish stroked his beard, his gaze riveted to the enemy, then nodded.

"Nay," Iain whispered. "They are too many."

"'Tis at worst three to one. We've gone up against less favorable odds and prevailed."

Iain moved a hand to his bow and rubbed the smooth, hardened yew between his fingers. He was the only archer. "Aye," he murmured, judging he could fell at least a half dozen of them before they reached the small creek at the bottom of the gorge. "'Twould no' be impossible, but is it wise?"

"That's why ye are laird and not me. 'Tis your decision."

He caught Hamish's wry grin out of the corner of his eye. A thin smile breached his own lips. Aye, it was his decision, and he wasn't about to start something he was not yet prepared to finish.

As he turned his mount, something caught his eye. A glint of polished steel crept across the ridge line. What the devil? He pulled the roan up short.

The light was flat, and Iain couldn't make out the rider's face as he picked his way carefully between thick stands of larch and laurel on the opposite side of the gorge. Grant warriors opened a path before him, goading their mounts to the side to let him pass.

The rider was large and sat tall in the saddle, his plaid covering his head. Another followed him: dark and small, sized almost as a youth, and attired all in black. A strange duo, for certain. Iain had a bad feeling about them.

Without warning the tall one spurred his mount from the shelter of the trees into the open. Iain's fist closed over his bow. A cold ray of sunlight breached the clouds and illuminated the cloaked figure.

Christ, it couldn't be. All the hairs on Iain's nape prickled. The warrior threw back his plaid and shook the water from his white-blond hair. Bile rose in Iain's throat as he met that familiar, cool blue gaze.

All at once he was transformed into that defenseless boy of twelve. Visions of that night crashed over him, unbidden, shattering his confidence and the strength mustered from years of unrequited bloodlust and rage. He closed his eyes and let the memory suck him in....

The air was cool and thick with the scent of new oak mingled with last year's crush. Iain stepped carefully, feeling his way in the dark, along the damp stone wall of the wine cellar. His father had asked him to remain in the great hall with Uncle Alistair and the other Chattan lairds when he took Reynold and Henry Grant belowstairs. But Iain felt uneasy. Something drew him, compelled him to follow.

The faint glow ahead grew into a warm yellow light as his father lit a wall sconce from the taper he carried. Iain ducked quickly behind the last row of casks, and stole along the wall, straining to hear their conversation.

His father's voice rose up in a shout. Heedless of discovery, Iain sprang forward toward the commotion. He turned the corner at the end of the row of casks and stopped dead in his tracks.

Henry Grant lay prone on the stone floor, his plaid dark with blood that seeped from a wound in his back. The warrior's face was shock-white, his eyes wide and still. Iain's father knelt over the body, gripping a dirk, blood dripping from its tip.

Nay! It couldn't be so. Iain refused to believe what his eyes made plain.

Metal flashed in the soft light as Reynold Grant stepped out from behind a row of casks, broadsword drawn and raised. Iain stared, unable to move, as Reynold looked from the body of his cousin Henry to Iain's father.

A slow smile spread across Reynold's face. "Grants! To me, to me!" His voice echoed shrilly off the stone walls of the cellar.

His father's eyes narrowed and a slow recognition overtook his astounded expression.

Iain stood, transfixed, his back pressed against the wet stones of the cellar wall. Reynold had not seen him. His father rose, then slid back to his knees, the point of Reynold's broadsword at his throat.

Saint Sebastian, he must do something! Iain checked himself for a weapon—a dirk, his bow, anything he could use to defend his father. He frantically scanned the room for anything he might wield. There was nothing! He stood motionless, helpless.

The chamber exploded with light. Grant soldiers bearing torches swarmed into the cellar, swords and daggers drawn. Iain knew they searched among the rows of casks for their laird's son.

Reynold hovered still as a statue, waiting. Rounding the last row of casks, the soldiers skidded to a halt behind him. All were silent, appraising the scene before them: Henry *dead on the floor, Iain's father kneeling over him, bloody dagger in hand.*

For a moment Iain heard only the sound of water dripping from the stones behind his back, and the wild beating of his own heart. Something made him turn toward the staircase.

John Grant stood alone on the bottom step, silent and grave, looking past his murdered son and his nephew, and into the face of a man he'd called friend. Colum Mackintosh.

Reynold spoke in what was almost a whisper. "The Mackintosh hath slain my cousin."

Iain watched in horror as Reynold plunged his sword into his father's throat.

The cellar erupted in anarchy. Soldiers charged down the staircase, a roil of bodies and weapons. The stench of blood quickly overpowered the familiar warm scents of wine and oak.

The voice of The MacBain rang clear above the rest, in prophecy more than declaration, "There willna be peace. This night, nor any other."

Hamish elbowed him out of his dream state. "'Tis The Grant himself," he whispered.

Shaking off his momentary stupor, Iain leveled his gaze at the blond warrior and tightened his grip on his bow. "Aye, that's him." He'd know him anywhere. Never would he forget those cold eyes.

He gauged the distance—no more than twenty yards—a ridiculously easy shot. He imagined the feathered butt of his arrow protruding from Reynold Grant's chest, his face a twisted death mask.

Iain also knew without looking that his kinsmen waited for his signal. The slightest nod from him and they would attack. He held his ground, unmoving, and waited to see what Grant would do.

The air was thick with anticipation—a gnawing, nearly overpowering hunger for blood.

Finally, the small dark rider moved toward his laird. Reynold Grant leaned over and whispered something to him. 'Twas time, then. Iain slipped the longbow from his shoulder.

To his surprise, Grant's henchman spoke. "Mackintosh!" he called across the ravine. "We ride in search of one of our own."

One of their own? He shot Hamish a sideways glance, then continued his stare down with Grant.

"And who might that be?" Hamish called back.

"A woman."

Every muscle in Iain's body tensed. His mount stirred beneath him. He nodded imperceptibly, his gaze still riveted to Grant's.

"A woman?" Hamish called out. "Who is she?"

The small man hesitated, darting his eyes toward his laird. "She's...but one of the laird's whores. Of no consequence, but a beauty, is she not? The laird would like her back."

Blood raged through Iain's veins, pulsing white-hot to his face. One hand shot toward his dirk. The other gripped his bow so tight he thought 'twould split asunder.

"Steady," Hamish whispered.

"He's willing to barter for her," the small henchman called back. "A bit of cattle, perhaps, or gold."

Reynold's head jerked toward his kinsman. Iain caught the almost invisible shrug of the small man's shoulders.

"This...whore," Hamish said. "What makes ye think she'd be here, so far from Glenmore Castle?"

"Ah," the henchman said. "She hath fled. 'Twas a...lover's quarrel, you see."

A thin smile crept across The Grant's face. Iain's blood began to boil.

"You'd best not turn your back on her," the henchman said. "She's quite skilled with a dirk."

Grant's smile exploded into a snarl. Iain studied the thick, dark line that scarred his face from eye to chin. The image of Alena streaked with bloody fingerprints, her gown torn away across her breast, flooded Iain's senses. A visceral rage seared his gut. By God, if the whoreson touched her—

Grant smiled at him suddenly. Iain had never in his life wanted to kill a man more than he did at that moment.

"Easy, man," Hamish whispered through clenched teeth.

The small, dark henchman rose up in his saddle. "So, will you barter?"

"Nay!" Iain shouted. "We havena seen such a woman."

The Grants, all save Reynold, inched gauntleted hands toward their swords. In a flash, Iain's kinsmen did the same.

Three to one.

Iain swore under his breath. 'Twasn't the time or the place to take him down. If he killed Reynold now—and, by God, he so lusted to do it he tasted blood—the whole of the Grant army would bear down on Davidson and Mackintosh alike, with a vengeance Iain didn't wish to contemplate.

Nay. Only when he had everything in place, when he knew he could win, would he raise his hand against this godless viper and smite his soul to hell.

Eighty riders sat motionless, livery creaking, awaiting their lairds' commands. The air was heavy and still. Iain fixed on the thudding of his heart and the gentle rushing of the creek at the bottom of the ravine.

And then to his surprise, Reynold Grant raised a cautionary hand. His smile broadened. Taking a last, long look at Iain, he touched a gauntleted finger to his brow in farewell, turned his steed, and spurred him back up the hill.

Iain exhaled. Christ, he didn't even realize he'd been holding his breath. Grant's soldiers waited until he was safely away, then followed their laird over the ridge top.

"Well," Hamish said. "I'll be damned."

"Aye, and every one of us." Iain slung his longbow over his shoulder and grimaced at his friend. "Let's go. I dinna like this place."

The sky cleared. Iain drove his kinsmen hard, riding through the night and all the next day, in hopes of reaching Braedûn Lodge by nightfall. There was little conversation during the journey and Iain used the time to sort out the mysteries that plagued him.

Grant. Iain was stunned the powerful laird didn't engage him. He'd had the advantage but didn't press it. Why? And what was a war party, headed by the laird himself, doing so far south? Reynold couldn't have known Iain and his men would be there. 'Twas a chance encounter, he was certain.

He tilted his head back and sucked in a breath. *Think, man.* The only route much traveled in that remote part of both their lands was the pass that joined the Macgillivray demesne to that of the Davidson's. His uncle Alistair used the route occasionally on his diplomatic journeys.

That was it!

Iain pulled his mount up short. Alistair, Margaret and their small party would be traversing the pass in a matter of days on their return to Braedûn Lodge. They traveled with an escort of less than twenty warriors. The question was, did Grant know this?

Hamish pressed his mount even with Iain's, interrupting his thoughts. "What is it?"

"Nothing," Iain said, and spurred the roan toward home.

Just past sunset the sky was transformed into a clear azure field flecked with the first evening stars. Braedûn Lodge lay but a half league away. Iain directed his stallion upward through the wood and the roan increased his speed, sensing his nearness to home.

Iain shook out his plaid and ran his fingers through his tangled hair. At least he was dry, if not clean. He rubbed a hand over his bare arm—'twas thick with the grit of three days in the saddle. His shirt was filthy and earlier he'd balled it up and jammed it under his saddle.

A small tarn lay just below the lodge. Iain left the main path and directed his stallion toward it.

"Iain," Hamish called, "where are ye goin', man? The house is just ahead."

"Aye, but I think I'll have a swim first."

Hamish's bellowing laugh rang in Iain's ears as he made his way to the water's edge. Aye, when had he ever stopped to bathe *before* reaching the house? His kinsmen continued on and he was left to his thoughts.

Foremost on his mind was Alena. Saint Sebastian, what would he do with her? There was no doubt in his mind she was the woman Grant sought. But why? What was she to him? As he stripped and dove into the cool water, he ground his teeth and fought back the image of Alena in Reynold Grant's arms.

Nay, there wasn't a shred of truth in the small hench-man's words. Alena was a maid, an innocent. But Grant had had his hands on her, Iain was sure of it. And she'd fought him off and fled.

Who was she? Why wouldn't she tell him, trust him?

The icy water cooled his body and cleared his mind. He strode dripping from the tarn and shook his head like a dog. In seconds he was dressed.

He mounted his stallion and spurred him up the hill toward the estate. Only a few warriors stood guard along the stone wall. They raised their weapons in silent greeting as he rode through the entrance.

Something was not right.

The main courtyard was all but deserted. Music and laughter echoed from the direction of the lodge. His horse moved instinctively toward the stable yard. Good God, 'twas ablaze with light! A huge bonfire had been built inside the enclosure. A dozen couples danced to a rollicking tune, spurred on by what appeared to be the entirety of his uncle's household, drinking and making merry.

''What the—''

And then he saw her.

Alena whirled light on her feet, her long, wild hair whipping about her like golden flames. She wore a gown of dark green wool. Iain recognized it as one of his mother's. The laces had been pulled tight to outline every voluptuous curve of her body.

His loins stirred; his heart slammed in his chest at the sight of her.

''Holy God,'' he breathed, and reined his horse to a stop just outside the enclosure. He dismounted, threw off his weapons, and secured them to the horse's saddle. Young Jamie appeared out of nowhere, snatched the bridle from Iain's hand and led the weary stallion away.

Iain moved slowly through the open gate and into the stable yard—a man in a trance—his eyes riveted to Alena, a vision not of this earth.

The music ended and she skidded to a stop, breathless,

her face flushed from the dance and the heat of the fire. Her cat-green eyes flashed surprise as she turned and caught sight of him. A radiant smile lit up her face, and Iain knew then that he would never give her up. Never.

Chapter Ten

Alena stood, transfixed, held captive by Iain's gaze. Her hard-won resolve of the past few days burst into flame and was reflected, bright and short-lived, in his eyes. It blazed to ash and drifted away on the cool night breeze.

He stood but a few paces from her and she drank in the sight of him. His chestnut hair, nearly auburn in the firelight, dripped water that ran in snaking rivulets down his bare chest and arms.

His outward expression was reserved, controlled, but she perceived an almost aching need, an unrequited desire smoldering just below the surface. He wore no weapons save one of the two dirks he kept belted at his side. She saw him as a warrior, nonetheless—a conqueror, and she the vanquished.

This was the man she wanted. He was the reason she had never married. She knew that now. She loved him fiercely. She always had. She always would.

"Iain," she breathed.

He stepped toward her, but she was yanked away into the crowd of revelers. Stumbling sideways, she caught Gilchrist's mischievous grin as he pulled her into his arms and guided her into the next dance. The music was lively and the young warrior spun her in so many directions she lost sight of Iain in the throng of clanfolk.

And then he was there.

Iain brushed his brother aside and swept her into his embrace. One hand splayed across the small of her back and the other caught her own as he slowed their pace and directed her toward the entrance to the stable.

He stopped at the open door but did not release her. They stood motionless for a moment, their eyes fixed on each other. She was conscious of the warmth of his hand on her back and trembled slightly as he inched it upward.

Jesu, he was going to kiss her! In front of the entire clan!

She slipped from his embrace and into the stable. Duncan, Gavin and the rest of the stable hands were busy unsaddling the lathered mounts that had borne Iain's party.

Without thinking, she brushed past them and darted through the labyrinth of structures connected to the main stable. When she reached the foaling shed, the last of the buildings, she stopped to catch her breath.

The door to the stable yard was closed and the window covered. All the same, a warm glow illuminated the shed from the small hayloft window overlooking the bonfire outside. The shed was empty save for some piles of fresh straw. Duncan must have boarded the mare and her colt elsewhere for the night.

Why had she run? She'd wanted Iain to kiss her, to touch her—more than she'd ever wanted anything. The knowledge of it thrilled her.

Quiet footsteps approached. 'Twas him. She held her breath and waited for him to speak. He stood behind her, so close she could feel his breath on her hair. A rush of excitement coursed through her as he ran his hands lightly up her arms. Succumbing, she melted into his solid warmth.

"Alena," he whispered, grazing the side of her face with his lips. He turned her in his arms.

"You came back."

"Did ye think I wouldna?" He smiled.

"I—I didn't know if...when you would."

He tilted her chin and brushed his lips across hers. "Oh, lass, I wanted to stay away, but I couldna." He kissed her lightly again. "I rode like the devil himself to get here this night."

"But Grant—"

"Shh...there's naught to fear from him. Ye are under my protection now."

She started at his words. What could he possibly know? Mayhap Duncan revealed some piece of information. Nay, even the old stablemaster didn't know the truth of her plight. Grant's men in the forest! Perhaps...

Her mind raced, but Iain's kisses distracted her from all rational thought. His hands moved over her back as he pulled her closer. She looked into his eyes and was at once and forever lost. He kissed her long, tenderly. She moaned softly in surrender.

He gripped her tighter and deepened the kiss, his tongue parting her lips and exploring her mouth with an urgency that she, too, felt. Her hands roamed his bare back, and he growled low in his throat with pleasure. She boldly returned his fervent kiss, darting her tongue into his mouth, teasing, tasting.

He moved his hands lower, caressing the rise of her buttocks, pulling her tight against the hardness of his growing passion. She thought she would go mad with desire. Pushing back against his chest, she broke the kiss.

"D'ye wish me to stop?"

"Nay," she breathed, and ran her hands brazenly over the tight musculature of his softly furred chest.

She didn't think he could possibly hold her any closer, yet he pulled her tighter still, crushing her breasts against him.

"Oh, lass, I dinna care who ye are. I want you."

"Iain," she breathed, and wrapped her arms around his neck.

"D'ye want me?" His eyes, cloudy with passion, searched hers.

"Aye."

"Say it. Say the words."

God help her, she longed to shout them. "I want you."

He bore her back in a powerful embrace and claimed her mouth with his. Before she knew what was happening, he swept her into his arms and strode to the ladder leading to the hayloft. Hoisting her over his shoulder as if she were a sack of grain, he climbed the short distance to the top and tossed her onto a bed of new straw.

She lay there breathless, her heart racing. Iain hovered over her, his body inches from hers, his eyes searching her face again in silent question. She breathed in the clean, male scent of him and was overcome by her own reckless desire. Without another thought she drew him down on top of her.

He possessed her mouth and she opened for him. Their tongues mated in wild abandon as he ground his hips feverishly against hers. She felt the full measure of his desire and reveled in her own newly discovered passion.

She was wanton, sinful, and she didn't care. Her body was on fire and only he could quench the flame. She could feel him trembling above her and knew he was close to losing control. She wanted him to take her, here, now. She willed it with her eyes, her body, her very soul.

He broke the kiss and gazed at her through slitted eyes,

his breathing ragged and shallow. "Stop me now, or I fear I willna have the strength to stop later."

She didn't want to him to stop. Not ever. She closed her eyes and arched against him. He showered her face with small, fervent kisses, brushing her forehead, her eyelids, moving down across her cheeks, the line of her jaw, her neck, until she thought she would die from pleasure.

He reached tentatively for the laces at the back of her gown. Her eyes fluttered open and met his. She smiled, and he kissed her softly on the mouth. He struggled to loosen the ties, and when they were free he yanked the gown off her shoulders, revealing her breasts.

She held her breath as his eyes roamed the creamy expanse of her skin, lingered on her taut, dusky nipples, and returned once more to meet her gaze.

"Ye are more beautiful than any imaginings I ever dared to conjure."

She slid her hands into his damp hair and arched her back as he drew her nipple into his mouth.

"Oh, sweet heaven." Joy surged within her.

The door to the shed crashed open, jolting her out of the near-dream state she'd succumbed to.

Iain pushed himself off her. One hand flew to the hilt of his dirk, the other pressed her flat into the straw. He willed her with his eyes to remain motionless. She quickly pulled the bodice of her gown back into place.

Jamie's breathless voice called up to them, "Iain! I—I mean, Laird. Gilchrist says ye must come quick!"

Iain hesitated all of a second. "Saint Sebastian to bluidy hell!" He swung his legs over the edge of the loft, shot her a brief, crooked smile and dropped to the ground.

She exhaled as she heard their footsteps leave the shed and the door bang shut behind them.

* * *

Iain adjusted his plaid and followed Jamie through the crowd, dodging dancing couples and clanswomen carrying trenchers of food and flagons of ale. He smiled thinly at the warriors who called out and raised their ale cups to him as he snaked his way through the merry swarm and out the stable yard gate.

Jamie sprinted ahead into the courtyard toward a group of men, Gilchrist among them, who crowded around the stone steps leading to the house.

Gilchrist turned and Iain caught his brother's grave expression. "The scouts," Gilchrist said, "returned from the northern border."

Iain elbowed his way to the steps. His two best scouts, bedraggled and filthy, rested on the smooth stone entrance. Their mounts were nowhere in sight. A Davidson warrior offered each of them an ale cup, hastily procured from a passing reveler. Iain waited until they had slaked their thirst before he spoke.

"Drake, what happened?"

"Laird—" Drake coughed and sputtered from what was clearly his first draught of liquid in some time. "Grant himself—the laird—"

"And the MacBain," the other scout added. "Due north o' Findhorn Castle."

"On Mackintosh land?" Iain knelt before the scouts and questioned them at eye level.

"Oh, nay," Drake said. "'Twas much further north—on MacBain land."

"Ye were there?" Gilchrist asked him.

"Aye, we didna expect to be, but we happened upon a large detachment o' Grant soldiers—a war party by the look o' them—better than three score."

"Led by Reynold Grant himself," the other scout said.

"I've only seen him the one other time…but I'd know him anywhere, that spawn of hell."

Iain knew the one other time to which the scout referred—the night Reynold Grant wreaked death and destruction upon the Mackintosh clan.

He swallowed hard. A huge paw of a hand clapped him on the shoulder. Hamish's great figure loomed over him. Their eyes locked and Iain nodded then turned his attention back to the scouts. "How long ago was this?"

"Four days," Drake said. "They passed from their own land west into ours and traveled half a day along the border between the Mackintosh and MacBain holdings. We tracked them until they turned north, and that's when they met The MacBain."

"The lairds themselves spoke, one to the other?" Iain asked.

Both scouts nodded.

"Hmph." Iain stood, and the small crowd of men parted as he paced a small circle. He looked up suddenly, remembering. "Where are your mounts?"

The scouts cast sheepish glances, first at each other, then at the stone steps below their feet. "Taken," Drake said quietly. "We tethered them about a quarter league from their meetin' place and approached on foot. There were so many warriors, of both clans, scouring the wood, we had to go far out o' the way to get back. By the time we'd returned to where we had left them, our steeds were gone."

"So they know ye were there," Iain said.

"Aye."

"But ye werena caught," Gilchrist offered, a little too brightly.

Iain scowled at his brother. He ground his teeth, and the group of warriors fell silent, waiting for him to respond. He knew 'twas a two-day ride at best from where the scouts had lost their mounts back to Braedûn Lodge. They wouldn't have been able to secure fresh horses from the few Mackintosh kinsmen who resided near Findhorn Castle. Too many Grants patrolled his father's old demesne.

Nay, the poor sods must have run the whole way to arrive on foot in only three days. Iain smiled at them. "Ye did well." They grinned in what he knew was relief and proceeded to drain their ale cups. "I must think on this. Gilchrist, Hamish—I'd have a word with ye."

He walked back toward the celebration, but stopped just outside the stable yard gate. Gilchrist and Hamish joined him. He watched the revelers absently, not really seeing them, considering the events of the past few days and the options at hand. "So, what think ye of this news?"

Hamish stroked his beard in contemplation. "Well, it appears Grant has swayed MacBain to his side."

"Perhaps," Iain said. "Perhaps not."

Four days—time enough to meet with The MacBain, then ride south to the place where Iain and his men had happened upon them. "And now the bastard thinks to meet with Macgillivray," Iain said. "Or mayhap murder the Davidson laird and his lady. 'Twould further his cause for certain."

"What?" Gilchrist gripped his arm.

Iain recounted their meeting with Grant along the southeast border, and his fears for both Alena's safety and that of their uncle and his party.

"Bluidy hell," the young warrior swore. "What will ye do?"

Iain studied his brother's face. He'd always thought of Gilchrist as a boy, but at ten and eight he was a man, a Mackintosh warrior. Iain was proud of how the ridiculously handsome lad had grown into a respected leader of men.

He was as quick with his wits as his sword, and 'twas far past time he tested both.

Iain eyed him. "What would *you* do?"

"Me?" Gilchrist croaked.

"Nay, Father Christmas. Of course, you. And be quick about it."

Gilchrist squared his shoulders. "I'd ride forty warriors south, tonight, and meet our uncle's party before they take leave of their Macgillivray escort at the border."

Iain nodded. "Aye, so do it. And take Hamish with ye. He knows well the route and the wee pass Alistair and Margaret must traverse between the two clan holdings."

Gilchrist turned to leave, his blue eyes alight with the promise of adventure.

Iain pulled him back by his shirt. "And Gilchrist, dinna leave tonight, man. Some o' the men ye must take just now rode in with me. Give them a rest. The morrow is soon enough."

He caught Hamish's look of relief and smiled. "And now, my friend, I'd like a word with my brother in private."

"Aye, Laird." Hamish reverted to the formal address he used when others were present. "Methinks I'll find my bed. 'Twas a long ride." He turned and strode toward the men's barracks on the opposite side of the courtyard.

"So," Gilchrist said, settling back against the fence. "What d'ye want to know?"

"To begin with, what in bluidy hell is *this?*" Iain waved an arm at the throng of revelers inside the stable yard, most of whom appeared to be exceedingly drunk.

"Oh. 'Tis a celebration."

"I can see that, ye dolt! But what are ye celebratin' and why on God's earth are ye doin' it now?"

Gilchrist grinned. "Well, 'tis on account of Conall's new

colt being born and all.'' He shrugged as if that should make perfect sense to Iain.

"A party for a horse. Christ, Gilchrist, is there no excuse too paltry for ye to break open every last hogshead of Alistair's ale and stumble drunk around a bonfire as big as a house?''

His brother's face fell. "'Twas really for Lady Alena that we did it. I—the whole clan wished to do something to show their gratitude for Conall, and the colt.''

Iain paused to watch the dancers. He hadn't seen his kinsmen so merry in months. "Aye, well, 'twas a bonny idea.''

"Alena thought so, too. She was most appreciative of—''

His hackles rose as he recalled Alena twirling brightly in Gilchrist's arms. "And about Alena... I asked ye to watch her, no' court her like a smitten youth.'' He elbowed his brother hard in the ribs.

"Och, I was but makin' sure she didna get lonely whilst ye were away.''

Iain shot him a hard look.

"Besides, 'tis another Mackintosh who's smitten, methinks.'' Gilchrist grinned and pulled a long green straw from Iain's rumpled plaid.

"Hmph.'' He scowled at the crowd. Then another interpretation of his brother's words struck him. He grabbed Gilchrist's arm. "Who? Which Mackintosh? Give me the man's name.''

Gilchrist dissolved into laughter, and Iain thought seriously about putting his fist through his brother's handsome face.

"Oh, brother,'' Gilchrist chuckled, "I wish our mother, God rest her soul, could have seen ye like this. 'Tis verra amusing.''

Alena had looked stunning in his mother's gown. Iain fought back a wave of emotion. "Go on, then, choose your men, and see you're away by dawn."

Iain narrowed his eyes as he spied Will leaning against the water trough. Hetty was standing not a foot from him. The two were holding hands, lost in each other's eyes, and looked for all the world like a pair of lovebirds. Iain snorted. "And take him with you," he said, nodding in Will's direction. "Christ—a celebration. War's brewin' and ye've organized a bluidy dance!"

Gilchrist smiled and ambled toward the house.

Iain leaned against the fence, staring blindly at the ground under his feet. A vision of Alena, lying naked and eager in a bed of sweet new straw, filled his mind.

"Bluidy hell, what was I thinking?" To bed her in the hayloft as if she were one of Gilchrist's willing milkmaids? Nay, he wouldn't dishonor her so. 'Twas more than one passionate night he desired from her—much more.

He pushed himself away from the fence and moved toward the stable yard entrance. As he strode through the gate he felt a sharp tug on the back of his thick leather belt. He whirled and looked down into the wrinkled, scowling face of Edwina.

She thrust a clean shirt into his hands. "Here," she said. "Dress yerself." Before he could respond she scurried into the night.

He pulled the shirt over his head, tucked it quickly into his kilt, then secured his plaid to his shoulder with the silver clan brooch. His gaze traveled past the bonfire to the small hayloft window of the foaling shed.

Let her still be there, he prayed silently to himself, and wove his way through the crowd toward the shed. He threw open the door and leaped onto the hayloft ladder. Three steps later he was at the top, staring blankly at an empty bed of straw.

She would tell Iain everything.

Gavin offered her a foot up, and Alena mounted the black stallion. She guided him around the smoldering remains of last night's bonfire and out through the stable yard gate. The sky was clear and the air warm. Summer had come, and with it unforeseen events that had irrevocably changed her life.

The courtyard was unusually quiet. She had noticed this morning that a sizable number of horses were missing from their stalls. Gavin had made no comment when she'd asked him about it.

Just before dawn she'd heard a commotion in the stable yard, but thought it only the remains of last night's revelers and had burrowed deeper into her bed, letting sleep reclaim her. She would ask Iain about it after she had answered all of his questions about her and Reynold Grant.

She tilted her head back and let the sun warm her face. She'd dressed this morning in her work clothes—worn breeches and light woolen shirt, her hair loose, as always— and wondered now why she had not donned a gown instead.

He'd called her *beautiful*.

She ran her hand absently along her throat and recalled his hot mouth on her skin. Her passion had nearly equaled his, and she wondered if he would think her too bold.

She spurred the black forward toward the main gate. Gavin had told her he'd seen Iain astride his mount, patrolling the outer wall of the estate. She wanted to speak to him right away. Now, in fact.

Midsummer's Day was but five days hence. Time was short.

She passed the armory, which was a bustle of activity. Three fletchers worked crafting arrows. She saw hundreds of them sheaved and piled in neat stacks outside the good-size building. The farriers from the stable worked alongside the man whom Duncan had said was the Davidsons' master weapons craftsman. Dozens of broadswords, dirks of all lengths, and double-headed axes lay in stacks at their feet.

They were preparing for battle.

She smiled weakly as she passed the laborers, but they didn't look up from their work. A chill ran up her spine as she considered the implications to both clans, Mackintosh and Davidson, of a full-scale war against Reynold Grant and his army.

She must stop it. 'Twas madness.

She must make Iain see the folly of engaging Reynold in battle. There was no possible way for Iain to win. Unless he had resources that were, as yet, unknown to her.

She approached the main gate and was surprised to see it closed. The huge larch log that normally lay propped against the stone wall was now in place across the heavy gate, barring entrance and exit. Half a dozen Davidson warriors stood at attention on the scaffolding that hugged the wall, looking outward toward the forest below them.

One of them, a man Alena recognized, turned as she approached. "I wish to go out," she said. "Can you please open the gate for me?"

Two other warriors turned and the three of them stared at her. Not one moved from his post.

Perhaps they didn't hear her. She would speak louder. "I wish to—"

"Nay, Lady," the man she knew called down to her. "I canna open the gate. The Mackintosh's orders."

"But I wish to see him—The Mackintosh. If you would but open the gate I could—"

"I'm sorry, Lady, but I canna. The laird instructed us no' to let ye out. For any reason."

A small crowd had gathered to watch her interaction with the guards. She was more than mildly irritated by their presence and the warrior's refusal to let her pass.

"We'll just see about that." She had it in mind to make a run at the low spot in the curtain wall at the back of the house, where once before she'd easily cleared the top on Iain's stallion. She started back toward the stable yard when she heard a scuffle behind her.

She turned her mount and saw that three of the guards had left their posts and were sliding the wooden bar back from its position across the gate.

Well, they must have thought better of preventing her exit. She whispered to her mount and he eased forward until he stood but a nose from the gate. The guards swung the huge doors inward and the black retreated, step by step, until the gate creaked past him, leaving him nose to nose with—

Iain's roan.

She caught the look of surprise on Iain's face before both horses reared. She clung desperately to her mount's back so as not be flung to the ground.

Iain was not as lucky. Several warriors sprang forward to assist him as he groaned from his sprawled position in the dirt just outside the gate. He waved them off and scrambled to his feet.

Alena sat quietly on the black, swallowing her laughter, and proffered the most innocent expression she could manage. Iain grabbed the bridle. The black started.

"Get down from that horse. Now."

From one minute to the next she never knew what to expect from him. Well, his rudeness she would not abide.

"Nay, I will not. He's my horse and I'll ride him when

I like.'' As soon as the words left her mouth she regretted them.

Iain's eyes blazed. She could see he was struggling with how to respond. At any moment he was likely to yank her from the beast's back and carry her off, as seemed his wont.

A tall Davidson clansman elbowed his way through the crowd and nodded at Iain. Alena recognized him as one of the warriors who'd been at table with Gilchrist on the day she'd asked to leave. ''She's right, Laird,'' the warrior said. ''The stallion is hers.''

Iain narrowed his eyes at the man. ''What?''

''Aye, 'tis true. Gilchrist made her a gift of the beast whilst ye were away south.''

Iain swore under his breath, then handed the bridle to the Davidson warrior. ''Aye, all right.'' He reached for her, but stopped just short of touching her. ''But ye will come with me now, lass.''

She breathed a sigh of relief and slipped into his waiting arms. He set her on the ground and waved the small group of clanfolk back to their duties. Their mounts were led away. Iain grasped her hand and pulled her along after him.

''Ye will never defy me again.'' His voice was sharp with thinly veiled anger, and something more.

''But—''

''D'ye hear me?'' He jerked her arm and she stumbled.

He turned to catch her and pulled her into his arms. She could feel his heart pounding. He grabbed her chin so she was forced to look into his stormy eyes.

''Dinna ye know how dangerous that black beast is?'' His voice was thick with emotion. ''I'm doin' my best to keep ye safe, but 'twould be easier if ye helped.'' He grazed his lips lightly across hers and released her from his embrace.

''But he's no danger. Well, not to me, he isn't.''

He grabbed her hand again. She struggled to keep up with his long stride as he pulled her toward the house.

"Even Duncan says so. He may not be fit for others to ride, but he responds well to me." She pulled Iain to a stop. "Let me keep him, please. I'll have need of a good mount."

He searched her face and she could see his resolve crumble. He growled and she knew she'd won. "Och, all right. But ye mustna ride him unescorted. No' as yet." She nodded her head enthusiastically. "And ye canna leave the estate. 'Tis too dangerous." She frowned and Iain eyed her sternly. "D'ye understand? 'Tis for your own safety."

He was right. She knew nothing of his recent dealings with the neighboring clans, but she'd heard talk of the Grants and the MacBains, and knew she should heed his words.

"Aye, I understand."

His expression softened and he smiled. "Good. Now, what have ye named him?"

"The black?" She'd given some thought to that. "Destiny," she said.

"Destiny?"

"Aye."

"'Tis a strange name for a horse."

She beamed a smile at him and felt a tightness in her chest. "Not so strange, methinks."

Iain grazed the back of his hand across her cheek. "I've something I would speak with ye about. About last night."

Her cheeks warmed. "There is something else I would speak to you of first." She must tell him who she was, and about Grant's threats to her family. Time was short.

"Come, lass," he said, and pulled her toward the stone steps leading to the house. He lifted her onto the second step so her eyes were even with his, and held her lightly around the waist. "Now, about last night, what we did—I did—in the hayloft. 'Twas wrong."

"But—"

He put a finger to her lips. "Shh. Now let me finish. 'Twas wrong, and I dinna want ye to think—"

The thunder of hoofbeats interrupted their conversation. Iain's hand shot to the hilt of his sword. He relaxed when he saw the riders come into view. A grin graced his ruggedly handsome face.

She knew now why so many of the stalls had been empty that morning. She guessed there to be at least fifty warriors clattering through the gate, heavily armed and in full battle dress. They approached the house and turned past the steps, heading for the stable yard.

A cry went up among the clanfolk in the courtyard. "Davidson! Davidson!" The warriors guarding the gate unsheathed their swords and lifted them in silent tribute.

Gilchrist led the company. Alena thought him magnificent in his studded-leather armor, his long, flaxen hair catching in the breeze.

With him rode Hamish, Will and two people she did not know but guessed to be Alistair and Margaret Davidson, the laird and lady of Braedûn Lodge. They sat astride twin white geldings, and Alena thought she had never seen so fair and regal a couple.

"Laird, Uncle," Iain called warmly to the tall, lanky man. "We didna expect ye for some days yet."

Gilchrist nudged his mount closer. "We met them on the forest road not two hours south of the house. They came up over the mountains, avoiding the pass altogether."

"'Twas wise, Uncle," Iain said.

"Aye." Alistair nodded, smiling broadly at his nephew. "I would speak with ye later on this and other matters."

Alena could see a slight resemblance between the two.

Alistair Davidson had tawny, flowing hair, just graying at the temples, and warm brown eyes. In the saddle he looked to be as tall as Iain, but not as heavily built. He had the same long, straight nose and finely chiseled features, which Alena now realized were bequeathed to Iain from his mother's people. She guessed the laird to be in his midforties. He appeared fit and a warrior still, yet he did not bear that rough, hardened edge about him as did Iain.

Iain nodded then turned to Margaret and bowed. "Lady, let me bid ye welcome home."

The lady of Braedûn Lodge was the most elegant woman Alena had ever seen. There had been few noblewomen at Glenmore Castle. John Grant, the old laird, had had no wife in Alena's lifetime. The little she knew of such highborn women came from the stories her mother had told her of the French court, from the days when Madeleine Todd, née Fouret, was a lady-in-waiting. Before she'd wed Robert Todd and had come to Scotland.

Margaret Davidson was cloaked in her clan's plaid and threw it off to reveal dark hair, coiled tight about her head in thick braids that bore the barest hint of silver. Her skin was pale alabaster, striking against her scarlet gown, and set off by clear blue eyes.

Alena thought, self-consciously, of her own freckled, sun-bronzed features and wild tangle of hair. She surveyed her inappropriate garments, wiped her hands on her breeches and struggled to meet the lady's penetrating gaze.

Iain surprised her by taking her hand in his and guiding her down the steps. "Uncle, Auntie, this is Alena." His voice projected a quiet reverence that made her blush. She, a stablemaster's daughter, presented to them as if she were some highborn maid.

Alistair and Margaret arched their brows and exchanged brief looks. For a moment they hesitated, and Iain squeezed her hand tightly in reassurance. Alena realized she was holding her breath and exhaled as the laird and lady smiled warmly at her.

"Alena," Margaret said, "we are most pleased." Her voice was engaging, almost melodic. Alena smiled up at her.

"She is here with us under my protection," Iain said.

Alistair studied her closely. "Ye are welcome in our home, lass." His eyes sparkled with what Alena thought a hint of recognition. She quickly averted her eyes from his discerning gaze.

The mounts fidgeted and nickered as Will and Hamish nudged their horses apart to allow two more riders to approach the steps.

Oh, no!

Father Ambrose sat before them on a swaybacked mare, mopping his sweaty brow with a frayed piece of cloth. He nodded at Iain then frowned at her; whether in recognition or disapproval of her attire, Alena didn't know. He was a young priest, newly ordained and sent to serve a number of clans. Alena had met him only once and prayed he would not remember what she looked like.

Her attention was drawn to the other rider, a small, lovely woman with delicate white skin and bound hair as black as a raven's wing. She had dark, wide-set eyes and rose-blush lips. She looked to be about Alena's age. She was beautiful, and something about the way she looked at Iain with those huge, knowing eyes made Alena uncomfortable. She bristled and let go his hand.

Iain smiled at the young woman and looked to Gilchrist for an introduction. "And who is this fair lady, brother?"

Gilchrist grinned from ear to ear, a mischievous glint in his bright blue eyes. "Iain, may I present Elizabeth Macgillivray—your bride."

Chapter Eleven

Alistair had truly gone mad this time.

Iain paced along the edge of the slate hearth in his uncle's apartment, purposefully kicking up the border of newly laid rushes covering the floor. "Aye, I want the alliance," he said, "but I willna take his daughter to wife to have it."

Alistair Davidson sat in the elaborately carved chair that was his favorite and drummed his fingertips lightly on the oak side table. His expression was unreadable, but Iain knew well what was his uncle was thinking.

Briefly, he glanced at his aunt Margaret who sat silent in the chair opposite her husband. She shot Alistair an *I told you so* look that told Iain she'd not been in favor of this plan.

"You're wearing a groove in the floor, lad. Sit ye down." His uncle indicated the richly padded stool tucked just to the side of the fireplace.

Iain continued to pace. "Why did ye have to bring her here? Ye knew I wouldna wed her."

Margaret smirked at Alistair. "Your uncle thought if you saw her, how lovely she is, you might agree to the match."

Iain snorted.

"Come, lad," Alistair said. "It doesna matter if she favors a toad. The important thing is Macgillivray offered her, and if ye wish the alliance ye'd best take her." He reached into the folds of his plaid and withdrew a rolled parchment. "Here's the marriage contract, and it's verra generous. He's offered lands, two small lodges and gold."

"Aye, and he'd have to, would he no', to unload that strumpet?" Still pacing, Iain dismissed the idea with a wave of his hand.

Margaret arched a dark brow.

Alistair promptly ignored the gesture. "I'll not have ye speak that way of Elizabeth. She's a widow—and young and bonny still, as ye can see. Can she help it if she's captured the attention of one or two warriors?"

"One or two? She's bedded most o' the chieftains across a half dozen clans."

Alistair scowled.

Margaret raised her other brow to join the first, pursing thin rose lips in her husband's direction.

"Hmph," Alistair muttered and shifted in his chair.

Iain strode to the window and peered down into the small garden tucked between the back of the house and the stone wall of the estate. What he saw did not surprise him. Gilchrist walked arm-in-arm with Elizabeth Macgillivray through the maze of herbs and summer wildflowers that had bloomed anew since the heavy rain.

Iain screwed up his face as she tittered in response to one of his brother's inane witticisms. "Look at the two o' them. Well, that didna take long, did it?"

"Huh?" Alistair rose.

Iain tossed him a thin smile. "Macgillivray's daughter— the chaste widow—and my brother, ever on the lookout for a new conquest."

Alistair glanced out the window. "Hmm…"

Iain returned to the hearth and dragged the padded stool to the table where his aunt sat. He plopped down as Alistair reclaimed his seat in the chair opposite.

"All right," Iain said, "what's to be done, then?"

Margaret rested a long elegant hand on his arm. "Iain, tell us about Alena."

Alena.

Iain recalled how she'd drawn away from him when she spied Elizabeth Macgillivray gloating like the bloody queen of Sheba from atop her fat mare. He'd read the shock, then pain, on Alena's face when the woman was introduced as his bride.

So help him, he was going to kill his brother. Ten and eight Gilchrist may be, but he wasn't too big for a thrashing. Iain pressed the palms of his hands against his temples and groaned.

He'd sensed the instant before Alena had bolted toward the stable yard that she was going to do it, and had grabbed her arm. She'd looked up at him with huge glassy eyes, her anguish a hot knife to his gut.

She'd wrenched out of his grip and snaked through the throng of mounted warriors crowding the stable yard gate. By the time Iain had made his excuses to his uncle and aunt and their guest, Alena was nowhere to be found.

"Bluidy hell," he muttered.

"You love her," his aunt said.

"What?" Iain looked up.

"And she loves you."

"I dinna know what—"

Margaret patted his arm, stilling his protest. "'Tis plain to see."

"Aye, lad, 'tis," Alistair said.

Iain glanced from one to the other. "Hell, I dinna even know who she is."

Alistair and Margaret froze in their chairs, each mirroring the other's shocked expression. They both spoke at once, but Iain waved them off.

He stood and resumed pacing as he related how he'd come upon Alena in the wood and rescued her from her Grant pursuers. When he revealed his encounter with Reynold, and his attempt to barter for Alena's return, his aunt's eyes went wide.

"Iain, there are things you must—"

"Margaret, enough!" Alistair boomed. "We willna speak more of this."

"But—"

"I would see it played out awhile longer."

"What played out?" What the devil was going on? Iain narrowed his eyes and studied his uncle.

"Now, lad, when your father died—"

"Was murdered," Iain said.

"Aye, well…from that day forward I've raised ye as my own and watched ye grow into a fine warrior—a leader, a laird."

Iain snorted.

"Aye, laird ye are—The Mackintosh—and ye'll reclaim what's rightfully yours. But ye must be canny, son. The time is right. Both Macgillivray and MacBain are open to the alliance, but ye must be willing to meet them halfway."

"Meet them I will, but I willna wed that woman."

Margaret looked hard at her husband. "Alistair, The Macgillivray is my cousin. 'Tis a good bond we have. He's for us and for Iain. With or without the marriage."

"Mayhap, but 'twould be a certainty if Iain wed the daughter."

"But 'tis not required," she said.

Iain eyed the marriage contract signed by the Macgillivray laird. "Hmph." He rolled it tight and stowed it in the folds of his plaid. "And what of The MacBain? Gilchrist told ye, no doubt, of his meeting with Grant."

"Aye," Alistair said, "and we knew of it already. We met with him ourselves just days before. He made it plain he was not committing—not yet, at any rate. He's not a man who joins easily with others."

"Nay, he's not." Iain recalled MacBain's reluctance to join the alliance the night his father had called the summit at Findhorn Castle. *There be men here who would as soon stick a dirk in yer back as call ye friend.* MacBain's words had been a black portent of the events of that night. Iain shook off the dark memory.

"And ye will remember that business with his sister."

"I remember it." MacBain's sister had been promised to Henry Grant. 'Twould have made a formidable alliance.

"When Henry was slain," Alistair said, "The MacBain was forced to marry her off to one of his lesser chieftains. Though your father was butchered in retribution, MacBain blames the Mackintoshes still for his ill fortune."

"The MacBain will be compelled to join us. I've something that will convince him of the truth of things." Iain's hand moved absently to the sporran belted at his waist. He rummaged inside and withdrew the small circlet of hair. 'Twas powerful, eternal. As was his vow.

The girl would be a woman now. Who knew if she'd kept the jeweled dagger? And if, by some miracle of heaven, she had, how on God's earth would Iain find her, know her? He smiled at the memory of her small dirty face and forever-tangled hair. He'd loved her then. She was bonny and brave and...

A sudden vision of Alena atop the black filled his mind's eye. Christ, 'twas madness. All of it. He rose to leave and his uncle followed him to the door.

"Are ye certain ye wish to make this war on Grant? 'Tis not necessary, lad. Ye've a home here, always, with us."

Iain smiled thinly. He studied Alistair's weathered face and rich brown eyes. "Aye, and I'm grateful to ye, Uncle, for all ye've done. But I must do this thing. For my father and for my clan. For Gilchrist and Conall." He squeezed the lovers' knot tight in his hand. "And for me."

Alena stared blankly from her window at the stable lads grooming mounts in the yard below. She was trembling, and fought the new bout of tears welling in her eyes. She made fists of her hands to stop them shaking, digging her nails into her palms until the pain sharpened her anguish.

A bride. Iain's bride.

At Gilchrist's words her stomach had lurched, her face had blanched—she'd felt it. She'd run blindly to escape the threat of Iain and the others seeing her reaction: the tears that had sprung immediate and unbidden to her eyes. She'd made her way to the back of the house and had rushed up the small stairway from the kitchen to the abovestairs corridor and the sanctuary of her room.

Both Hetty and Edwina had tried to coax her belowstairs for the midday meal, but she would not go. She could not go. Iain had come twice to her room already, but she'd barred the door and ignored his pleas to speak with her.

She was a fool.

Had she really thought Iain Mackintosh could love her? She had, and her naivete sickened her. Aye, his desire was plain, but that's all it had been—lust. And she'd been ready to spread her legs for him like some common whore.

She turned from the window and leaned back against the cool, stone sill.

Iain must have known about Elizabeth Macgillivray all along. He'd even tried to tell her this morning that what had happened last night—their fierce and unbridled passion—had been a mistake. *'Twas wrong,* he'd said. *I dinna want ye to think…* What? That it meant something to him? Why would it? He was a laird and she was a stablemaster's daughter. A servant. Nothing.

Alena had overheard from her window the conversations in the stable yard below about the proposed alliance with Macgillivray, the strength a match between Iain and the laird's daughter would bring. Not to mention the lands, the wealth—all the things Iain had told her so long ago he wanted, and would wed for.

So where did she fit in?

What had he said when they were children? *Ye can fletch my arrows, lass, see to my warhorse…* And take care of his *other* needs, too, she supposed.

She sank to the bed and toyed with the fabric of her borrowed gown, rubbing the soft nub of pale green wool between her fingers. Hetty had insisted she change. Alena had complied, so shocked by the arrival of *Iain's bride* she'd scarcely noticed Hetty had wrestled her out of her breeches and shirt, slipped a gown over her head, and had combed out her ever-wild hair.

Alena examined her callused hands, made so from years of work. Work she loved. She snorted. All the gowns in Scotland would not make her a lady the likes of Elizabeth Macgillivray.

The woman was beautiful and rich. A worthy bride for Iain. One who would bring him the sorely needed manpower he must have if he were to challenge Reynold Grant for the return of Findhorn Castle.

Iain needed the alliance. Without it, he had not the numbers to wage a war and win. But Iain would challenge Grant with or without Macgillivray's help. Of that Alena was certain.

She closed her eyes against stinging tears and for the dozenth time told herself she must be strong. Iain would marry Elizabeth Macgillivray and have his alliance. She would return to her clan and wed Reynold Grant. 'Twas the only solution.

As Reynold's wife and as mistress of Glenmore Castle she would be in a position to influence her husband's actions and certain events. Perhaps she could persuade him to give up Findhorn Castle. Should Iain gain the support of the Chattan clans he would be a formidable force, one Reynold might think twice about challenging.

She recalled the cold brutality that burned like a thin, icy flame in Reynold's eyes. Nay, Grant was a man who'd not willingly give up anything of value, least of all his enemy's vanquished holdings.

And Iain would not be satisfied until blood ran hot from his sword. *I willna rest until every last one of them is dead.* Stalwart words for a boy of twelve, but a vow Alena knew he meant to keep. Jesu, was there any way out?

She took some comfort in the fact that, as Reynold's wife, she would be able to protect her parents. She drew breath and exhaled slowly, getting a grip on her turbulent emotions.

"Bear up. There's more at stake here than your foolish heart."

She knew what she must do. She must leave right away. But how?

The demesne was teeming with warriors, scores of Mackintosh and Davidson clansmen. She was certain she could outride any man, but did not want to create a situation where she would be pursued.

Nay, 'twould have to be a stealthy departure, one best achieved at night while most were abed. The demesne was heavily patrolled and the walls of the estate guarded, but she would find a way. She must.

A soft knock sounded at the door of her chamber, and Alena froze. 'Twas not Iain's sharp, insistent rapping, nor was it accompanied by Hetty's rattling of the door latch. 'Twas someone else. "Who is there?" she asked.

"Margaret Davidson," the calm, musical voice answered. "Might I speak with you, child?"

She hesitated a moment, then slipped the bar from its position across the heavy oak door. She opened it cautiously and peeked out. Margaret Davidson, the mistress of Braedûn Lodge, stood alone in the corridor, her arms piled high with clothing.

Alena swung the door inward—what else could she do?—and stepped aside as Margaret glided into the room and moved purposefully toward the bed. She tossed her burden onto the plaid coverlet as Alena quickly rebarred the door.

A smile, bright as the summer sun, graced Margaret's smooth, lineless face. "Alena, child, let me look at you." Her voice was warm, almost tender, as she floated toward her and took Alena's hands in hers.

Without warning, Alena felt a sharp longing for her own mother and fought the tears glassing her eyes.

Margaret scanned her features with both an interest and a recognition Alena found unnerving. The lady squeezed her hands then let them go. "You are lovely, and Ellen's gown suits you remarkably well."

Embarrassed, she brushed her hands over the soft green wool. "Oh, I...didn't mean to wear her... Edwina and Hetty thought—"

"Edwina and Hetty were right. And Iain, as well." Margaret waved at the pile on the bed. "And here are some other things of Iain's mother's I thought you might like.

They are beautiful clothes and are in need of someone with your stature and grace to do them justice.''

She peeked over Margaret's shoulder at the garments on the bed. "Oh, I could not. 'Twouldn't be proper. Mayhap Iain's…betrothed—'' the word stuck in her throat ''—would want them.''

Margaret dismissed the notion with a wave of her hand. She moved gracefully to the bed and began to unfold and smooth the gowns she'd brought with her. "Nonsense, Elizabeth has gowns enough to clothe the whole of Scotland.''

Alena remembered the half dozen horses laden with trunks that had pressed into the courtyard behind Lady Elizabeth and Father Ambrose. "Oh, but of course she would.'' Her cheeks grew hot. "How stupid of me.'' She moved to assist Margaret who was busy inspecting the garments that now covered Alena's bed.

"Besides, methinks Elizabeth Macgillivray wouldn't cherish them as might another. Ellen was very dear to me and to her sons. I'd not see her things cast off onto the rag heap.''

"Oh, nay. They are beautiful and far too fine for me.''

"Nonsense. Now here's a lovely thing.'' Margaret untangled a white garment from the twisted pile of gowns and lightly shook it out.

Alena gasped. The shift was made of the barest whisper of fine, sheer silk and had long, translucent sleeves. A chain of delicate lavender thistles joined with soft green stems was embroidered along the low rounded neckline. "'Tis lovely,'' she whispered. "Like the gossamer wings of a dove.''

Margaret's eyes shone as she held the garment aloft. "'Twas Ellen's—the night rail she wore to her bridal bed. Now there was a fine marriage, the one betwixt Ellen and

Colum Mackintosh.'' Margaret's smile faded to a wistful sort of frown. ''She was like a sister to me, but she was ne'er the same woman after Colum was...after he died.''

Margaret paused, then her face brightened again. She turned the delicate shift in her hands. '''Twas only worn the once—and not for very long, methinks.'' She arched a brow and her eyes twinkled with mirth.

Alena smiled awkwardly, her face flushed with heat. She knew little of such things. But she would have known more were she and Iain not interrupted in the hayloft last eve.

'''Twill bring good fortune and many sons to the lass who wears it.'' Margaret thrust the night rail into her hands. ''Here, you've the figure for it.''

''Oh, nay, I—''

Margaret forced Alena's hands to close over the thin fabric, stilling her protest. She handled the shift gently, turning it over and over, stroking the fine, soft weave.

A pristine and naked emotion welled inside her. She clutched the night rail to her breast, fighting a tide of despair and regret for the marriage bed that would never be, the sons she'd never have.

Iain's sons.

Margaret's hand on her shoulder brought her to attention. The lady's eyes were drawn to the trunk that lay open at the foot of the bed, where Alena's borrowed clothes and pale yellow gown were folded neatly as if in preparation for something. Margaret frowned and in inquiry raised a thin brow.

''Oh,'' Alena said. ''I thought to move into the stable, so as to make space for the Lady Elizabeth.'' *And to better my chances of slipping away in the night.* ''There are few rooms here for guests, and as she is to be Iain's...bride—''

''The stable?''

''Aye.''

Margaret studied her. ''I've heard naught but praise for the magic you've worked with Duncan's mounts. I admire women with skills. 'Tis even better when they rival a man's.'' A corner of her mouth curved in a wry smile. ''Sewing and keeping the house are fine for some, but not all.''

She met Margaret's appraising gaze. The lady's eyes sparkled like deep blue pools. She felt drawn into them and comforted, somehow, as if this woman understood her, and approved. She smiled back, then laid the gossamer night rail on the bed.

''You might be good with horses, child, but I'll not have you sleeping with them. You will sleep here in this room. Elizabeth has already been installed in a small chamber belowstairs. 'Twill suffice.''

''But—''

''Besides, I want you close to us…to Iain.'' Alena caught her even gaze. ''My nephew told us of how you came to be here, how he came upon you in the wood.''

Alena looked away and began to arrange the pile of gowns on the bed. Her hands trembled and she worked quickly to hide her discomfort. ''Aye, 'twas most fortunate for me he happened to be hunting in that place.''

''And most fortunate for him, methinks.''

Her mind raced, searching for a new subject—something that had naught to do with her or with Iain. ''Your accent,'' Alena said abruptly, '''tis unusual.''

''I was born a Macgillivray, in the Highlands, but grew up in the Borderlands with my mother's people. When I wed Alistair I came here to the Davidson stronghold, which is not far from my birthplace.''

Alena nodded politely. A Macgillivray. Margaret would have some stake in this marriage between Iain and one of her clan. And yet she seemed to dismiss Lady Elizabeth at every turn.

"And *your* speech," Margaret said, interrupting her thoughts. "'Tis Scots and yet 'tis...different."

"Oh, aye," she said absently, her mind still working on the Macgillivray connection. "My mother is French and she—" Jesu, would she give herself away to this woman so easily? She glanced quickly at Margaret and caught her raised brows.

No matter. Margaret Macgillivray Davidson was a high-born lady and would not know of Robert and Madeleine Todd, stablemasters to Clan Grant. Alena forced herself to relax and continue with her work.

"Ah, yes, that would account for it." Margaret's voice was placid, unsurprised. She finished with the gowns and folded her small white hands in front of her. "Now, we missed you at the midday meal. You will join us for supper." 'Twas a command, not a request.

Jesu, how would she muster the strength to sit at table with Iain and his bride and not betray her feelings? Her mind searched for a suitable excuse but she could think of nothing that would not create suspicion. Resigned to it, she nodded her assent and forced the words from her mouth. "I'd be honored, Lady."

"You must call me Margaret." She stepped closer and grazed long fingers over Alena's cheek, letting them rest for a moment on her chin. Her eyes were warm and... *knowing*.

Jesu, Margaret knew her!

She felt it in the depths of her soul. But how? How did she know her? Duncan? Nay, he gave his word he wouldn't yet speak of it, and Alena trusted the old man.

Father Ambrose? He must have recognized her and made his knowledge known. If so, they would all know she was a Todd—and of Clan Grant. But nay, this wouldn't explain the lady's recognition of her.

How could this be?

Alena's mind raced. "Um, Father Ambrose...he will be at table this night?"

"Aye. We do not often see him. 'Tis a pleasure and a blessing to have a man of God among us."

"Aye, it is." Then, of a sudden, the obvious purpose of the priest's visit slammed into her. She turned away and grasped the carved oak bedpost with both hands. Her throat went dry and her voice was but a rasp. "He is here to perform...the wedding?"

Margaret did not answer.

"Iain's—I...I mean, the laird's wedding?"

"Ah, aye." Margaret's voice was lilting, almost cheerful. "'Twould make sense to take advantage of his presence, would it not?"

Alena felt the hot sting of tears and for the third time that day fought for control. "Then Iain...does intend to wed?"

"From all I've seen and heard this day, it appears my nephew has every intention of marrying—and quickly."

Alena sucked in her breath and closed her eyes against the hot torrents brimming there. White-knuckled, she dug her nails into the burnished wood of the bedpost.

Margaret's footfalls moved toward the door. "But there is one question yet unanswered, child. Who shall be the bride?"

Chapter Twelve

She was late.

Iain ground his teeth and drummed his fingers impatiently on the huge oak table. The great hall was teeming with warriors who swilled their ale and related wild tales of the events of the past few weeks.

Alistair had taken his customary place at the head of the table on the dais near the hearth. The wood fire blazed and crackled behind him, casting a warm glow on the rest of the diners. Margaret sat on the bench to her husband's left while Iain fidgeted in the seat to his uncle's right, which afforded him a view of the wide staircase and entry.

Much to his displeasure, Elizabeth Macgillivray, attired in a revealing scarlet gown that left little to one's imagination, had been seated next to him. She'd spent the past quarter hour attempting to engage him in trivial chitchat. Fortunately, his brother Gilchrist sat opposite them and was all too happy to secure the lady's attentions.

Iain's gaze drifted farther down the table to Father Ambrose who was wedged uncomfortably in between Hamish and Will with no way to politely escape their litany of bawdy jokes and made-up tales. Iain snorted in mild amusement then turned his attention to his ale cup, which he'd barely touched.

He'd tried all afternoon, without success, to see Alena alone. Three times he'd requested entry to her chamber—the third time his patience worn so thin he was tempted to grab an ax from the wall and split the door asunder. But he was refused on each occasion. Now he was desperate to speak with her, to make her understand there was no truth to this bride business.

He cast a sidelong glance to Elizabeth. Aye, she was pretty and alluring in that gown, but she held no interest for him. Normally he'd welcome the opportunity to bed a willing lass and think himself lucky to have one so fair. But her hair was all wrong. 'Twas dark, as were her eyes.

When Iain closed his own eyes he saw cascades of tumbled wheat and flax, and eyes the color of spring moss. Not pale, white skin, but burnished gold with a spray of freckles across the nose. Not some pretty plaything, weak and helpless, but a woman bonny and braw with a passion to match his own. A woman not afraid to take risks. A woman like Alena.

God help him, but he'd have her and no other.

He drew a breath and focused his eyes on the staircase. Where the devil was she? He was about to send Edwina in search of her when a pale yellow swirl at the top of the landing caught his attention. She floated down the staircase like some bright apparition, and he wasn't the only man in the room to notice.

She wore her hair loose, a firefall of burnished gold in the warm glow of the hearth fire. She approached their table, head held high and eyes darting from one clansman to another, purposefully avoiding his gaze. The honey-silk gown she'd had on when first he'd seen her in the Highland wood suited her. Simple and elegant, 'twas a startling contrast to Elizabeth Macgillivray's garish attire.

The gown had been cleaned and repaired, all traces of Reynold Grant's despoilment gone. Iain stiffened, remembering the bloody fingerprints that had covered it the day he'd found her. Christ, he should have killed the whoreson when he'd had the chance.

He bristled at the nods of approval and lusty grunts drifting from the end of the table where half a dozen warriors sat transfixed by Alena's presence.

Awkwardly, he pushed back the bench with his thighs, jostling the Lady Elizabeth who proceeded to spill her wine. He stood to offer Alena a seat, but she ignored him and walked tentatively toward the other end of the table.

Gilchrist shot to his feet. "Lady Alena. Will ye honor me?" He indicated a place on the bench between his seat and Margaret's.

Alena hesitated, studying his brother's irresistible smile, then accepted the seat, which placed her directly across the table from him and Elizabeth. Her cheeks flushed a demure peach, and she lowered her eyes to avoid both his gaze and Elizabeth's noticeable scrutiny.

"We are so pleased you have joined us, my dear," Margaret said, and affectionately patted her arm.

Alena flashed his aunt a thin smile. "Thank you, my lady."

Alistair said nothing but watched her with interest. He glanced at Iain and cocked a brow.

"Hmph." Iain looked evenly at his uncle for a moment, then lifted his ale cup and drained it in one swift motion.

"Alena," Gilchrist said, "have ye met the Lady Elizabeth Macgillivray?"

Iain narrowed his eyes at his brother and made a mental note to murder him as soon as the meal was done. Alena looked up, and for a moment her eyes met Iain's. His heart-beat quickened and he fisted his hands in his lap.

"I am pleased to meet you, Lady," she said.

Ignoring Alena's greeting, Elizabeth slid closer to him on the bench. "So, this is the horsewoman. She is the talk of Braedûn Lodge, is she not?"

Iain kept his eyes on Alena. "Aye, she is a woman of skill and knowledge where beasts are concerned."

Alena's cheeks flushed and she again riveted her gaze to the table and the steaming trenchers of food before them.

"Ah, beasts." Elizabeth drew herself up, her lips a hair-breath from his ear. "But what of her skill with men?" she whispered.

To his astonishment, he felt Elizabeth's slippered foot graze his booted leg. He ignored her outrageous boldness. He was desperate to speak with Alena alone, but willed himself to get through the meal.

He noticed Elizabeth staring at Alena, her dark gaze in-specting, scrutinizing. She cleared her throat—a high, del-icate sound. "Alena, 'tis an unusual name for a Scot. What is your clan?"

Her wine cup halfway to her lips, Alena froze. Iain leaned forward, as did the others at the table, straining to hear her answer over the din and raucous laughter echoing off the stone walls.

Alena sipped at her wine and met Elizabeth's cool gaze. "I hale from far away."

"Aye, well that would explain it—and your clothes." Elizabeth smirked and flashed her dark eyes at Iain. "I havena seen a gown like that in years. 'Tis truly a relic." She tittered, covering her mouth with a small white hand.

Alena lowered her cup. Her expression hardened to stone; her eyes burned a green, catlike fire. She drew a breath and Iain felt a stirring in his loins as he watched the gentle heaving of her breasts 'neath the close-fitting gown.

"Aye, 'tis old," she said. "'Twas given me by someone I hold dear." Her voice was deadly calm, and Iain thought her magnificent.

Elizabeth giggled. "A lover?"

Gilchrist shot him a mischievous grin.

The chatter at the table again ceased, and all waited for her reply. Iain realized that he, too, was waiting.

"Nay," she said. "The gown was a gift from my mother."

He exhaled, relaxing the taut muscles of his face. His heart raced, and he caught himself smiling stupidly at Alena's response. He glanced at his uncle and aunt, who, for the second time this day, exchanged identical looks of surprise. They studied Alena with renewed interest as she began to pick at the roasted meat on the trencher she shared with Gilchrist.

"'Tis the loveliest gown I've e'er seen," Iain said quietly, willing her to look at him.

At last she lifted her eyes and met his gaze.

With his own eyes he projected his awe of her strength and innocent perfection, his intense desire, his love and his torment—reaching out to her, bidding her to see.

And she did see.

He read it in her face, so startlingly beautiful, framed with a fire-gold halo that spilled like some alchemist's molten treasure over shoulder, breast and waist. He felt her recognition and something else—something that shook him to his very core.

She loved him.

He knew it, breathed it, drank it in like a thirsty beggar who'd wandered for years in a wasteland. Their eyes locked and Iain was barely cognizant of the others watching them.

A second later she broke his gaze and the moment vanished. Oh, but she couldn't take it back. And he would never forget it.

She turned her attention to the end of the table where Will and Hamish sat beside Father Ambrose. Iain looked past the pouting Elizabeth to better see their faces.

The two warriors were busily stuffing themselves with meat and bread, washing it all down with huge gulps of ale. The priest sat quietly between them, silent, his eyes on Alena.

Iain had met Father Ambrose but a few times. He was new to the Highlands and to the church, recently ordained, so Iain had heard. He was a young man, thin and nervous looking. He supposedly traveled among the clans, performing weddings, baptisms, last rites and the like. He might be able to provide some useful information about the comings and goings at Glenmore Castle if he, perchance, had passed that way. Iain would remember to ask him.

Alena didn't look at the priest, but kept her eyes moving as if she were afraid to hold his gaze. Something was odd about her reaction to him, and Ambrose's fixation on her.

"Hamish," Ambrose said suddenly. "'Tis said that Reynold Grant bartered with your laird for some unnamed woman. His lover, I think she was."

Iain choked on his wine. Alena jolted to attention and riveted her gaze on the priest.

"'Tis said he offered gold for her return."

Hamish looked up from his trencher, still chewing, and caught Iain's stony expression. He glanced briefly at Alena then said, "Aye, well, Iain told him—The Grant—that we'd no' seen such a woman."

Alena didn't move a muscle. Her face was blank, but her eyes grew wide with trepidation. Iain longed to hold her, calm her fears. And to find out the truth of things.

Hamish smiled, still chewing, and pointed his knife at the priest. "But if we had, d'ye think our laird would give her up to his sworn enemy, just like that?"

Ambrose glanced speculatively at Iain. "Nay, I don't think he would." He sipped his wine and said, "So, there's to be a war."

The table went dead quiet. All eyes turned on the priest.

"And where did ye hear that, Father?"

Ambrose flushed, as if he just this moment realized he'd gone too far. "Why, the...t-talk's all over the Highlands. And at Glenmore Castle."

"I'd have a word with ye, Ambrose." Alistair's face was stone. "Later."

"And, Father," Iain said coldly, "whilst we are honored to have a man of God among us, ye'd best be moving on. I'm certain there's many a clan could profit from your services."

Elizabeth Macgillivray squeaked beside him.

The priest flit his eyes to her, to Margaret and Alistair, then back to Iain. "But surely—"

"The morrow should prove a good day to travel. My brother, Gilchrist, and a score of warriors will see ye safe to our border."

Elizabeth shifted on the bench beside him and screwed her reddened lips into a pout. "But—"

"On the morrow." Iain held his cup aloft for the serving maid who sprang forward to refill it.

The corners of Gilchrist's mouth curved in a wry smile, and for a moment Iain met his brother's gaze.

He returned his attention to Alena who'd gone shock-still with the news of Grant. He tried to coax a glance from her but failed. He was reluctant to speak to her directly for fear, once he started, he'd pour his soul out in front of his family, his clan and their guests.

Nay, he must wait until they were alone. And then he'd speak his heart.

She was in some deep trouble, that much Iain knew. He must persuade her to trust him, to enlist his help. She wouldn't be forced to reveal the truth, and he no longer wished to force her. He loved her. He wanted her to trust him, to seek his aid, and his love.

And he wanted to trust her—with his heart, his pain, his plans for his clan and his hopes for the future. But what future could there be for her with him? In truth, he could very well be dead within the week, should he face Grant as planned.

His warriors were more than ready, itching for battle, and loyal to his cause. Mackintosh and Davidson alike supported his claim, but their numbers were small compared to Grant's vast army. Even if they could reclaim Findhorn and rout the Grants from off his land, the vermin would return and in huge numbers.

He needed the support of all the Chattan clans, and to count on the Macgillivrays and the MacBains was foolish. They would require more than Iain's words to condemn Reynold Grant for his past sins. Proof was needed of his treachery, and of the innocence of Iain's father on that night long ago.

He must find that jeweled dagger!

'Twas the only way now. But how?

"When will ye make your move, lad?" Alistair whispered.

He met his uncle's gaze. "In two days, perhaps three. There is something I must do first."

An image of the girl clutching the plaid-wrapped dirk to her breast flashed briefly in Iain's mind. He turned and caught Alena watching him.

Bloody hell, what was he going to do?

"Iain." Alistair tugged on his shirtsleeve. "There is something ye need know."

"Tomorrow," he said, not listening.

"Aye, tomorrow then."

Alena lowered her eyes. She pushed back from the table and abruptly stood. "Laird, Lady," she said to Alistair and Margaret. "I bid you pardon me. I'm very tired and would retire now."

His aunt smiled at her. "But, child, you've hardly touched your food. Won't you stay awhile longer?"

"Thank you, Lady, but nay."

She turned to leave and Iain saw his chance.

He shot from his seat. "Alena, I'll escort ye to your chamber."

He bolted 'round the table, but she moved to Gilchrist's side and placed a hand on his shoulder. "Oh, nay, Laird. Do not trouble yourself. Your brother has already offered."

Gilchrist grinned and cocked a wiry, blond brow. "Oh, aye," he said, rising quickly from the bench. "I'd be honored, Lady." He extended his arm to her.

Iain offered his hand, as well, but Alena stepped away and wouldn't meet his eyes. She took Gilchrist's proffered arm and pulled him quickly to the staircase.

Iain watched them ascend, his gut churning, until the hem of her gown disappeared with a swoosh at the top of stairs.

In another hour the moon would set. 'Twas nearly time.

Alena leaned against the window frame in her chamber and stared at the bright orb that just last night had beamed full and glorious, as had her heart.

Iain's love words, his heated kisses, their bodies writhing together in desperate need—it all seemed a lifetime ago, crushed by the cruel events of this day.

She felt chilled suddenly, and briskly rubbed the goose-flesh from her arms. Hetty had helped her undress and had insisted she don the gossamer night rail Lady Margaret had given her that afternoon. Alena had resisted at first, but then relented, knowing 'twould be the only time she'd ever wear it. She ran her hands over the nearly sheer silk and felt her nipples harden beneath the wispy fabric.

"Jesu, give me the strength to leave him."

She recalled Iain's curious behavior at supper. He'd actually shunned Elizabeth's attentions. Every time Alena had looked up from the table, Iain was staring at *her,* not at the small dark beauty who'd soon be his wife.

Lady Elizabeth Macgillivray. Beautiful and rich, but she was also snobbish and mean-spirited. Alena bristled at the recollection of Elizabeth's rude remarks about her gown. No matter. Alena would soon be gone from here, and Iain would have his bride and his alliance.

Her tears welled again and she battled them into submission. She could not allow herself to think about the future. A future without Iain. She must focus on this night alone, on her escape. 'Twould be dangerous, but she would succeed.

The demesne was heavily guarded, but Alena was certain she could slip over the low spot in the wall at the back of the stable yard without being seen. With Destiny as her mount, once she was safely away from the lodge no one would be able to stop her. She recalled the lay of the land, spread out before her that day atop the ancient ruins.

"Aye, I'll find the way home."

Shivering, she padded to the bed. Earlier she'd tried to sleep but had just lain there, her mind racing. Nay, there would be no sleep for her tonight, nor tomorrow—not until she reached the Clan Grant demesne and her parents' cottage.

For the tenth time she inspected the things she meant to take with her. She would wear the breeches, boots and wool shirt she'd borrowed from young Jamie, and a plaid for warmth. But 'twould be too dangerous to ride into Grant territory wearing the Mackintosh colors. One of her kinsmen might kill her before he recognized her as one of their own. She'd take a Davidson plaid. She'd need the warmth and 'twould be safe enough.

She rolled the pale yellow gown, her mother's gift to her, into a small bundle and laid it aside along with the plaid.

"Now all I need is a bit of food and a wineskin of ale." 'Twould be foolish to try and ride that distance without some sustenance.

Earlier that day she had collected some bread and cheese from the kitchen. She'd also lifted a half-full wineskin from off one of the mounts in the stable yard. Unfortunately Hetty had found her stash, hidden under the bed, and had taken it away with her that evening, muttering something about vermin.

"Blast the girl!"

Well, she'd just have to get more. She considered waiting until 'twas time to leave but discarded the idea at once.

Should someone see her, 'twould be too difficult to explain what she was doing in the kitchen, dressed for a journey, in the wee hours of the night. Nay, she would go now, in her nightclothes. Should someone see her, she could simply say she was hungry.

She grabbed the plaid, shook it out and whirled it 'round her shoulders, pulling it close about her. She padded to the door and lifted the latch. All was quiet.

It had been quite a celebration that evening to welcome home the laird and lady. Most of the men had still been hung over from the festivities in the stable yard the night before. They should all be abed now, and sleeping soundly, she hoped.

Still, this was no time to risk discovery. She stepped into the drafty corridor and, instead of turning left toward the main staircase that led to the great hall, she turned right, intending to use the small stairway at the opposite end of the corridor—the one the servants used between the upper floors and the kitchen.

She crept quietly along the corridor, keeping close to the wall. There were no torches alight on this floor, only the pale glow of the tapers and the hearth fire from the great hall below to light her way. It took a moment for her eyes to adjust to the darkness.

She passed a door on her right and stopped to listen. 'Twas Iain's chamber, she was sure. She'd seen him come and go from it several times. She gripped the plaid tighter about her and closed her eyes for a moment, fighting the overpowering urge to simply walk through the door and into his arms.

She forced herself to take a step, then another, moving quickly to the end of the corridor. She reached the stairs and put a hand out to steady her descent. The last thing she needed was to pitch forward into blackness and break her neck.

Creeping silently down the curving stair, she felt the pleasant warmth of the kitchen hearth fire rise up to meet her. A warm glow softened the darkness and the smell of fresh bread buoyed her spirits. At the bottom of the steps she stopped and peeked tentatively 'round the corner into the kitchen.

The room was empty.

One of the Davidson dogs snored comfortably by the hearth, surrounded by a litter of clean, white venison bones. She stepped gingerly past him and headed for the larder.

A chill suddenly gripped her. A light breeze billowed the hem of her thin night rail. She stopped and turned to see from whence it came. Scanning the room, she saw nothing. She turned back toward the larder but before she could take a step she felt the breeze again.

This time she padded silently 'round the kitchen, looking for the source of night air. Ah, there it was! The small door leading to the garden stood open. She'd best close it against the chill night.

She reached for the latch and froze.

Iain sat on a bench, not twenty feet from her, resting against the smooth stones of the garden wall. Highland heather, a tangle of wildflowers and fragrant herbs surrounded him. In the ghostly moonlight he resembled more fairy spirit than warrior.

In his hands he cradled a circlet, a child's heartfelt gift: a braid of hair bound with a strip of tartan, the soft moonlight illuminating the marked contrast of chestnut against gold.

The plaid slipped from her shoulders to the floor as she gripped the door frame for support. The tears she'd fought so desperately welled again, unbidden and unstoppable.

She watched as he fingered the lovers' knot affectionately, almost reverently, and was certain her heart would break from the magnitude of his tenderness.

"Jesu, help me to be strong."

He looked up then, his own eyes dark and glassy, his face a mask of despair. The face of a boy who wept for his father, the face of a warrior who knew no peace from his inner torment.

And in that moment she was lost forever in a fierce, immutable love that smote to dust her hard-won resolve.

Chapter Thirteen

She was really there.

A woman, an angel—some ethereal creature all gossamer and silvered gold in the moon's pale light. A gentle breeze lifted wild tendrils of hair from off her face and molded the diaphanous silk of her night rail to every curve of her body. She drew a breath and her breasts swelled against the milky fabric, nipples taut and ripe.

She was the Madonna.

Venus rising from a turbulent sea.

Iain crushed the circlet in his fist and before he could rise she rushed toward him, an angel in flight. He opened his arms, and she fell to her knees before him.

She wept, silver tears reflecting the moonlight. Her pain was replete, visceral, and he hungered to embrace it and fuse it with his own so they might burn together, bright against the dark promises that would keep them apart.

She tried to pry his fingers open, and he resisted, suddenly fearful of losing her should she find the token he bore. She persisted, and for some reason he relented; he opened his hand and the lovers' knot sprang forth. She studied it for a moment with a kind of awe, then looked up at him, eyes luminous silver in the milky light.

Oh, how he loved her. He cupped her face with shaking hands. Nay, she would never understand. How could he tell her? How could he not? "Alena," he breathed, and leaned in to kiss her.

"Nay." She pulled back from him, her eyes huge and liquid.

He started to speak, wanted to tell her everything, but her fingers pressed lightly against his lips, stilling his words. "Do you not know me?"

"What?" He searched her face, brushing her tears away with his thumbs.

"Look at me!" Her hands trembled as she lifted the circlet, chestnut and gold, between them as if it were some holy relic.

Anxiety gripped him. He felt as if all he knew, the infallible tenets that had shaped his life, were suddenly suspect. He ran his fingers through her hair, fisting a handful of spun gold, and drew it toward him.

Her eyes begged him, implored him to see.

And then he did see.

"Lass," he breathed in wonder, his eyes darting back and forth from her hair to the braided circlet she held in her hand.

She grasped the front of his plaid and pulled him toward her. In a dream state he slid from the bench to the ground. Was it possible? She swayed in his arms and he steadied her, bracing himself against the faltering of his own liquid limbs.

She murmured his name, tears brimming, her face contorting in anguish.

His own eyes welled again. He gripped her shoulders tight, afraid to believe. Afraid not to. "It *is* you!"

"Aye." She tucked the circlet into the folds of his plaid, over his heart. "It's me." Her hands cupped his face and in her eyes, her gentle touch, he read an almost painful longing.

"But...how? When did you know me?"

"From almost the first I saw you." Her mouth bloomed in a smile. "You've not changed all that much, you know."

He grinned and pulled her into an embrace, recalling the perpetually dirty face and wild, tangled hair of the sprite he once knew. "You have." He drank in the sight of her, accepting what his heart knew as truth. "I canna believe I didna see it. I felt it, but..."

He claimed her mouth in a desperate kiss, needing to touch her, taste her, prove to himself she was real. Aye, she was his. She always had been. 'Twas meant to be.

He breathed in the warm scent of her and felt his heart swell with tenderness. Her tears were hot, salty on his lips as he peppered her face with small, fervent kisses. "Dinna weep, love."

"But you weep."

"For joy," he said, stunned by the magnitude of his feelings. He kissed her again.

She wiped his tears away and smiled up at him, her face radiant in the moonlight. Oh, that he could freeze this one moment in time forever.

"So tell me, what is your name?"

Her smile broadened and her eyes lit up. "'Tis Alena."

They both laughed.

"I am glad, for 'tis the name that haunts my dreams and the one I whisper in my prayers."

She drew herself up for another kiss. They knelt on the hard, stony soil of the garden, but she seemed not to care. He lifted her. Their lips met and she trembled in his arms.

He must know. He had to ask it.

"Alena," he whispered against her lips. "What is your surname, your clan?"

Her body went slack in his arms. Her voice was the barest whisper. "Please, let us not speak of it this night."

Her face clouded with doubt and what he knew was fear. Nay, he wouldn't force her. He must win her trust. "Oh, lass, I dinna care if ye are the devil's own daughter. I love you."

"I have *always* loved you."

He held her for a moment, committing to memory her fresh, innocent beauty, the adoration in her eyes. He wanted her more than he'd ever wanted anything in his life.

Then he bore her back and kissed her thoroughly. Her arms shot 'round him and she returned his kiss with an ardor that surprised him. He was all too aware that the thin silk of her shift was but a flimsy barrier between him and her bare flesh. He rolled his hips against her and watched her response. Her eyes were vitreous, passionate, her lips wet and parted, swollen from his rough kisses.

The ache in his gut, the anxiety that gripped him at the thought of ever losing her, laid bare to him the magnitude of his love. "Marry me, Alena. Marry me."

Her soft brow furrowed. 'Twas not the response he'd expected. He moved a hand over the curve of her waist and upward, cupping her breast, and felt the sharp beat of her heart beneath his hand. "Say you'll marry me."

Her eyes glassed with new tears. "'Tis my heart's desire, but—"

"Then it shall be so, as soon as this business with Grant is done."

"Nay! Promise me you will not go against him. He is very powerful. I'm afraid for you, Iain."

"Dinna worry about such things."

"But—"

"Hush now," he murmured against her lips. "Ye must trust me, love, to do what's best."

He would protect her with his life, with all he commanded—no matter who she was—and wouldn't have her anxious over events far beyond her control.

His mouth moved over the moonlit curve of her neck, her skin afire against his lips. She moaned softly and he blazed a trail of brief, delicate kisses across her collarbone.

"Iain," she breathed. "Make love to me."

Oh, he intended to. He couldn't help the low, guttural sound escaping his throat. He gripped her tighter and grazed his teeth along her bare shoulder. Her hips surged against him and his desire flared, his body stiff with need. Before he realized what he was doing, he'd slipped the gossamer night rail from off her shoulder.

The silky fabric slid and caught on the hardened tip of one perfect breast. He tasted his way lower and her breaths grew short, like the panting of some wild, beautiful creature. He willed himself to stop, but his body ignored the plea.

With his teeth he drew the silk over the edge, revealing her small areola. 'Twas lovely, virginal—a smooth, dusky ivory in the moonglow. He circled it with his tongue, then drew the ripe nipple into his mouth and began to suckle.

She gasped and gave her weight up to him, her body quivering in his embrace. His own body quickened, his loins afire, as he gripped her tighter, kneading her buttocks and grinding his hips against her.

"Aye," she cried, and dug her nails into his shoulders.

He was seconds away from losing all control. His head pounded, his blood screamed through his veins. His only thought was to bear her back onto the cool ground and slake his desire within her yielding body.

Mustering all his discipline, he pushed himself away from her, his passion barely in check. "Nay, love. No' like this. No' here in this place."

Her face bloomed in a seductive fusion of innocence and passion. His need was all-consuming, but his determination to honor her, love her as she deserved to be loved, stayed his hunger. "We should wait for the wedding."

With a trembling hand he slid her shift back onto her shoulder, covering her exposed breast. "In the marriage bed where I was born—I and my father before me—there I will make you mine." He kissed her softly on the mouth and felt a joy the likes of which he'd never known.

But she could never truly be his, could she?

A surge of emotion welled inside her and she choked back a sob, her eyes clouding again with tears. A vision of Reynold Grant flashed briefly, hideously, in her mind. She held tight to Iain, willing the image away. "I do not wish to wait. Make love to me, Iain. Now, tonight."

"Oh, lass." His eyes grew dark and searching, his desire all too evident. "Are ye sure?"

She was never more sure of anything in her life. She moved his hand to her breast, her eyes locked on his, and pressed it against her body. "Aye."

They came together in a desperate embrace, doubt and fear reborn into hope and unfettered joy. His mouth seared her skin with frenzied kisses. His hands were everywhere, fondling, stroking, and her desire exploded into furious passion.

He swept her into his arms, and the shock of it left her breathless. He shot to his feet and carried her back into the kitchen. She clung to him, breathing in his musky, male scent, allowing her lips to roam the hot pulse point of his neck.

He tightened his grip on her, then tripped over the dog who lay slumbering on the hearth. "Bluidy hell!"

She laughed and held on tight as he recovered his footing, ducked into the stairwell, and bounded up the steps with her in his arms.

"Hurry," she whispered against his neck, no longer shocked by her own wantonness, not caring about anything beyond this one night, this moment in his arms.

He bore her silently down the dark, empty corridor. Shifting her weight in his arms, he fumbled with the latch of his bedchamber door. A second later they were inside.

She'd never seen his room and her first impression was that it was small, much smaller than the one she occupied. 'Twas sparsely furnished with a simple bed flanked by a chest on one side and a plain wooden chair on the other. Atop the chest rested an elaborately carved box, a cup and an ewer. There were no tapestries on the walls, nor were there rushes on the bare, wooden floor. A fire burned low in the hearth and cast a warm glow about the otherwise spiritless place.

Iain carried her to the bed and set her gently down beside it. He looked at her with longing, his eyes indigo pools, his face handsomely ruddy in the firelight. She would always remember him so, no matter what happened.

He slipped the belt that held his broadsword from off his shoulder and leaned the weapon against the hearth. Then he removed the two dirks sheathed at his waist. She'd never seen a man undress before. She watched in fascination as he tugged off his boots and tossed them out of the way.

Her heart thrummed in her chest as he unbuckled the wide leather belt that held his plaid in place 'round his waist. He hesitated for a moment, then cast it aside. The plaid slipped to the floor, leaving him naked but for his shirt.

She yearned to let her eyes roam the long, muscular expanse of his legs, but willed herself hold his gaze. The night was still; silent but for the crackling of the fire.

He undid the laces of his shirt then paused. "Are ye sure?"

She nodded.

"Do ye know what…to expect?"

"Oh, aye. I've seen it many times."

His brows shot up in surprise, and she knew he'd mistaken her meaning. Her cheeks flamed. "With horses, I mean."

The corners of his mouth twitched in a smile. His eyes sparkled with tenderness. "Oh. Well, it's no' quite the same."

Without preamble, he stripped the shirt off and cast it aside. He stood naked before her, his body bathed in the hearth fire's golden radiance.

Her eyes widened of their own accord. She held her breath, transfixed by the virile beauty of the warrior who stood before her. She did let her eyes stray then, slowly roaming the landscape of his athletic form.

His dark hair was long enough to frame his broad shoulders, and she let her eyes wander from there to his muscular, sun-bronzed chest. 'Twas lightly furred with ruddy-brown hair that formed a triangle whose point curled downward toward—

Her breath escaped in a ragged gasp as her gaze took him in, fully erect and frighteningly beautiful in the dancing firelight.

A sudden flash of heat surged from her core through belly and breasts, flushing her cheeks with warmth. Her nipples burned against the silk of her night rail.

She tore her eyes away and met Iain's steady gaze. In it she read desire, hunger—a barely leashed, feral energy that caused her heart to skip a beat.

"Are ye afraid?"

"Nay," she lied. He took a step toward her and she

tensed. Her reaction registered in his eyes. "Well, maybe a little."

The edges of his mouth curled in a smile. "Dinna worry. 'Twill be all right." He grazed a finger along her cheek, then trailed it down her neck and across her shoulder to the edge of her shift. She shivered in anticipation.

He slid the silken fabric off her shoulder, revealing the swell of her breast, then trailed his finger across her collarbone to the other side. Her heart pounded, her breathing grew rapid as he paused, his eyes drinking her in.

He flicked the embroidered edge of the gown and it slid to the floor, sparking a thousand tiny nerves as it silked across her skin. A soft cry escaped her throat, and he responded with a low growl.

His eyes roamed her nude body, then finally lit on hers. She searched their depths for some sign of approval. "Truly," he whispered, "I dinna deserve such a woman."

Without reservation she stepped into his arms. He kissed her long and tenderly, his hands exploring, stroking, teasing. Her skin ignited under his feather-light touch and she could not control the soft moans that escaped her throat. Growing more and more bold, she ran her hands across the heated expanse of his tightly muscled back and buttocks.

He groaned and swept her off her feet, bearing her back onto the bed. 'Twas covered with animal hides and she reveled in the feel of the soft, cool fur against her heated skin. He stretched out next to her and continued the gentle stroking, his hand moving slowly over her breasts.

Her nipples burned as he teased them with his fingertips to tight, hard peaks. She fisted a handful of his hair as he leaned down to suckle each in turn.

"Oh, sweet heaven."

He kissed her softly on the mouth, then raised his head to look at her. His hand trailed lower, coming to rest in the triangle of golden curls that shielded her sex, the soft woman's place that now throbbed with a need she'd never before known. She held his gaze as his fingers delved deeper. The sensation was something she was completely unprepared for. She gasped and arched against his hand.

"'Tis hot," he breathed, his eyes burning into her.

With a shock, she felt his velvet hardness pulse against her thigh. What had she expected? She didn't really know, and no longer did she care. She closed her eyes, sinking deeper into the furs. His fingers teased her, and she thought she might go mad with the pleasure of it. When his mouth closed over her nipple, she abandoned herself completely to his loving.

As his strokes grew faster, his suckling harder, the room seemed to close in on her. She dug her nails into his shoulders, her strangled moans rising up into a soft, high keening.

"That's it, love," he whispered against her breast.

She felt a growing tightness, a deep welling inside her, a converging of raw emotion and acute sensation akin to nothing she'd ever experienced.

He abruptly took his hand away and her eyes flew open, her need screaming in on her. She hovered on the edge of something wondrous, but she knew not what it was or how to reach it—only that he would take her there.

"Nay, do not stop."

He smiled, then spread her legs, positioned himself between them. "I dinna intend to stop."

To her astonishment he lowered his head, eyes riveted to hers, and slipped his tongue inside her. She bucked in his arms from the unexpected bliss.

His warm breath silked across her thighs and over the sensitive petals of her flesh, cooling her skin. She sank deeper into the furs and closed her eyes, letting him take her where he would.

He teased the white-hot center of her, stirring in her a pleasure, a madness, she'd not thought possible. The tightness surged again, the deep centering of all perception, all emotion, and swept her toward some unknown pinnacle.

She gripped the bed furs as she reached its startling peak and was borne unto a place outside her body, yet grounded there. Wave after wave of pleasure crashed over her. She was conscious of crying out, but the sound seemed far away and muffled by the roaring in her head.

Iain slid on top of her, covering her body with his own. His desperate need was revealed in the intensity of his expression and in the furious beat of his heart as he settled his weight upon her.

Instinctively she wrapped her legs and arms around him, clinging to his heated body, desperately needing to hold him, to be one with him, to be his. He kissed her tenderly, with a reserve that she knew came hard for him. His arm slipped 'round her waist and held her fast. They moved in unison, their bodies melding, until she felt his silken hardness nudge gently at the entrance to her body. Between fervent kisses he whispered words of love, and her heart soared.

"Hold me tight, love," he breathed.

He kissed her fiercely, and she opened herself to him, wrapping her legs around his hips. His grip on her tightened and with one, quick thrust he sheathed himself within her.

Her passion dissembled into sharp, brilliant pain. She cried out, pushing against him with the whole of her body, but he held her fast, pinning her to him to still her struggle.

"Easy, love. That's the worst of it."

She trembled in his arms as he showered her face with small, delicate kisses and whispered sweet words of comfort and love. After a moment the throbbing within her subsided and she began to relax, reveling in the dark pleasure his assault wrought from her body.

He kissed her long and lovingly, and she read in his face, his eyes, his struggle to lie still, as if to let her body adjust to his invasion. Velvet lightning seared her insides as he shifted his weight to his forearms. She thrust her hips upward in an unconscious response. He moaned and surged against her, deepening his penetration, then withdrew.

"Am I hurting you?" His voice quivered.

"Nay," she breathed, and thrust against him, sheathing him tight.

His eyes glassed with passion. Her hands moved over his back, his trembling arms and broad shoulders. He was hot—an inferno—and sheened with sweat. She knew he struggled to control himself, that he was intent on being gentle with her.

But her own passion surged, his slow thrusts renewing her need, and she arched harder and faster against him, urging him to abandon himself to their increasing rhythm.

"Oh, lass, dinna do that. I...I—"

"Aye," she breathed, and thrust upward, hard against him. "More."

He bucked in response, his thighs spreading her legs wider. Abruptly he grabbed her wrists and pinioned them, one-handed, above her head. "Ye dinna know what ye ask." He began to thrust in earnest then, his eyes heavy-lidded and locked on hers.

His scent aroused her: strong, feral, male. She grazed her mouth along his neck and shoulders and tasted the slick saltiness of his skin.

She felt the tightening again, and her eyes grew wide with new discovery as his thrusts consumed her, controlled her, drove her toward that wondrous peak. Her breaths grew short, her heart slammed in her chest as she arched against him, desperate for release.

And when he drew her nipple into his mouth, gently biting and sucking, she matched him thrust for thrust, frantic, desperate, her nails digging into his back.

At long last, when she thought she could bear no more, he moved his hand between them and teased her into madness. She cried out, and raked his back from nape to buttocks.

The fire burned low in the hearth, comfortable coals casting a dim, warm glow about the room. Alena lay awake, eyes closed, as Iain absently stroked her face and whispered sweet love words in her ear. His body still blazed with the heat of their lovemaking, and she drifted warm and fulfilled in his embrace.

"Where are ye goin', love?" he said sleepily as she disentangled herself from his arms.

She slipped from the bed and padded across the cool floor to the pile of clothes Iain had discarded by the hearth. Rummaging in the folds of his plaid, her hand closed over the circlet, the gift she'd given him so many years ago. She bolted back to bed, suddenly chilled, and burrowed under the furs, nestling in Iain's arms. She cradled the memento. They both looked at it and smiled.

"A lovers' knot," he said. "That's what ye called it."

"Aye." She fingered the fine hair, auburn and burnished gold in the fire's glow, and ran her fingers over the rough strip of plaid that bound it together. "You kept it all these years." Her love for him filled her heart to aching. She turned in his arms and looked into his dark, sleepy eyes. "Why?"

His smile broadened. "To remember ye by." He laughed. "No' that I'd forget that dirty face and wild mane o' hair.'' His smile faded and his face grew somber. ''And because I loved you.''

The look of pain in his eyes unsettled her. ''What is it, Iain?'' She stroked his face, and he closed his eyes and pulled her closer. ''Tell me.''

''It's just that...I loved you...and had promised to come back for ye.''

''Aye, you did promise.'' She searched his face, almost wishing he'd make something up to ease the hurt that kindled still beneath her newfound joy.

''And I did. But blast if I could find ye.''

''You did?'' She bolted upright, pushing the furs aside.

He looked at her as if she'd said something daft. ''Of course I did. Lay back down. It's cold as—''

''But when?'' A thrill shot through her.

He pulled her back down into his arms and tucked the furs around them. ''I dunno. Lots of times. But, I didna know who ye—''

''Lots of times?'' She looked at him, incredulous. ''Truly?''

''Aye, truly. Why would I—''

She didn't let him finish. He was not prepared for the onslaught of small, violent kisses that raged from her lips. Her joy was immeasurable. He kissed her back, pleased, though she could tell he was confused by her behavior. And then the truth of things dawned in his eyes.

He held her at arm's length and frowned. ''Ye thought I didn't. Come back for ye, I mean. Ye thought I just...''

She nodded.

''Oh, lass.'' He pulled her into his arms again and held her tight. ''If ye only knew...''

''It doesn't matter now.''

''Aye, it does.''

''You *did* come back.'' Only he couldn't find her. Of

course he couldn't! How could he have? He didn't know who she was. What, did she think he would just stroll into Glenmore Castle and ask for her? Something in his eyes still troubled her. "You would have kept coming 'til you found me."

"But that's just it. D'ye no' see?"

No, she didn't see.

"I meant to come back. But when I found ye in the wood and brought ye home with me...well, everything changed."

Now she was truly confused. "Everything changed?"

"Because I fell in love with ye."

He cupped her chin and squeezed it gently. "I fell in love with *you, Alena,* but still I loved the girl and had made the vow."

"But—"

"I didna know ye were both the same person. How could I know when ye did everything to keep it from me?" He cocked an accusing brow at her.

"Ah, now I see." She smiled.

"Och, lass, ye dinna know the pain that wrenched my gut. I wanted ye so, but I had no right to love ye. I couldna drag ye into all this trouble with Grant. Christ, I could be dead on the morrow."

But she was already a part of it, he just didn't know it. She closed her eyes and held him tightly.

"And I had to return," he whispered, stroking her face. "I'd made a promise."

She met his gaze, deep as a summer midnight. "I used to go there, to our place."

"For years Alistair would no' let us leave Davidson land. I was furious, and young. When I was older I saw the wisdom in it. 'Twas no' safe. Young as I was, I was The Mackintosh, and we were hated everywhere. But I did go back. Many times."

Looking into his eyes, she was reminded of him as a boy, that chill morning he made the vow. He had that same faraway look.

"And I must go again. The time is right to move against Grant, and for me to claim what's mine." He hugged her tightly to him, grazing his lips across hers.

"But, Iain, you must not—"

"Aye, love. 'Tis already in motion and canna be stopped. Even now, what's left of my clan, the few crofters and loyal kinsmen who live near Findhorn Castle, prepare to join us in war." Her stomach tightened as he nodded. "Aye, I was there just ten days ago."

"At Findhorn Castle? But—"

His mouth curved in a mischievous smirk. "'Twas when ye thought me ruttin' at Inverness."

She hit him playfully on the arm. "You…"

He laughed, but his expression darkened.

Fear touched her heart. "Iain, you are too few—Grant will cut you down. Trust me, I know this to be true. His army numbers hundreds, and with the aid of his cousin, George, near a thousand."

He searched her face, brow furrowed. "And that which I left with ye to safeguard… D'ye have it still?"

She sat up in the bed. "The dagger—the one with the jeweled hilt?"

"Aye." He gripped her arm.

"Iain, what does it mean? To whom does it belong?"

"You *do* have it."

She nodded. "'Tis in a safe place. No one else knows of it."

He pulled her back into his arms, and she pushed away the dark thoughts that raced through her mind.

"Ah, lass, the sun rises and sets with ye, my bonny, braw wife."

His words cut her like a knife.

He rolled on top of her and kissed her thoroughly with a tenderness and love she felt in the depths of her soul. She clung to him and closed her eyes tight against the sting of tears. He thrust his hips against her and she opened her legs to him, losing herself in his gentle loving.

Iain burrowed deeper beneath the warm furs and allowed himself to float in that tranquil state between sleep and awareness. Their lovemaking had left him sated, replete, suspended in an incredible calm from which he had no desire to surface.

Alena had fallen asleep in his arms after their second, spirited coupling. He'd watched her for a long time afterward, marveling at the miracle of finding her, his incredible good fortune, before drifting off himself.

She'd been bold that second time. He grew hard again recalling how her lips had seared his skin, how she'd lovingly explored his body with her mouth. He'd never known such pleasure, had never felt such love.

She was his now, and all the armies in Scotland would not take her from him.

He cast an arm out, blindly, in search of her. His hand skimmed the spot where she had lain. 'Twas empty and cool. He groaned and slid across the bed. ''Come here, love.''

Running his hand over the coarse linen sheet, he finally connected with something familiar. A smile broke across his face as his fist closed over the lovers' knot, forgotten amidst their passion of a few hours ago.

He groaned again and stretched, his eyes drifting open. 'Twas dark yet, just before dawn. A dim, gray light outlined the window, which he never covered.

She was gone. He could feel it.

He sat up in bed and blinked the sleep from his eyes, quickly scanning the room for confirmation. Aye, she was gone. He felt at once a sharp longing for her, the need to touch her, hold her, prove to himself that last night was real, that her love was true.

He lifted the braided circlet to his mouth and brushed the fine hair over his upper lip. His fingers smelled of her— musky, arousing. He smiled again, recalling her passion, her sweet innocence.

Ah...he understood now. She had returned to her own chamber, fearful of the embarrassment of being found in his room. Her maidenly sensibilities charmed him, but she had naught to fear. She would be his wife and all his clan would honor her. For truth, they loved her already—as did he, with all his heart.

He threw off the furs and rose naked from the bed. He would go to her now, slip quietly into her bed and take her in his arms. He would love her again, pleasure her once more before the sunrise.

Reaching for his plaid, he noticed something amiss on the chest flanking the bed. The hearth fire had all but gone out. 'Twas so dark he could only make out the outlines of things in the room.

Where was the damned candle? He felt blindly along the edge of the chest—ah, there it was. He moved to the hearth, taper in hand, stirred up the ashes until he'd uncovered a glowing coal, then lit the wick. The room burst into soft light.

He turned toward the chest and froze, his heart skipping a beat. The finely carved box lay open, its contents scattered across the rough wooden top. ''Bluidy hell.''

Bits of his mother's jewelry, his father's ring, a few odd rocks he'd collected when he was a boy. Nothing was missing except—

The contract.

The rolled parchment signed by the Macgillivray laird offering his daughter in marriage. Offering the alliance.

Iain stood there, stupefied, his eyes riveted to the disarray of objects. Who would take it? Why would someone take it? 'Twas of no value to anyone, save—

"Grant." His voice was the barest whisper in the dead quiet.

He kicked his shirt aside, grabbed his plaid from the floor, and dressed.

Though Iain hadn't signed it, the contract was proof the two clans meant to align. Grant would know Iain meant to raise the Chattan: Mackintosh, Davidson, Macgillivray. Only MacBain wavered in his support.

Grant would know Iain was coming—coming for what was his. But who among them, Mackintosh or Davidson, would steal the parchment, betray his plans to their enemy? He shook his head, bewildered. Nay, not one of his kinsmen would do such a thing.

Who then?

A cold fear gripped him. He secured his dirks to his belt and took up his sword. Nay, it couldn't be so. He wouldn't believe such a thing.

His mind raced as he threw wide the door and raced down the dark corridor to her chamber. Grasping the door latch, he stood there motionless, eyes closed, his heart hammering in his chest, not wanting to believe what in his gut he already knew.

She'd never told him her surname. And he hadn't pressed her because somewhere deep inside him he already knew what she was.

He swallowed hard and opened his eyes. Hand shaking, he tripped the latch and pushed open the door. A small flame danced atop a beeswax taper that rested on the table, bathing the room in a warm glow.

Alena's bed hadn't been slept in. The silk night rail lay, carefully folded, along with the rest of his mother's clothes, on top of the mattress.

She was gone.

Iain moved to the bed and grazed his fingers over the delicate silk of the embroidered shift. A lump rose in his throat.

Perhaps she was at the stable. Aye, that was probably it. She was passionate about her work and always rose early. But as he turned and fled the room, taking the steps at the end of the corridor two at a time, he knew in his heart he wouldn't find her there.

He raced past clansmen slumbering in the great hall, pulled open the huge front door, and ran toward the stable, the chill air raising gooseflesh on his bare chest and arms.

All was quiet. He slowed his pace to a walk and strode quickly across the training yard. The gray light of dawn gave an unearthly cast to everything it touched, the morning awash in a sea of shadows and pale, flat light. He yanked open the door to the stable and froze.

"What the—"

Duncan sat before him on the earthen floor, his back to a post, his arms crudely bound behind him with a leather bridle. He was gagged with a strip of tartan that had been cut from his own plaid.

"Saint Sebastian to bluidy hell!" Iain scanned the shadows for intruders, his sword raised.

Eyes wide, Duncan beat his head against the post and made excited, muffled sounds through the gag. Seeing no one else and nothing out of order, Iain knelt and jerked the gag from the stablemaster's mouth.

Duncan coughed and sputtered.

"Where is she?" Iain grabbed the front of his shirt.

"G-gone."

Christ, he knew it! With one quick jerk he hauled Duncan to his feet. "Where? How, man?"

"On Destiny, the black, not three hours ago."

"But—"

"Her name is Alena Todd. She is the daughter of the Clan Grant stablemaster."

"What?" Iain fought the sudden urge to wretch. He jammed his sword into the hard-packed earth and grabbed the old man by the shoulders. "Nay."

"Aye, 'tis true."

Bile rose in the back of his throat. A cold pain balled within him. His body went slack and he took a step back to steady himself.

She had…betrayed him.

Hamish's words came rushing in on him. *She could be a spy, in league with Grant.*

Iain shook his head, staring dumbly at Duncan, who struggled in vain to free himself of the tethers still binding him to the post. He was aware of the heat of his own blood screaming through his veins. Rage ignited his gut, searing away his momentary anguish.

"Nay!" He lunged at the nearest wall, smashing his fist into the brittle wood, chips flying, the pain jolting him to the shoulder.

"But, Laird!" Duncan shouted. "Iain, there's more."

He wasn't listening. His body burned so hot he felt a sheen of sweat break upon his skin.

"Ye must stop her, man."

"Nay," he said through gritted teeth, fists white-knuckled against the wall. "Let her go. Back to her *laird*."

"But, Iain, ye dinna understand. Grant means to—"

"Enough!" he roared, and butted his forehead viciously

against the wall. Ignoring Duncan's pleas for release, he stumbled down the row of stalls, kicking in timbers as he went. Horses reared, snorting and neighing, beating the ground with their hoofs. He passed the black's empty stall and paused, seething.

Destiny she'd named him. Ha! 'Twas cold, premeditated mockery at his expense. He kicked at the stall and continued down the row.

In the last enclosure his own roan stallion struggled against his tether, alarmed by the racket and the anger in his master's voice. Iain released him from his restraint and grabbed a bridle off a hook on the wall. Securing it to him, he vaulted bareback onto the beast and spurred him back down the row of stalls.

Duncan struggled with the leather ties that bound him, his face red with anger. Iain didn't care and had no intention of releasing him. Foolish old man. He'd let the woman best him and get away. Christ, she'd duped them all.

"Laird, ye must stop her! She means to—"

"Nay! I know well enough what she means to do, but it doesna matter. She's no' worth pursuing, and I'll need every man to stand with me against The Grant. 'Tis time."

He leaned from his mount and jerked his sword from the hard-packed earth. Duncan's protests were stifled as the roan burst into the stable yard and Iain kicked the stable door closed behind him.

In the pale light of the approaching dawn, he drove the roan toward the back of the yard and up and over the low spot in the stone wall. Just as *she* had done, no doubt. Unseen by the sentries, he urged the stallion into a gallop, up the hill and into the forest. He needed time to think, to clear his head, to get a grip on his anger.

He didn't rest until he broke through the forest at the top

of the ridge an hour later, his horse lathered and wheezing, himself breathless, his rage unabated.

During the fast, furious ride he'd turned over in his mind every moment he'd shared with her these past weeks. He'd recalled every detail, every seemingly innocent thing she'd said from the moment he'd rescued her in the wood to their passionate coupling of the night before.

It all made sense to him now. She was a ruthless vixen, Grant's pawn, and well versed in the game. 'Twas lies, all of it.

He reined the exhausted stallion to a halt before the blackened ruins of the ancient keep. Dawn shattered the still, cerulean night, a few scattered stars yet visible. He inhaled deeply of the cool air and looked out over the quiet landscape, shocked into wakefulness by the first blinding rays of the summer sun.

Slipping from the stallion's back, he let his knees buckle, and thumped cross-legged on the ground. He buried his head in his hands and gripped his hair, his eyes squeezed shut.

He'd let himself love her and she'd— Christ, he still couldn't believe it.

"Ye fool! Ye bluidy, besotted fool!" His shouts echoed off the barren landscape, startling larks and small hares who rested nearby.

He'd believed her, had cast off his natural suspicion and succumbed to her charms, her lies. What had he been thinking? He was laird, and yet he'd allowed himself to become vulnerable, and in a way he'd never thought possible.

He'd trained relentlessly, had become a warrior, skilled and shrewd. He'd shaped his uncle's soldiers and what was left of his own kinsmen into an efficient, tightly knit army, albeit a small one. For years he'd planned his revenge, controlled and directed his overpowering bloodlust, waiting until the time was right to make his move.

Now, mere weeks before execution, his carefully laid plans were compromised—not by an army or even a warrior, but by a woman, a stablemaster's daughter.

"Saint Sebastian to bluidy hell!"

He'd never forgive himself. Never. But he'd have his revenge. By God, the River Spey would rage scarlet with their blood before he was done.

Squinting at the brightening sky, he fisted handfuls of the rocky earth where he sat. He drew a deep draught of air and fought to control his emotions. He must think. He needed a plan.

Alena would have given Grant the dagger. 'Twas the only proof of Iain's father's innocence, and his only hope of unequivocally aligning the Chattan clans against Grant. She would also give him the marriage contract, proof of Macgillivray's support. Iain would lose that element of surprise, and Grant would know from Alena's information how many men he commanded, the number of mounts they possessed, what weapons they had.

No matter. He would forge his alliance and strike them down. Avenge his father's murder and the decimation of his clan, take back his castle and his lands. This was *his* destiny and no one would keep him from it.

There was only one way now.

Iain ground his fists into the earth. He would marry Elizabeth Macgillivray—today.

Chapter Fourteen

Leaving him was the hardest thing she'd ever done in her life.

Alena wiped hot tears away with the back of her hand and guided Destiny onto the forest path leading north toward Glenmore Castle. She'd ridden the black hard, half the night and all this morn, stopping only once to water and rest him.

In the wee hours before dawn she'd crossed out of Davidson territory. Her dark hunting plaid blended easily into the muted colors of the forest, and Destiny moved almost stealthily, as if he knew they were in danger.

At this pace she'd make Glenmore Castle by dawn tomorrow. 'Twas soon enough. She would have this one day to herself, to reflect on all that had happened these past weeks.

She ached for Iain's touch, his sweet words of love. During the hard ride the night before she wouldn't allow herself to think on him, fearful she might surrender to her emotions and turn back toward Braedûn Lodge. But today she inhaled the cool, green scents of the forest and let her tears flow unchecked.

Their lovemaking had been passionate yet tender, and

she was not prepared for the emotions Iain's declaration of love wrought within her.

Wife, he'd called her. *Wife.* Would that it were so.

She'd lost herself in him then—reveling in his tenderness, his passion, in his strength. She'd loved him that second time with a desperate, wild abandon.

Before she'd slipped quietly from his chamber she'd turned to take in one last image of him, stretched naked on the fur-covered bed. His body was relaxed, sated, his face strong, so beautiful in sleep, the fall of his chestnut hair a burnished aura about his shoulders in the dying firelight.

She loved him fiercely, without reserve, and would give her life to keep him safe. Aye, would that it were so easy. Instead she would endure his hatred, his certain marriage to another, and her own submission to a man so frightening she shuddered to think on it.

She recalled the thin, spidery letters of the marriage contract between Iain and Elizabeth Macgillivray. 'Twas a stroke of genius on her part to have taken it. As soon as he was freed, Duncan would reveal her identity. Iain would wed the Lady Elizabeth and have his alliance. It must be so. There was no other way.

Then what?

She would give herself to Reynold Grant and wed him on the morrow. Midsummer's Day. She'd insure her parents' safety and, as wife of the laird and mistress of Glenmore Castle, she'd do what she could for her clan.

But one question still nagged at her. Why did Reynold want her? Why? She'd been over it a hundred times in her mind and could not fathom a reason. She was the daughter of a stablemaster. Why would a great laird make such a match? He had nothing to gain from it—no lands, no wealth, no alliances.

Reynold plotted some foul treachery, of that she was

certain. He'd actually tried to barter for her return! Jesu, she'd almost swooned at the supper table when the priest related the tale.

But none of this explained her importance to Reynold. Perhaps Iain was the link. Could Reynold know of their childhood friendship? She did not see how he could. No one had known of it, save Duncan. And if Reynold *had* known, of what consequence was it? She knew little about the Mackintoshes, certainly nothing that could help the Grants defeat Iain.

But wait… Of course! She possessed something of Iain's—something important.

The jeweled dirk!

She tensed, and Destiny jerked to a stop. The stallion's sweat-covered coat steamed in the late-morning chill. He snorted and thumped the ground with an impatient hoof.

Aye, that was it! Reynold must know she has it. But what *is* it? *Whose* is it? When she'd questioned Iain about it he didn't answer. Whatever its significance, Alena knew she must never let the dagger fall into Reynold's hands.

And what of Iain? If he possessed it, how would he use it?

She spurred Destiny on and wrinkled her brow as a chilling thought occurred to her. Iain lusted for blood. Not just the return of his castle and lands. She recalled the clansmen stockpiling weapons in the courtyard at Braedûn Lodge.

Aye, and Reynold Grant's blood alone would not sate him. She could see that now. Iain would raise the Chattan against *all* her people.

Until every last one of them is dead.

Iain guided his spent mount down into the wood toward Braedûn Lodge. The sun was high and he threw back his plaid to let it warm his bare chest and arms.

He was calmer now, and could think clearly without rage blinding his judgment. 'Twas a lesson he'd learned from his father, God rest his soul, and had worked to instill in his brothers. Though he hadn't practiced it well himself this day. In his anger he'd left poor Duncan bound to the post in the stable.

The roan picked his way carefully down the forested slope. Iain allowed his mind to wander, sifting through the details of Grant's treachery. 'Twas clever of Reynold to have sent a maid to woo him—and one whom he knew, or had known. One he would trust.

He brushed his hair away from his face and breathed in the fresh scents of the forest. Still, some things didn't make sense, and nagged at his mind as he rode.

Why didn't Alena reveal herself from the start? 'Twould have saved weeks. The masquerade only delayed his trusting her completely. If he'd known she was the girl from his past earlier, he would have allowed her close to him sooner. He might have told her more of his plans. As it was, he hadn't told her much, nor had his men.

He wrinkled his brow and unconsciously urged the stallion into a trot. Other things about her, what she'd said, her reactions to him and to others, didn't make sense were she Grant's pawn.

The day he'd found her fleeing from the soldiers, 'twas fear he'd seen in her eyes, the look of a trapped animal as they closed in on her. Aye, and that last night at table she'd visibly paled when Father Ambrose had recounted the chance meeting with Reynold and the laird's attempt to take her back.

Nay, her reactions had been pure—not an act for his benefit, but truth. Christ, what did it mean?

He recalled her face twisted in anguish in the soft moonlight of the garden. Her lips had trembled when she told him who she was. And her tears... Aye, they'd been real and wrought from a bright fusion of pain and joy, as were his.

He gripped the roan's back tightly with his thighs and urged him faster through the wood. His mind began to race, pummeled with memories of her voice, her touch, the things she'd told him, and those things left unsaid.

When he'd asked her to marry him she'd said, *'Tis my heart's desire, but...* But what? Their lovemaking had been more wondrous than any he'd ever experienced. 'Twas as if their two bodies shared one heart, one soul. He'd never felt like that with anyone before—nay, he'd not even thought it possible.

He loved her.

And she loved him.

Like a bolt of lightning the truth struck him. She *did* love him, and yet she'd gone back to Grant. Why?

He kicked the stallion, a short command escaping his lips. The roan reared, then burst into a gallop down the long, wooded slope, dodging trees and bushes as Iain spurred him into a mad race toward home.

He glanced at the sun streaming through the trees. "Bluidy hell." Aye, he'd been a fool, all right, but of a different sort than he'd first suspected. Why hadn't he listened to Duncan? The stablemaster had tried to tell him, begged him to listen, but he wouldn't.

He'd let her go. Christ, he'd let her go! He'd never forgive himself if anything happened to her, if Reynold touched her, harmed her in any way.

He leaned forward and urged the roan faster. By God, he'd get her back safe or die in the trying. He pushed all thought from his mind and focused on the ride ahead of him. The slope began to flatten but the trees were thick and the ground uneven; he'd dare not push the stallion faster.

Shouts sounded from the woods ahead. He strained his eyes to see. Riders! He moved a hand instinctively to his bow. A shout went up again, and he recognized his kinsmen: Hamish, Will and one of his uncle's warriors.

They nearly collided when he didn't slow his pace. Hamish's dappled gelding reared. The other two mounts sidestepped out of Iain's way as he thundered past them. He looked back and waved them follow.

Hamish drove his mount until he nearly caught him up. "She's gone!" he shouted over the thunder of hoofbeats.

"I know she's gone, ye mullet!" Iain shouted back.

"But, Iain, ye must—"

"Aye, man, now let's fly!" He spurred the stallion faster as the trees began to thin. His kinsmen fell into pace behind him.

Less than an hour later the foursome burst from the wood. Iain drove the roan clear over the low spot in the wall at the back of the house and landed hard in the stable yard, knocking the breath out of him. Hamish and the others pulled up short, then spurred their mounts around to the main gate.

Directly ahead of him, not twenty paces away, Father Ambrose sat atop a fat mare, dressed in traveling clothes, his meager belongings strapped to the back of the saddle. Duncan was adjusting the bridle. Both men looked up at him, mouths agape, eyes wide.

Iain dropped neatly to the ground. He threw off his bow and quiver, patted the heaving chest of his mount and strode toward them.

Duncan was the first to react and stepped toward him, hands on hips. "Weel, it's about time ye—"

Iain shot him a hard look and pushed past him, stopping before the mare. He looked into Father Ambrose's wide brown eyes and read fear. Aye, he ought to be afraid.

Iain grabbed him by the front of his robe, hauled him from the saddle and dumped him on the ground. The terrified priest crab-walked backward in the dust. Iain leaned down and yanked him to his feet. "All right, priest, tell me what ye know."

Father Ambrose looked to Duncan for help, but the old man stood silent, stroking his white beard, one brow cocked.

"Alena!" Iain roared, and prodded the priest's chest with a finger, driving him backward. "Alena Todd of Clan Grant—the stablemaster's daughter."

Hamish and Will burst through the stable yard gate and slipped from their mounts. They rushed to Iain's side but he waved them back, his eyes focused on the priest.

Father Ambrose trembled under Iain's glare. "I—I do not know her."

Iain grabbed him roughly by the neck of his robe and leaned down so his forehead touched the quivering priest's clammy skin. His voice was low, his rage barely controlled. "Speak now, priest, or prepare to meet your maker."

Father Ambrose nearly swooned in his grasp as Iain gripped the hilt of his dirk. "All right, all right! Don't be rash. I'll tell you what I know."

Hamish and Will edged closer. Duncan stepped up, flanking them. Gavin, who was leading the roan into the stable, dropped the stallion's reins and joined their huddle.

"I—I carried the message to her parents that she was here, safe with ye, just as Gavin bade me." His eyes darted quickly to the stableman, then he lowered his eyes.

"There's more," Iain said. "I see it in your face. What else?"

"The…the laird is to take to wife an unwilling bride— a woman of his own clan—on Midsummer's Day. I can't say for certain, but it must be the same woman, aye?"

Iain felt his jaw go slack. "Midsummer's Day? Saint Sebastian, 'tis tomorrow!"

"Aye, tomorrow, ye dolt!" Duncan spat, elbowing Iain roughly, his eyes bright blue fire. "I tried to tell ye, but ye were a ravin' madman! Now ye've lost another three hour!"

Iain spun on him. "Ye knew! Ye knew her and her parents—that she was a Grant? Ye knew all this time and ye didna tell me?" He shot a murderous look at Gavin. "And you?"

Gavin shrugged and lowered his eyes.

"Aye, I knew her," Duncan said, and met his furious gaze. "But she begged me no' to tell ye. She wanted to tell ye herself, in her own way. I promised her I'd get word to her parents. I knew naught of all this—Grant's plans, his treacheries—until yester eve. 'Twas then I put it all together. And then…weel, everything happened so fast." He paused and dropped his head, blankly studying the dusty ground. "I've failed ye, Laird. I should have come to ye straightaway."

Iain fisted his hands at his sides, working to control his emotions. He clapped a hand on Duncan's shoulder. "'Tis done now," he said quietly. "And the blame's no' on your head but mine. Now go. I'll need a fresh mount, the swiftest ye've got."

He turned toward Hamish and Will, but Duncan grabbed his arm. "There's more, Laird."

"More? What bluidy more?" Duncan hesitated, all eyes on him. "Speak man!"

Duncan reached into the folds of his plaid, drew forth a rolled parchment and placed it in Iain's hands. "I saw her hide it in the hayloft of the foaling shed. She didn't see me, and after Gavin cut me loose I found it."

Iain didn't have to read it to know 'twas the marriage

contract offering him Elizabeth Macgillivray. Rather than take it with her and risk Grant finding it, Alena had hidden the document here, safe among his own clan. A wave of emotion swelled in his chest.

He crushed the parchment in his hand and cast it to the ground. "Will," he said. "Go and find my uncle. Hamish, raise every man, Mackintosh and Davidson. 'Tis time."

"Aye, Laird," both answered in unison and raced from the stable yard.

Iain jogged after them and turned at the house, taking the steps two at a time.

"Laird," Hamish called after him, "to where do we ride?"

He leveled his gaze at the warrior. "Glenmore Castle."

A crooked smile broke across his friend's ruddy face. Hamish drew his broadsword and raised it high. "Excellent!" he cried, and ran toward the men's barracks.

Iain burst through the door to the house, raced up the stairs and down the corridor toward his chamber. The door was ajar. As he stepped through it he collided with Hetty. "What the devil now?"

The lass screamed and jumped back into the room, her eyes like a frightened hare's. Edwina stood hunched just inside the doorway, hands on hips, her gaze narrowed at Iain, her wrinkled face twisted into a scowl.

'Twas then he noticed his bed had been stripped. Hetty clutched the bundle of sheets in her arms. He followed Edwina's gaze to the traces of blood, crimson against the ivory linen.

"Get out!" he bellowed.

Hetty jumped and they both scurried from the room. Edwina shot him a hard look as she turned into the hallway.

He knelt before the chest flanking his bed and plucked his father's gold ring from the items scattered across its top. He studied it for a moment, swallowing hard, then jammed it onto his finger. In one swift motion he swept the wooden surface clean and the rest of the items clattered to the floor.

Eleven years the chest stood closed.

Iain released the latch and threw back the lid. There it was. His father's bloodstained plaid—the one he wore the night Reynold Grant plunged a broadsword into the soft flesh of his throat. Iain ran his hand over the rough, woolen fabric, black and hardened with dried blood, then pushed the garment aside.

The bright glint of steel winked at him from the bottom of the chest. He gripped the hilt of his father's sword and drew it from its resting place. Marveling at the weight of it in his hand, he rose and held it aloft.

For this one day he'd lived his whole life.

For the sake of his mother and young brothers he'd swallowed his pride and had accepted his uncle's charity, living under his roof, plotting, waiting, until the time was right. The years of training, sacrifice and single-mindedness—all would come to fruition this day.

He was The Mackintosh, and the time had come to raise the remnants of his broken clan and strike down those who had wronged them. 'Twas time to reclaim what was his: Findhorn Castle, his father's lands, and the valiant woman who would be his wife.

His and no other's.

Iain gripped the sword and felt the blood scream hot through his veins, flushing his face with the heat of vengeance. "By God, I'll get her back, and let no man who values his head stand in my way."

Alistair appeared in the doorway, breathless. "She's gone, then?"

"Aye." Iain pulled his own sword from its sheath and

cast it onto the bed behind him. He sheathed his father's weapon in the empty scabbard.

Alistair leveled his gaze at him. "Come with me now, nephew. There's more to this tale ye've yet to hear."

Dawn blazed through larch and laurel, casting cold fingers of light across the forest floor. The previous day and night had seemed the longest of Alena's life. She'd ridden progressively north and eastward, and was now but a half league from Glenmore.

The lack of sleep and hard ride had finally caught up with her and with Destiny. She was exhausted and so was the stallion, though he had not faltered, not once on the long journey.

For the past hour she'd been followed by mounted warriors. Directed, really. They were her own kinsmen and rode just within her sight, but did not approach her. At first she'd made for the training stable and her parents' cottage. She was desperate to see them, to make certain they were safe. But the soldiers wouldn't allow it. They herded her like a sheep to the slaughter toward Glenmore's keep.

Toward Reynold Grant.

She needed all her courage now, all her strength. She must be canny and sharp, have all her wits about her. Above all, she must show no fear. She had something he wanted and that gave her power. She would wield that power now, for her parents' sake.

And for Iain's.

For Iain she'd ride into the mouth of hell and stand before the devil himself. A high, shaky laugh escaped her lips. Aye, that was exactly her plan.

The keep loomed cold and gray before her. She had stopped some time ago—long before the soldiers appeared—to water Destiny, and had changed from breeks and shirt into her yellow gown, the one she'd worn the day she'd fled Glenmore's keep.

The warriors closed in on her as she approached the curtain wall and rode as her escort. She knew most of them, she realized, and smiled thinly as they flanked her. Only one returned her smile. The rest looked away, their faces stone.

She spurred Destiny forward through the main gate and into the bailey. Everywhere she looked she saw the defeated faces of her kinsmen. The old laird, John Grant, had passed only months ago, but already his nephew Reynold had worked unspeakable evils on his own clan in his lust for dominance and power.

She'd overheard Gavin tell of it one night in the stable. The news had come from traveling tinkers out on the forest road. Duncan had not repeated the tale to her, and she hadn't asked. She didn't want to know.

She longed for things to be the way they were before the old laird's death, before Reynold's treachery, and Iain's love. Nay, 'twas far past time for such regrets. She had to face the facts.

The clashing of steel on steel jolted her from her thoughts. A crowd was gathered in the courtyard just outside the keep. She urged Destiny forward and breached the knot of clansmen. 'Twas early morn, and she was not prepared for what she saw.

"Jesu," she breathed. Her stomach twisted in fear.

Reynold Grant stood panting, stripped to the waist, a sheen of sweat about his face and torso. In one hand he wielded a broadsword, in the other a dirk. His blond hair spilled loose about his shoulders, a few sweat-soaked tendrils clung to his face. He was the image of what a warrior should be. If Alena did not know him for the cruel manipulator he was, she might think him almost handsome.

A few steps behind him an older clansman, not a warrior but a farrier, lay in the dirt, gripping a battered wooden shield. His eyes were pure fear.

She reined Destiny to a halt and mustered her courage. A thin smirk bled across Reynold's face when he saw her. Her gaze was drawn to the angry red scar jagging from cheekbone to chin. She remembered when she'd cut him, and unconsciously moved her hand to the dirk belted at her waist.

Perkins stepped from the crowd. "Take her!" he cried. The mounted warriors rode forward.

"Nay!" Reynold sheathed his sword and cast his dirk to the ground. "Let her come."

She fought desperately to control both her fear and her revulsion. She nudged Destiny forward until the stallion stood but a pace away from him.

Reynold cocked a white-blond brow, his face a mask of cold satisfaction. "So, ye've come back."

"Aye," she said, forcing herself to hold his gaze.

"I knew that ye would. Smart lass. How did ye get away?"

The crowd fell silent, leaving only the sounds of birds overhead and a dog barking somewhere in the distance. She ignored his question.

A malevolent smile spread across his face. His gaze roamed over her as he moved closer. He smelled of sweat and blood. Her stomach lurched.

"No matter. You're here, and a bonny bride ye will make." He sauntered around the stallion, grazing a hand across the animal's flank. Destiny snorted at his touch. "'Tis a fine mount ye have. A wedding gift is it, from Iain Mackintosh?"

Alena gripped the reins and bit back a comment.

Reynold grabbed her ankle.

Her heart leaped to her throat. Destiny stirred beneath her.

Reynold's eyes locked on hers. "The wedding is tonight."

She gritted her teeth as he ran a sweaty hand under her gown and up the length of her bare calf. She willed herself not move. She must be calm, purposeful, and not give in to her fear. "My...my parents. Are they well?"

"Oh, aye. Fat and flourishing. And they'll continue so, now that you're here."

Thank God for that! She forced herself to relax. "I would spend this last afternoon with them...if it please you. After that you may do as you wish with me."

He withdrew his hand from her leg at last, and ran it along his scarred face. "Oh, I intend to, lass."

Against her will her eyes widened. He read the panic she felt and laughed. "I'm not a monster, ye know."

She begged to differ but held her tongue.

"Verra well. Have your afternoon. Ye shall come to me at sunset. A priest is come from Inverness to witness our vows. I'll send a suitable gown to your parents' cottage. See that ye wear it."

"But I have a gown." She indicated the pale yellow silk.

"That rag? Dinna insult me. Ye shall wear the gown I've chosen. Now go."

He turned and unsheathed his sword. Metal flashed in the afternoon sun. He eyed the farrier who now stood cowering against the stone wall of the keep, his battered shield poised in defense across his body. "There's other sport to be had this day."

Aye, and it sickened her. She leaned forward, fisting handfuls of Destiny's mane. She would leave before this *sport* recommenced, yet she had to know if her suspicions about Iain and the dagger were right. "Laird," she called out. "There is one question yet unanswered."

Reynold stopped dead in his tracks, regarding her with what seemed mild amusement bordering on contempt. "Ask it, then. I haven't all day."

She held his gaze and drew a breath. "Why me?"

The question clearly surprised him. He handed his weapon to Perkins, and as he approached her she could see in his eyes he was ready to bare the truth. "Dinna be so modest. Surely ye know by now. The secret is out."

'Twas as she'd suspected! The dagger was her trump card, and she must use it smartly. She decided to toy with him a moment longer. "The secret about what I have?"

Reynold frowned. "What ye *have?* Nay, lass, the secret about what ye *are.*"

What I am? What on earth did he mean? "What am I?"

He smiled at her confusion. "Why, Angoulême, my sweet. A highborn daughter of France."

Chapter Fifteen

"Angoulême?" Alena searched the grim faces of her parents, or rather, the man and woman she'd always thought of as her parents.

Robert Todd glanced out the cottage window at the sentries sent to ensure her return to the keep at sunset. With a tug he pulled the drapery closed. "Aye. Alena of Angoulême, daughter of Beatrix. You be she, lass."

She shook her head, not wanting to believe it. "But I am *your* daughter."

"Nay, *ma petite,*" Madeleine Todd said. "Your father—I mean, Robert—is right."

Even if it were true, what did it mean? She knew little of politics—of anything, really, outside her clan. Her gaze strayed to the pallet in the corner by the hearth. A deep purple gown trimmed in gold lay strewn across it. Reynold's gift to her.

"It matters not," she said. "You know why I've returned." She nodded at the gown.

"No, you cannot!" Madeleine's soft eyes glassed with tears. "He's a terrible man."

"I must," she said, and looked from her mother's anguished face to her father's grim expression. "'Tis the only way to keep you safe."

"We are safe enough," Robert said. "Ye willna do this thing."

She reached across the table and grasped his weathered hand. "You do not understand, Father. I *must* wed Reynold. If I do not—" she struggled to keep her voice steady "—he will cast you out from Clan Grant. You and mother. And…there are other reasons I must be his bride."

A sharp, fleeting image of Iain flashed in her mind, tugged at her heart, and she prayed for strength.

Her father began to shake. He let go her hand and fisted his own into tight, white-knuckled fists. "Throw us out? Robert Todd, stablemaster here for forty years, and friend to his uncle for longer than that. And he would cast us out?" Alena nodded. "And that was his threat to ye, lass?" Her father's eyes blazed in quiet fury. "That's what made ye return?"

"Aye. And though 'tis possible we could leave this place and be welcomed elsewhere…" She thought of Iain and of the kindness afforded her by the Davidsons and the Mackintoshes. "There are now other reasons which compel me to see this marriage take place." She rose from the table.

Her mother's eyes widened, almost in desperation. She watched her father as he reached across the table and grasped his wife's hand. They exchanged solemn glances, brown eyes locked, then turned their gazes on her.

She had the strangest feeling some silent decision had passed between them. 'Twas not the first time she'd seen them so. A chill of premonition tingled its way up her spine.

Robert Todd's voice resonated low and urgent. "Ye need no' wed him, lass. Aye, a daughter of Angoulême ye be. But ye are also another's daughter."

"My *father's* daughter, you mean."

He nodded.

She had not dared ask earlier. The revelation of her mother's true identity had been more than enough to comprehend in one sitting. And now, studying their grave faces, she didn't want to know. "Wh-who is he?"

Robert hesitated. "Your father was...John Grant."

The room spun. She reached for the edge of the table to steady herself. "The old laird? How can this be?"

Robert Todd's face seemed to have aged years in the past few moments. "Sit down, lass. 'Tis time ye knew the whole of it."

Madeleine rose from the bench and helped her back to her seat, then stepped quickly to the hearth. Alena watched in fascination as she counted the hearthstones from the bottom up, her hand coming to rest on the sixth stone. With a grunt she pulled it free.

A kind of horror gripped her as Madeleine drew a rolled, yellowed parchment from the crevice and offered the document to her. With trembling hands she accepted it.

"Read them," Robert said.

"There are two, *ma petite,* one rolled inside the other."

She unfurled the brittle paper and separated the two documents. One was written in French, the other in her native Scottish. She chose the latter and spread it carefully on the table.

As she began to read, a roil of emotions churned inside her. She was helpless to fight the tears which sprang to her eyes.

"'Tis written in the hand of the old laird, John Grant," she said, awed. "Aye, here is his signature and his seal at the bottom. 'Tis dated mere months ago!" She choked back a sob and looked up at them. "It says here that he, John

Grant, is my father.'' She shook her head, not wanting to believe it. ''Nay, 'tis not so.''

Tears welled in Robert Todd's eyes. He reached out a craggy hand and grasped one of hers. ''Aye, lass, John Grant was your father, and my friend. He penned that document the very hour we broke the news to him. Insurance, he'd called it, in case... Well, ye know what happened afterward.''

''But...'' She pulled her hand away, stunned, and turned to the woman she would always think of as her mother. ''What does it mean?'' A wave of nausea washed over her. ''Mother?''

Madeleine's eyes glassed, and Alena saw her battle the torrent of tears threatening to erupt. ''Read the other, *ma petite*,'' she said, her voice thin and shaky.

Alena spread the second parchment with trembling hands and quickly scanned its contents. Her gaze was riveted on the signature and seal at the bottom. *''Beatrix d'Angoulême,''* she breathed. '''Tis true then.''

''Your *maman*,'' Madeleine whispered.

She read the document carefully, translating from the French. *'''Alena of Angoulême, sole heir of my fortune and my estates...'''*

''That is you, *ma petite*. Your *maman* wrote this on her deathbed, not an hour after you were born. I was her lady-in-waiting, her friend.''

Alena sat there, barely able to speak, her thoughts racing. She shook her head in denial but could see the truth of it in their eyes. ''Tell me about her. Tell me about my... mother.''

''She was a beauty,'' Madeleine said, her brown eyes alight with the memory.

''Aye, she was, lass,'' Robert said, ''and your da, John Grant—from the moment he looked upon her he loved her.

'Twas over twenty years ago now, the laird and I traveled to the French court of Philip the Second. John's first wife, Henry's mother, had died the year after her son was born.''

Alena had heard the story when she was a girl. The old laird had not taken another wife. She had always wondered why, and was now about to hear the answer.

"John took me with him to France. We were to buy horses, Arabians from Spain, sold through someone he knew in Angoulême."

"That's where I first met your father—I...I mean, Robert," Madeleine said.

"Aye, and 'twas where John Grant met Beatrix of Angoulême. I'd known the laird long years. We were lads together when my own da ran the stable here and his da was laird. I'd ne'er seen John so taken with a woman before—not even his wife, whom he loved. He was well into his thirties when he met yer mother, and she...weel, she was but ten and nine."

"Like me," Alena said.

"Aye, but ye are even bonnier, and she was a rare beauty. Ye have her hair, all spun gold in waves down to yer waist. But ye've got John's eyes, green like a cat's."

She unconsciously wound a tress of hair around her hand. 'Twas true, she looked nothing like Robert and Madeleine Todd who were both small and dark. She always wondered about the dissimilarity. She was tall and fair, as John Grant once had been—as Reynold was now.

Cousins. A small shudder coursed through her.

Madeleine edged closer along the bench, eager it seemed, to tell her everything now that the secret was revealed. "They loved each other, your mother and father. But she was betrothed to another—a rich comte, a man of great power in France. She was titled and wealthy in her own right but would not go against her father's wishes. So they met in secret, Beatrix and John Grant. Robert and I carried their letters back and forth and arranged for their trysts.''

''Aye, and that's when I first came to love ye, Maddy.''

Madeleine blushed. ''Beatrix sent John Grant away, determined to wed the comte according to her father's plan. But when it was learned she was with child, she was sent away to have the babe in secret, and I with her. Her parents were furious she wouldn't reveal the father's name. A few months later you were born.''

''And...my mother?''

''Dead at childbed.'' Madeleine paused to let her take it all in. ''I feared for you, *ma petite*. Of what would become of you. So I did a foolish thing.''

''No' so foolish,'' Robert said, and shot her a half smile.

''I took you and I fled. I crossed the channel, and from England sent word to Robert.''

''And you told the laird, and he sent for me.'' He had wanted her! Somehow, that made it all bearable.

''Nay,'' Robert said. ''The laird never knew about ye. Nor did I, 'til a few months ago.''

''What?'' Her head spun, each new detail jerking her emotions into a roil of confusion.

''I kept it all a secret.'' Madeleine grasped her hand. ''For fear of losing you, *ma petite*. I swore on your mother's deathbed I would care for you, protect you, always.''

Alena grazed a hand across her cheek. ''And so you have.''

''In the letter come from England, Maddy lied—said *she'd* had a babe. And naturally I thought...''

''You thought I was yours!''

Robert nodded.

''But, all this time? All these years?''

''I never told the secret,'' Madeleine said. ''It was...''

"'Twas wrong, Maddy," Robert said. "Dead wrong. But I dinna fault ye for it."

"I loved you." Madeleine's tears broke, and Alena embraced her.

"And I you. Both of you."

"Robert came to England and brought me, and you, back here to Scotland. I married him the day we arrived at Glenmore Castle."

"Aye, you've told me many times you could have wed any number of wealthy Frenchmen," Alena said, marveling at the tale.

"'Tis true, *ma petite,* but none of them captured my heart as did Robert Todd, stablemaster to Scotland's Clan Grant. And you…you are like my own child, wrought from my own body, so close was I to your mother."

"And the laird, John Grant…he never knew then, that he was my father." Remorse welled inside her. The old laird had been a good man. He'd always been kind to her and the Todds. A flood of random memories washed over her.

"Oh, but he did know, in the end," Robert said. "The day ye turned ten and nine Maddy came to me with the secret. I went straightaway to the laird with a copy of the parchment ye hold there." He nodded at the French missive. "That very night John Grant was killed."

She remembered the mystery surrounding the old laird's death. A chilling thought occurred to her. Aye, 'twas the only explanation that made any sense. "Reynold must have known! He must have found out, and…"

"Aye, and killed him," Robert said. "Why, I can only guess. But I suspect he was after the match with ye, and the laird wouldna approve it."

"He killed him! His own uncle."

"Your father," Robert said.

'Twas too horrible to comprehend.

"So you see, *ma petite*, you do not have to wed Reynold." Madeleine wiped away her tears and smiled. "Not now."

"Aye, I see."

"We must go to the council." Robert pushed back from the table. "The elders. We must tell the tale and show the documents. They will know what to do."

Alena rerolled the parchments and stuffed them into the pocket of her gown. Today was the solstice, Midsummer's Day, the longest day of the year. As such, sunset was hours hence. She was exhausted, in desperate need of sleep, and time to think. But there was no time.

She didn't want to be highborn, neither French nor Scots. She wished to live quietly, with the only parents she'd ever known. Raise and train horses, be of use to her family and her clan. There was one other thing she wished—so much her heart ached with the wanting—but 'twas impossible now.

Iain would truly hate her, if he knew the truth. The irony of the situation made her laugh amidst her tears. Think what it would have meant, if she'd wed him. Iain would have aligned with a powerful clan, indeed. One who boasted near a thousand warriors amongst all its families.

Clan Grant.

Iain would have wed her, Alena Grant, cousin of his most hated enemy.

Nothing went as planned. An hour later Alena spurred Destiny up the hill toward the keep, surrounded by Reynold's men. The sentries had not allowed Robert and Madeleine Todd to accompany her. Now what would she do?

The day was cool and clear, the scent of summer heather thick in the surrounding forest. She had donned a simple gown of soft, rose-colored wool and arranged it as modestly as she might whilst riding astride. Her hair was plaited and hung in a thick, gold rope over her shoulder. She pushed it away and unconsciously checked the position of the dirk belted at her waist and the rolled parchments hidden in the deep pocket of her gown.

They rode in silence for a time, then the senior soldier reined his mount in line with hers. ''Lady, ye are no' sportin' the gown the laird commanded ye wear.''

''Nay, I am not.''

A thin smile creased the warrior's mouth. ''He'll no' be pleased.''

''I expect he will not, but 'tis of no consequence as there will be no wedding today.''

The soldier raised a brow but did not question her.

Her statement was bold, but she had to do something, trust someone. She knew this man, this captain in Reynold's army, and wondered whether or not he might aid her. She must find out, and quickly.

''You are Owen, are you not?'' she said. ''One of the laird's captains.''

He smiled at her, surprise and delight in his eyes at her recognition of him. ''Aye, lass.''

''How long have you served the laird?''

''Reynold, ye mean?''

She nodded.

''No' long. Since the old laird's passing. A pity, that, God rest his soul. He was a great man.''

''Aye, he was that—and more.''

''Before he died I was his senior soldier. Now I serve his nephew.''

Spurred by his comments, she decided to be bold. ''And what think you of Reynold's leadership?'' She fixed her gaze on him and watched for some reaction.

He nudged his mount closer. "Ye've witnessed his *leadership* with your own eyes. What would any man who loved his people think of such a laird?"

She allowed the corners of her mouth to turn up just slightly. Owen held her gaze. "So," she said. "Should another challenge his position and the council back him, you would support a…change?"

The warrior casually scanned the blank faces of his men. Alena knew they listened but he did not seem to care. "I would support this…change," he said. "In fact, there is talk already afoot."

"Is there?" Heartened by this news, she drew the rolled parchments from the pocket of her gown. "Owen, if John Grant had had another child, besides Henry, would you serve that issue with the same loyalty as you showed the old laird?"

Owen narrowed his eyes. "I would."

She separated the parchments and handed him the Scottish missive, tucking the French document back into her pocket. She watched as he unfurled it.

Owen scanned the parchment and nearly fell off his mount. He looked at her, astonished.

She edged Destiny closer and grasped his forearm. "Will you help me, should I need you?"

He placed a gauntleted hand over hers, his expression grave. "I would protect ye with my life. But what think ye to do?"

She frowned as she took the document from him and returned it safely to the pocket of her gown. "I know not—yet. I cannot predict how Reynold will take this news of my paternity."

"Methinks he willna be pleased."

"I must reach the council, the elders. They will know what to do."

"They meet today, as we speak! In the great hall."

She urged Destiny into a trot, and Owen and his men stepped up their pace. She pressed further. "Know you George Grant?"

The warrior's brows shot up. "Reynold's cousin—aye, and your cousin, as well, I suppose."

She nodded.

"He's a bit young, but he's led his own, near five hundred folk, since his father died two years ago. He is the one, truth be told, who thinks to unseat Reynold."

"Think you George would come to my aid should anything happen this day?"

Owen's expression hardened. "Aye, lass, methinks he would. But rest easy that no harm will come to ye whilst I yet live."

"My thanks, Owen. You are a good man."

This news of George's intentions buoyed her courage. They rode the rest of the way in silence and she felt strangely comforted by the way Owen and his warriors closed in around her, protecting her, it seemed, though the captain had uttered not a word to his men.

The main gate lay open and the party entered the bailey, riding directly to the keep. Few folk were about and she thought it strangely quiet. Two of her father's stable lads rushed from the small castle stable and steadied their horses whilst Alena, Owen and his men dismounted.

"Keep them close at hand, lads," Owen said, eyeing the boys. "Come," he said, "we shall all go together."

Alena followed the warrior up the stone steps to the keep. They were met at the door by Perkins and two dozen of Reynold's henchmen. "He's abovestairs, in his apartments." Perkins eyed Owen suspiciously. "I shall take her from here."

"But—"

Owen shot her a cautionary look. "Fine. I will go with you."

There were too many of Reynold's men, she realized. More than enough to subdue Owen and his warriors should it come to that. Jesu, how would she ever get to the council?

Perkins whisked her up the staircase, Owen and his men in their wake. He pushed her down the corridor to the door she remembered as the entrance to Reynold's chambers.

"Perhaps I should go in alone," she said with more conviction than she felt.

"Nay, lass, I will accompany you." Owen turned to his men. "The rest of ye remain here. And keep your ears and eyes open."

The warriors nodded. Perkins knew something was afoot. He narrowed his eyes at her before knocking on the huge wooden door.

"Come." The voice was Reynold's.

She tripped the latch and entered the room, Perkins and Owen on her heel.

Reynold sat at his writing desk, a cup in his hand. Three other warriors Alena didn't recognize leaned casually against the far wall. All eyes were on her.

Reynold stood and moved 'round the desk to face her. "Owen," he said, his icy gaze leveled at her, "I see ye've brought my bride."

"Aye, Laird," Owen said from behind her.

"Ye have arrived earlier than I expected, but no matter." He smiled, and Alena felt a chill snake up her spine. "'Twill give me time to get to know my wife before we speak our vows."

She stood her ground as he approached her.

Reynold lifted his hand. She heard the leather and metal of Owen's garments and weapons creak behind her. Neither of them moved. Reynold grazed a finger down the side of her face. Her anger stirred, as did her fear.

"Ye are not wearing the gown I had fashioned for ye." He scowled at her for a moment, then his features softened. "No matter. There's plenty of time before the ceremony for someone to fetch it." He edged closer. Just as she stepped back, the door behind them burst open.

A soldier entered and, from the look of him, Alena could tell he'd been riding all night. "Laird," he said, breathing hard. "Our sentries on the western border were found dead yester noon. A dozen of them."

Reynold approached the soldier, grabbing him by his plaid. "Who did this and where are they now?"

"We…we know not, Laird. By the look o' the ground ye can tell there were many. Riders they were, two score or more."

Reynold released him and the frightened soldier took a step back. "We found a bonnet with this pinned to it." He reached into his sporran and drew out a silver badge: a cat reared up on hind legs. Attached to it was a sprig of red whortleberry.

Alena choked back a gasp, her eyes riveted to the badge.

Reynold spun toward her. "Mackintosh, our neighbors. Remind me, wife, to thank them for the hospitality they showed ye." He called for Perkins, and the wiry man appeared at his side. "Is all in place?"

Perkins grinned and shot her a dark look. "Aye, Laird. Four hundred ride to Findhorn Castle as we speak. They will be there long before The Mackintosh arrives."

Her heart skipped a beat. "What treachery is this?"

Reynold snorted, towering over her, hands on hips. "What, think you to reprimand me? I am but preparing a warm welcome for our neighbors. A welcome into hell."

He laughed and Perkins and the others joined him. She heard Owen's deep voice behind her, chuckling with them.

Her blood boiled and her cheeks flushed hot. She fisted her hands at her sides and willed herself remain silent.

Reynold ran a hand up the sleeve of her gown, and she tensed, returning his icy stare. "Oh, aye," he said. "We heard of his movements on the border yesterday. He thinks to recover Findhorn Castle. Let him think again. To challenge me with that ragtag pack he calls a clan? What a farce. Even with his uncle's support, they number but a fraction of my army."

Reynold meant to annihilate them. She could see it in his eyes. She must do something, but what? "I—I must go. Back to my parents' cottage." She turned to leave. "There are things—"

Reynold grabbed her arm. "Nay, I want ye here where I can enjoy you." He pulled her to him and, before she could protest, he kissed her hard, his tongue thrusting against the hard line of her lips.

She pushed herself away from him, stumbling backward into Owen's arms. Her face burned with rage. The warrior steadied her but made no move to assist her. She looked up at him and he cast her a cool, even glance, his expression unreadable.

Reynold laughed. She held her ground and shot him a murderous look. He reached out, ripped her dirk from the sheath at her waist, and flung it to the floor behind him. "We'll not have a repeat of our last meeting, *wife*."

"Do not call me that."

"Why not? 'Twill be fact soon enough." He turned to one of the soldiers who lounged against the stone wall of the chamber. "Get the priest."

She felt a smile curl at the edges of her mouth and, with more confidence than she felt, let it break across her face.

''There's not a priest in all the Highlands would wed us against my will. Now or any other day.''

His cool eyes roamed over her. He broadened his smirk. ''And why is that, my sweet?'' He reached out to stroke her hair and his hand closed over the thick braid.

She looked up into his finely chiseled face. She could see the resemblance now—the high cheekbones and long, straight nose. It sickened her, and she almost lost her nerve. His fist tightened and he pulled her close, until his face was inches from hers. Her eyes locked on his.

''Because I'm John Grant's daughter.''

For a long moment the only sounds were the crackling hearth fire and the creaking of the warriors' leather battle garb.

Reynold blinked, and the malevolent smile fled his lips.

She had him. She could see it in his eyes. He loosened his grip on her hair. Before he could recover his composure, she drew the parchments from the pocket of her gown and thrust them at his chest. '''Tis true, *cousin.*''

He grasped the documents and unfurled them. He glanced only briefly at the French missive, then turned to the other. 'Twas as she had suspected. He already knew of her French lineage, her connection to the court of Philip the Second. 'Twas the sole reason he'd wished to wed her.

But he hadn't known she was his uncle's child.

As Reynold scanned the document written in her father's hand his face blanched. His eyes widened as he read it again, slowly this time. Then he stared at her, his expression a cold fusion of horror and fascination. He shook his head almost imperceptibly. ''Nay,'' he whispered. '''Tis a lie.''

'''Tis the truth. You've only to look at me to see it is so.'' She plucked the documents from his hand and, meeting no resistance, quickly rerolled them and stuffed them back into her pocket. She glanced briefly at Perkins who had read enough over his laird's shoulder to understand his position. A thin smile cut his pock-marked face.

"Now," she said, "I'm going to the council."

She turned to leave, but Reynold grabbed her braid and jerked her back. She winced with pain, her scalp burning, and looked to Owen for help. She saw caution in the warrior's eyes as he took a step forward and moved his hand to the hilt of his broadsword.

"This changes nothing," Reynold said. He half dragged her back toward his writing table and flung her to the floor in front of the hearth. She landed hard, the breath rushing from her.

"Perkins, find that bloody priest! And the rest of you, out! All except you." Reynold pointed at Owen. "Come here and hold her. I dinna want her leaving."

Fear balled up inside her. She scrambled to her feet as Owen moved quickly behind her and grabbed her arms. Sweet God, would he not help her?

Reynold shrugged off the leather strap belting his broadsword to his back and set his weapon on the table behind him. Perkins and the other soldiers left the chamber.

"Now, *cousin*," Reynold hissed, moving toward her, "prepare yourself for your vows."

Hot tears stung her eyes. She fought to control the fear that racked her body and caused her heart to beat wildly in her chest. Surely the priest would hear her and would believe. Surely he could not force her.

Owen gripped her shoulders and while Reynold's back was turned pressed his lips to her ear. "Courage," he whispered, and squeezed her once, firmly.

She almost swooned with relief. She blinked back her tears and tried to prepare herself for whatever Owen intended to do.

Reynold turned and towered over her.

"You are too late," she blurted.

"Too late for what?"

She tipped her chin and glared up at him. "I—I am no longer a maid. I have made a gift of my virginity to another. Your enemy." 'Twas risky to bait him like this, but she didn't care. Mayhap the revelation would buy her time.

Reynold narrowed his eyes. His face contorted, flushed crimson to the roots of his white-blond hair. "Whore," he breathed.

She read Reynold's intention a split second before he slapped her hard across the face. The blow stunned her. In a protective move, Owen pulled her back against his chest.

Reynold raised his hand again.

"Enough!" Owen roared, and shoved her sideways. He drew his sword, metal screeching, and pointed it at Reynold's chest. He glanced at her. "Run, quickly—that way!" He pointed to an interior door on the other side of the room. "The council meets belowstairs. Find them! Tell them."

"Perrkiins!" Reynold yelled.

The door to the corridor crashed open and Owen's men burst into the chamber. In the momentary chaos Reynold jumped backward, grabbed his sword, and unsheathed it in one quick motion.

Alena bolted to the interior door and jerked it open. She turned in time to see the flash of metal as Reynold plunged his broadsword deep into Owen's shoulder.

Owen crashed back against the stone hearth, his face a mask of shock. "Run, lass," he choked as he slid to the floor.

She hesitated, wanting desperately to help him. Reynold whirled on her, bloodied sword in hand. As Owen's men surrounded him, she fled into the connecting chamber.

Doors and hallways, room after room, all ran together as

she raced from the echoes of shouting warriors and the ring of metal against metal. She ran down the corridor, away from the din, then spun toward a tiny stairwell she saw out of the corner of her eye.

Lifting her skirts, she bolted down the steps, stumbling on the uneven stones. By the time she reached the bottom the keep was in an uproar. Soldiers charged through the front entrance and up the main stairs.

Alena raced past them, ignored and undetained, as they hastened abovestairs in response to their laird's cries. She burst through the door to the great hall. Jesu, 'twas empty! Where was the council?

There was no time. In truth, she half suspected Reynold controlled them, anyway. She shot out the door and into the courtyard, stumbling down the steps. Destiny waited, ears cocked, restlessly stamping the earth whilst a stable lad tried to calm him and the other nervous mounts.

"Stop!" The voice belonged to Perkins.

Without thinking, she leaped atop the stallion's back, spurred him forward and looked back only when Destiny had set his sights on the main gate and was racing toward freedom.

Perkins danced wildly in the courtyard, shouting and waving his arms toward soldiers and horses. He threw himself on one of the mounts and started after her, leaving battle-dressed soldiers in his wake.

Destiny thundered out the open gate, nostrils flared, breath steaming, every muscle straining. Alena leaned low over his sleek neck and urged him fly like the wind.

Only one thought possessed her, consumed her, drove her like a madwoman southwest into the wood...

Four hundred Grant soldiers pushed on toward Findhorn Castle and would lie in wait for Iain Mackintosh and those who rode at his side.

Chapter Sixteen

He was too late. He could feel it.

Iain pushed the thought from his mind and reined his sweat-soaked mount to a halt just outside the cover of the larch wood. He slipped from the saddle with a grunt. They'd ridden hard nearly two days and a night and the exhaustion was beginning to show in his men's faces and stiff bodies.

Forty of his best warriors, Davidson and Mackintosh, watered their horses in the brook at the edge of the wide, low glen. Waves of wild grasses, heather and wildflowers undulated in the breeze, rippling with color and scenting the air with the unmistakable fragrance of high summer.

'Twas Midsummer's Day and, by his reckoning, they were still hours from Glenmore Castle. He swore under his breath. If Grant had so much as touched her, Iain would make certain he died a slow, horrible death.

They'd been forced to follow a circuitous route across the vast Clan Grant demesne to avoid sentries and the scores of soldiers who patrolled the southwest border. The detour had cost them hours. There had been no other way. Stealth was required if Iain was to get her back. He hadn't the manpower to lay siege to Glenmore. He squinted at the sun, judging the time—nearly midday. "Damn!"

Hamish knelt by the muddy edge of the brook and examined innumerable deep hoof prints and the occasional boot print marking the soft earth.

Iain looked out over the glen and could plainly make out the trampled swath running east to west, confirming his suspicions and the news his scouts had conveyed. "How many?" he asked, casting Hamish a sideways glance.

"Hundreds," Hamish said, rolling a clod of soft earth between his fingers.

"How long?"

The warrior wrinkled his nose and touched the tip of his tongue to the ruddy-brown clay. "A day, maybe less." He rose with a grunt and looked to Iain with raised brows.

"Aye. They've arrived at Findhorn, then."

The edge of Hamish's mouth curled in a half smile. "Mayhap, but they dinna know they are expected."

"Let's hope that's the case. Alistair led his warriors out two days ago. He's certain to arrive first. "

"Aye, but will Gilchrist be able to convince Macgillivray and MacBain to join us?"

"They'll come—but when and with how many I canna say."

"Ye dinna know for sure they'll support ye," Hamish said quietly, out of earshot of the other men.

Iain met his friend's steady gaze. Hamish was right, but there was no turning back now.

The Chattan. The four. 'Twould be the first time since his father's murder all the clans would meet. "Christ," Iain breathed, and turned to mount his steed.

A shout went up among his men.

He pulled himself into the saddle and adjusted the long-bow resting casually over his shoulder. He reined his mount toward the group of warriors, but couldn't see what caused the commotion.

"Hell and damnation!" Hamish hurled himself onto the back of his mount and pointed a beefy finger off in the distance. "Iain, look man!"

Iain shaded his eyes and scanned the wide glen in the direction Hamish had indicated. He rose in his stirrups as his gaze lit on a lone rider astride a black warhorse, skirts flying, charging at breakneck speed across the open meadow.

"Alena!" he cried, and kicked the roan forward.

A score of warriors broke from the cover of the trees on the opposite side of the glen and bore down on her in hot pursuit.

Iain charged forward through his own pack of clansmen, scattering their mounts. "Come on!"

In well-practiced moves, his men leaped onto their saddles and spurred their steeds forward, flanking him.

The wide, grassy meadow dipped gently in the center. Iain urged the roan faster toward Alena and her pursuers who were clearly visible now, yet more than a furlong away. As the riders closed in on her, Iain's throat constricted. He leaned forward in the saddle urging the roan faster still.

Hoofbeats thundered. His heart slammed in his chest. His gaze narrowed, blocking out the sky, the waves of wild grasses and bordering wood. His only focus was the woman he loved, the brave lass who would willingly give herself to a beast for the sake of her family, her clan and for him.

A flash of metal jolted him upright. Iain watched in horror as a rider broke from the oncoming pack—a small, dark man, sword drawn and wielded high above his head. Panic seized him as the rider closed the distance to her.

Iain's blood raged, every muscle in his face and neck

taut as a bowstring. His cry of fury and anguish roared over the thunder of hoofbeats and the battle cries of his men.

Destiny faltered, recovered, and Alena's pursuer was suddenly on her, both of them racing toward the center of the glen, his broadsword poised to strike her down.

A hundred yards to go. Iain was out of time.

His own men drew their weapons, metal glinting in the afternoon sun, but too late.

He jerked the reins, pulling his stallion up short. The horse reared, nearly flinging him to the ground, but Iain dug in with his knees. Eyes riveted to Grant's henchman, he stood in his stirrups and drew an arrow into his bow.

Instinctively his warriors spread out, laying open a clear path for his shot. Fifty yards, forty. Destiny thundered toward him, Alena clinging to the stallion's back.

The henchman raised his sword.

Iain nocked the arrow and sighted down the shaft. Her life hung in the balance and with it his very soul. He loosed the arrow.

The henchman swung his weapon down. At the last moment he jerked and pitched sideways off his mount, the feathered tip of Iain's shaft protruding from his chest.

The bow slipped from Iain's hands and he collapsed into his saddle, shaking with relief. Sweet God, he'd almost lost her! He was suddenly aware of tears stinging his eyes. He shrugged off the wave of emotion and spurred his mount forward, his gaze locked on hers.

The roan and the black nearly collided. Alena flung herself toward him and in their desperate attempt to embrace, both she and Iain slipped awkwardly to the ground. He pulled her to him and her arms went 'round his neck. She choked back an anguished sob against his chest.

His own control shattered. He gripped her tightly,

burying his face in the warmth of her hair, his own tears spilling hot into the golden nest.

They knelt together like that amidst the tall grasses and brilliant waves of summer flowers, barely aware of the battle that raged not a hundred feet from them. He covered her face in small, fervent kisses while running his hands lightly over her body, instinctively checking her for injury.

Pulling back, he gazed at her through glassy eyes. Her face was radiant, lit from within, belying the suspicion and doubt that had racked his soul. How could he have questioned her love? He choked back a ragged sob and pulled her tightly against his chest.

Awareness came crashing in on him as Destiny reared and stumbled. The battle raged around them, swords ringing, the stench of blood sharp and shocking against the fragrant summer heather.

He pulled Alena to her feet, grabbed the stallion's reins and thrust them into her hands. ''Get to the trees. Now!'' He lifted her onto Destiny's back.

''But—''

''Do it!'' he ordered, and slapped the stallion's rump. He watched her as she spurred the black into a gallop and made for the wood. Then he vaulted onto his mount, drew his sword, and cast himself headlong into the battle.

'Twas over quickly.

Alena watched the fighting from her position in the larch wood. Iain, Hamish and the others vanquished the soldiers whom they outnumbered two to one, without one injury to their own.

Guilt and shame twisted her belly. She had wanted Iain to strike them down—her own kinsmen—Grant warriors, many of whom she had known since childhood. Tears stung her eyes. She drew a steadying breath, sickened by her own feelings.

She watched as Iain dismounted and stood over Perkins's crumpled body. He kicked at it and, seeing no movement, placed a booted foot upon the henchman's chest and jerked his arrow free. He snapped the shaft in two and cast it to the ground.

A short time later Iain left his men to join her amidst the larches and bays bordering the glen. To her relief, he reined his mount beside hers and pulled her into his lap.

Her heart soared. She wrapped her arms around him as he claimed her mouth in a deep, yet tender kiss. She gave herself up to his comforting strength and let her body go limp in his embrace. She felt and shared his desperation and his relief.

After a moment she broke the kiss and looked up at him. His face was streaked with mud and sweat; a few bloodied fingerprints trailed across his forehead. She wiped them away, then let her fingers trace the angular line of his jaw.

"They are all dead, then?"

"Aye."

A shudder coursed through her. "They were my kinsmen."

With a gentle touch he tilted her chin up. Clear, blue eyes willed her to his gaze. "They would have killed ye, love. They nearly did."

She nodded, her eyes welling. On her own, or under another's influence, she was a threat to Reynold. If he couldn't control her and use her for his own purpose, he'd surely kill her.

Her tears broke and she clutched Iain to her, burying her face in the warmth of his chest. She shuddered in long, uncontrollable sobs, powerless against the emotions racking her body.

Iain rocked her gently in his arms, the roan stallion swaying under their weight. He whispered sweet words of love and comfort against her hair, stroking her back, calming her, enveloping her in his warmth. He tilted her chin again and kissed her tears away.

"I—I had to warn you," she said, her voice shaky.

A bittersweet smile graced his mouth. "Oh, my brave, bonny lass." He tightened his embrace.

She drew herself up in his arms, the urgency of her mission buoying her strength. "Reynold has dispatched four hundred warriors to Findhorn Castle. 'Tis a trap, Iain. He means to—"

He pressed a callused finger to her lips, stilling her words. "Shh-hh… 'Tis all right, love." He kissed her forehead. "I know what he plans and we've seen their tracks. Ye mustna worry."

"Then—"

"Aye. Alistair rode a hundred men north to Findhorn two days ago. And Gilchrist has gone to raise the Macgillivrays and the MacBains."

She stiffened in his arms. "The Macgillivrays? The alliance." A sick feeling washed over her. "Then…then you've married her."

Iain's face darkened. "Married who?"

"Elizabeth Macgillivray."

A sharp laugh burst from his lips. "Nay. I sent her back home with Gilchrist."

Joy shot through her and she watched Iain's eyes as he read her every thought, her innermost feelings, the truths she could no longer conceal. Still, she worked to restrain herself. "Oh, it must have been disappointing for her."

He laughed again. "Well, she didna appear overly distraught." He leaned down to kiss her and she parted her lips for him, tasting the salty slickness of his tongue as it played at the edges of her mouth.

She drew back suddenly. "Iain, there is much I must tell you. Reynold and I—"

He gripped her shoulders and his expression sobered. "He didna harm ye?" His gaze roved over her, inspecting her for signs of damage.

She shook her head and cupped his face in her hands. "Nay, nay, he did not."

His indigo gaze bore into hers and she beat back the memory of Reynold's manhandling, fearful Iain would read the truth in her eyes. He leaned in for another kiss.

"You came for me," she whispered.

"Did ye think I wouldna?"

"I—"

Hamish burst through the trees and rode past them, a satisfied grin contrasting sharply against the sweat and dried blood that caked his ruddy face. He nodded once at Iain and kept moving, urging his gray gelding deeper into the forest.

"Come, love," Iain said, taking up his stallion's reins. "We must away. 'Tis no' safe here."

She stilled his hand. "Iain, I told Reynold nothing. I—I wanted you to think I had, but—"

He dropped the reins and embraced her, silencing her with a gentle kiss. "Hush, now. I know ye didna."

"I would never—"

He stilled her with another kiss, then pressed his lips to her ear. "Later."

He took up the reins and she repositioned herself in front of him, astride the roan.

Will came up behind them and reached for Destiny's reins. He smiled at her as he urged his mount forward, the black trailing behind looking remarkably refreshed after the short rest.

"'Tis a fine animal," Iain said.

"Destiny, you mean?"

Iain studied her. In his eyes she read not only love, but remnants of the fear and anguish she'd seen as she thundered toward him, racing for her life. And his.

"Aye, Destiny," he whispered, and enfolded her in his arms as the roan bore them deep into the wood.

After dark they stopped at a small crofter's cottage, nestled deep in the Highland forest that ran along the border of Grant and Mackintosh land. The croft was unoccupied but Alena could tell from its cleanliness and the stores of food near the hearth its owners must not be far.

"Someone lives here." She knelt and lit a fire in the hearth. The dry twigs and peat caught at once. Flames crackled into life.

"Aye, one of my kinsmen," Iain said, closing the door behind them. "He is likely gone to Findhorn Castle to join up with Alistair and the rest of our warriors. We are safe enough here, for tonight."

She peeked out the small window. Iain's men busily made camp outside in the clearing surrounding the cottage. She smiled, noticing Will had already started a fire and had a few wild hares spitted and roasting across the coals. She unfurled the deerskin window covering and the cottage took on a warm glow, the radiance of the small hearth fire lending a comforting charm to the spartan surroundings.

Iain sat heavily on the pallet in the corner and tugged off his worn muddy boots. He watched her as he removed the silver clan badge securing his plaid to his shoulder, and pushed the woolen fabric to his waist. His face was drawn, etched with the burden of responsibility, but his eyes were warm and danced in the firelight.

"Come here," he said, and opened his arms to her.

She moved across the hard dirt floor and into his embrace. He gathered her into his lap and held her tightly, nuzzling against her breast. Ah, he felt good! She ran her hands through his thick chestnut hair and clutched him to her.

"Why did ye no' tell me the truth?" he whispered. "Christ, 'tis a wonder ye werena killed." His arms tightened around her. "I could no' have forgiven myself if…"

He looked at her with shimmering eyes and she cupped his face in her hands. "I love you, Iain."

"And I you," he murmured, his voice husky with emotion. He bore her back on the bed and claimed her mouth in a relishing kiss.

She felt as if she were melting into him, losing herself beneath his comforting weight.

He pulled back a bit to look at her, and frowned. "I've got blood on your bonny face." He licked his thumb and wiped it across her cheek. After surveying his stained, muddied garments and dirty hands, he stood up. "I'm no' fit to touch ye."

"I'm not much better, myself," she said, examining the sorry state of her gown and the dirt caked under her fingernails.

Spying a bucket on the floor next to the food stores, she scrambled from the pallet and lifted it onto the table in front of the hearth. She sniffed at it cautiously, then tasted a drop from her fingertip. "'Tis water." She smiled, satisfied.

She rummaged through the cottage for a few minutes until she found what she sought: a pile of clean linen, which she set on the table next to the bucket of water. She turned to Iain, beckoning. "Come, I shall wash you."

His eyes sparkled—dark gemstones in the firelight. A slow smile spread across his face. She watched, her heart fluttering, as he rose from the pallet and pulled off his shirt.

He moved toward her and she let her gaze rove over the taut, burnished muscles of his chest and arms, the dark ringlets of hair glistening with perspiration. Her cheeks flushed hot. 'Twas silly. She'd seen him unclothed before. All the same, a warmth spread through her as he inched closer, so close she could feel his breath on her upturned face.

She ripped a square of linen from the stack on the table and dipped it into the cool water. Turning to Iain, she hesitated, unsure of where to begin. He smiled at her, his eyes warm and filled with love, assuaging her mild embarrassment.

Gently, she sponged the dirt and dried blood from his face. He watched her for a while, then closed his eyes and tilted his head back as she moved the cloth lower over his neck and shoulders. She remoistened the square of linen and drew it in a circular motion over the hard muscles of his chest.

He reached out blindly and grasped her waist, pulling her closer as she continued the slow, deliberate strokes. He rolled his head forward and, through slitted eyes, fixed his gaze on her. She inched the cloth lower over the taut muscles of his abdomen.

"Ye set me afire with your touch," he whispered huskily.

Her hands began to tremble as she moved closer and wrapped her arms around him, sponging the muscles of his back. His scent aroused her and she unconsciously let her lips wander over his softly furred chest, breathing in his maleness, tasting the saltiness of his skin. His body was an inferno stoking her own rapidly growing desire.

She wanted him, needed him to possess her so she might forget, for a time, the impossibility of their situation.

He moaned and pulled her tight against him, his mouth desperately searching out hers and claiming her lips once more. She sagged against him, letting him bear her weight in his strong embrace. Parting her lips, she welcomed his tongue into her mouth. His hands moved to her braid. He untied the ribbon securing it and ran his fingers through the plait, freeing her hair.

He broke the kiss abruptly and held her away from him, his eyes dark, glazed with desire. "Now you," he whispered, and worked loose the laces at the back of her gown.

She closed her eyes as he tugged the gown from her shoulders and pushed it down over her hips. It slipped to the floor, a pool of dusky rose at her feet. Iain took her hands and she stepped away from it.

He loosened the ribbon tie of her thin shift. The sensation of his rough fingers on her warming skin sent sparks to her breasts. His gaze was fixed on the dusky peaks straining against the fabric.

He remoistened the cloth and handed it back to her, then tore a strip of linen for himself and dipped it into the bucket. Jesu, he meant them to bathe each other! He pressed the wet cloth to her collarbone, and rivulets of cool water snaked down her body under the shift, shocking her.

Her breath caught and her eyes grew wide, meeting his smoldering gaze. "Iain," she breathed, and moved her own square of linen to his chest.

With one hand he fumbled with the wide leather belt that bound his kilt, unbuckled it, and cast it away. The plaid slipped to the floor and he kicked it behind him, standing naked before her.

She allowed her gaze to roam over him, drinking in his long, well-muscled legs, narrow hips and flat belly. Her eyes were drawn lower and her cheeks flushed hot with the memory of their last lovemaking.

Iain continued his ministrations, gently pulling the front of her shift open and drawing the damp linen over the rise of her breasts.

She stepped closer and let her cloth slide over his hips to the small of his back, then sponged the taut muscles of his buttocks and the backs of his thighs.

He moaned with pleasure and she thrilled at the power wielded in her touch. He yanked the thin shift down over her hips, letting it drop to the floor.

Closing her eyes, she sucked in her breath and rolled her head back. She was his now. Nothing could change that. Even if he did not want her after what she had to tell him, still she would be his.

Their hands moved over each other more urgently, washing the dust and perspiration from their skin. Suddenly he dropped the cloth. He lifted her in his arms, and pulled her down on top of him onto the small pallet that would serve as their bed.

"I need ye, love," he murmured as he ran his hands over her hips, positioning her on top of him. "I need to be inside ye."

She could feel his heart beating in his chest and let her lips brush over the soft, dark hairs. Her mouth grazed his nipple and he groaned, his face tight with need.

He pushed her up so that she sat astride him, then positioned her hips until she felt the tip of his velvet hardness throb against her.

"Oh…" Her own desire bloomed. She was ready.

Their eyes locked. He held her fast and thrust upward, sheathing himself inside her. She gasped with pleasure and threw her head back, pushing down against him. Her breath caught again as he thrust his hips a second time. She rolled her head forward and caught his passion-filled gaze, his eyes mere slits, a wild, feral look to them.

He tightened his grip on her and began to move her slowly back and forth astride him, each time withdrawing then thrusting upward again.

She felt flushed, light-headed, and grasped his arms for support. She moved at the rhythm he set and immediately felt the deep centering again, the focus of all sensation: heat, pleasure, a complete surrendering of her body and her soul.

Her gaze was fixed upon him and he began to thrust harder, his body taut, his hands clamping down on the soft flesh of her hips. The room closed in upon her, the only sounds the crackling of the fire and their short, sharp breaths.

He pulled her closer and laved her breasts, suckling greedily on one inflamed nipple, then the other.

They blazed up together.

"Oh, Iain, please…I—"

She bucked astride him, her body white-hot, as he moved his hand between her legs, shattering all her mysteries.

His shuddering release and strangled cry pushed her higher still, as she seized her own fulfillment and became one with him in that secret place where only he could take her.

Hours later she wrapped Iain's plaid around her and tossed another faggot onto the fire, which had burned to glowing embers. The dry larch caught immediately. Its bright flame bathed the cottage in a soft light.

Iain sat naked on the edge of the pallet they'd made their bed. "Ye look bonny in the Mackintosh tartan."

She smiled.

"It suits ye. I would see ye always dressed so."

Her emotions churned. Love, joy, desperation and visceral fear all roiled within her. She rose and stood with her hands outstretched toward the crackling fire.

She must tell him.

He joined her in front of the hearth, snuggling up behind her, and wrapped his arms 'round her waist. She laid her head back on his chest and felt the comfort of his chin rest lightly on her head.

"Marry me, Alena."

She tensed in his arms. She knew he sensed it, and did not want to meet his questioning gaze when he turned her to face him. "Iain, there is something you must know."

He tilted her chin up so she had to meet his eyes. "What, more secrets?"

Her heart, replete with love, felt as if it were breaking. More than anything she wished to be his wife. She mustered her courage. "I am not who you think I am, Iain."

"Ah, but ye are." He smiled, ran his hands through her hair and cupped her face. "And now that I see it, never again can I look on your bonny face and no' remember the wee lass I once loved, and love still."

His words stirred a bittersweet joy within her, but pain and fear burned bright at its edges like some dark halo, a portent of despair. "Nay, I do not mean that. I mean... Iain, the Todds are not my true parents."

There. She'd said it. There was no going back.

She pulled herself from his embrace and retrieved her woolen gown from the floor. He watched her, his expression unreadable, as she drew the rolled parchments from the pocket of the gown. Her hand trembling, she thrust the documents toward him.

He took them but, to her surprise, made no move to unfurl them. He cradled them in his hands, weighing them it seemed, as if to determine their value.

She drew a breath and exhaled slowly. "Iain, my mother was not some lady's maid, but Beatrix of Angoulême."

His expression did not change, and for a moment she was certain he had not heard her. Or perhaps he knew nothing of French nobility. Why would he? She hadn't. Then his face softened. "I know, love."

"You *know?*"

"Aye. Alistair told me, not an hour before I rode for Glenmore Castle."

"But how did Alistair—" Her words died on her lips as she recalled the day in her chamber when Margaret Davidson had come to see her. Her instincts had been right. The lady had known her.

"The priest told him. On their journey to Braedûn Lodge."

"Father Ambrose!" The priest *had* remembered her. "But how on earth did he find out?"

"The day he carried news of you to the Todds, he overheard them talking about your tie to Angoulême."

"And yet he revealed nothing whilst at Braedûn. Why? He owes no loyalty to me or mine."

"Aye, but he owes much to Alistair. And my uncle can be a verra persuasive man. He bade Ambrose keep the secret until he could decide what to do."

"And had I not left, what would he have done? What would you have done, had you known then?"

Iain smiled. "I know not. It doesna matter now, love."

But it did matter. Her body grew suddenly cold. "You knew before you came for me," she whispered, barely hearing her own voice, "that Beatrix of Angoulême was my mother."

"I did. What of it?" He moved to embrace her but she stepped back and pulled the plaid tighter across her chest. The light went out of his eyes and they seemed cool now, almost hard, in the flickering firelight. "Ye have powerful allies, now, should ye wish them," he said evenly.

"What do you mean?"

He looked away from her into the fire. "King John, of course. Of England."

He was making no sense. "I don't understand."

He snorted and tossed his head, a gesture of impatience she knew well. He grasped her by the shoulders, crushing the parchments in his hand. "Lass, his *wife,* the child bride John took not three years ago. Isabella."

She shook her head, now completely puzzled. This meant nothing to her. She knew naught of the dealings of English kings.

"Isabella of Angoulême—your mother's youngest sister—your *aunt.*"

A sudden wave of nausea gripped her. "But, my moth— I mean, Madeleine Todd, she told me naught of this."

"Perhaps she didna know. The lass was born after your mother's death at childbed."

She felt light-headed all of a sudden and swayed in Iain's arms. He tightened his grip on her. "This Isabella, she would be almost of an age with me?"

"It seems she would, though I dinna know for certain."

"And you knew all of this," she said, pushing back from him. "Before you came for me. Before you sent Elizabeth Macgillivray away."

He tried to pull her back into his embrace but she resisted. "I did, but—"

"I see. That is why you wish to wed me. 'Twould mean a great alliance for you. Not only with France, but with England, as well."

She turned to the hearth, gripping the rough stones for support. Tears stung her eyes and she could not bear to look at him. "My God, what would you be worth to our own King William should you bring him such a prize?"

"Alena." His hands lit on her shoulders.

"Nay! Do not touch me!" She tried to pull away but he held her fast.

In their struggle the plaid slipped from her body and he caught her up, naked, in his arms. She beat against him, pleading with him to let her go, her tears flowing unbidden, her emotions unchecked.

He shook her, his face twisting in what she sensed was pain. "Bluidy hell, woman! Think ye I care a whit about alliances with England or France?"

He was shaking. She brushed her tears away and looked into his eyes. They were soft now, darkest blue in the firelight. Her breathing steadied, as did his, and they stood there for a moment studying each other, the silence like a great distance between them.

"Don't you?" she whispered. "Wish such an alliance, I mean."

"Don't *you?*" He abruptly let her go and stared into the fire, fisting his hands at his sides. She watched as his knuckles went white, as if there were some great struggle going on inside him.

"Ah, lass, d'ye no' see what this means?" His voice was thin, shaky. She had never seen him like this. "Ye could choose for your husband among the most powerful men in England or France."

It took her full second to comprehend his words. Her heart soared. She placed a hand on his muscled forearm. "Nay. There is only one man for me, and he is neither French nor English."

He fixed his sapphire gaze on her, one hand closing over hers.

"And our marriage would bring him everything he's

ever wanted—lands, riches, a titled lady for his bride.'' At least she could give him that. Small compensation for what she had yet to tell him.

His face softened and a half smile graced the corner of his mouth. He knelt and retrieved the crumpled parchments from the floor where they had fallen, forgotten, in their struggle.

''I dinna want a titled lady for my bride.''

''Don't you?''

''Nay,'' he breathed. '''Tis a stablemaster's daughter I love. And it's her I'll wed. Her and no other.''

He looked at her, his eyes an ocean into whose depths she longed to cast herself, and she knew then there could be no more secrets between them.

''Iain, there is more.'' She took the parchments from him and unfurled them. Placing the Scottish missive on top of the other, she thrust them back into his hands. ''Read it.''

He scanned the document written in John Grant's hand. His eyes widened. She watched him, waiting, for what seemed an eternity, her heart balled in her throat.

And then slowly his face turned to stone.

Chapter Seventeen

Nothing in the whole of his life had shocked him more than what was written on that parchment.

"Grant's...*daughter*," he breathed.

"Aye, but I knew it not until just this day." Alena retrieved the plaid from the floor and wrapped it around her.

One look at the grief in her eyes and he knew she told the truth. Iain rolled the missives together and set them on a nearby table. "So, then, Reynold and ye... Ye are..." Christ, he couldn't get the words out.

"Cousins." She looked away, and he did not blame her. Had he more presence of mind, he would have concealed from her his first reaction. God's truth, he wasn't sure what he felt.

"By marriage," she said. "Not true cousins."

A hundred odd thoughts occurred to him. The one he could not ignore was a question. *What to do now?*

"Come." She offered her hand, tentatively, as if she wasn't certain he would take it. He did. How could he not? "Sit down on the bed," she said, "and I will tell you all I know."

And she did. And he listened, and he believed.

"What now?" he said.

"Mayhap I can use my position to help my clan. Reynold has done them much harm." She looked up at him, her green eyes luminous and catlike in the fire's glow. For a moment Iain feared what he saw there. "Do you understand?" she whispered.

"Aye." But he didn't. What could she mean to do? "Nay, I—I'm no' sure."

His thoughts whirled in his head like some mad dervish. He grasped her hands and squeezed them in his. 'Twas then he realized she was trembling.

Christ, he was a fool! She didn't wish to leave him. She needed him. Now, more than ever. And he didn't intend to fail her. Suddenly his mind was clear.

"Aye," he said. "I do understand. And whatever needs doing, we will do it. Together."

"Do you mean that?" Her face lit up.

"Aye, I swear it."

She threw her arms 'round him and pulled him down on top of her on the bed.

As she peppered his face with kisses, he was distracted by the weight of another promise he had made and also intended to keep. But for now, for tonight, he would push all thought of it from his mind. He stripped the plaid from her body and lost himself in her love.

Hours before dawn, Iain dressed then sat lightly on the edge of the bed to pull on his boots. Alena stirred under the furs. Gently, he grazed the dove-soft skin of her cheek. Their second coupling had been tender, replete with emotion. 'Twas as if, though unspoken, they understood the fragility of their newly forged bond.

Love welled inside him, constricting his throat and stinging his eyes, as he watched her emerge from that deep lovers' sleep they'd shared after their bodies had exhausted themselves in the giving.

Her eyes fluttered open, and he leaned down to kiss her on the mouth. "I must go," he whispered, brushing his thumb across her lower lip.

She wrinkled her brow, frowning, and pushed herself up in the bed. "Where?"

"To Findhorn Castle to join my clan."

She threw the furs off and scrambled to the edge of the bed. "Nay, you cannot go! You must not!"

In the dim light of the near-exhausted hearth fire he thought her the most beautiful creature he'd ever seen. Her wild hair cascaded from her shoulders, a golden waterfall through which her rosy nipples peaked. Her face was radiant, sleepy, and he couldn't help but cup her chin in his hands.

"Ah, ye dinna know how ye tempt me, love, to stay here with ye under the furs." He kissed her softly then rose from the pallet in search of his weapons.

As he adjusted his plaid and donned his broadsword, she quickly dressed and slipped on her shoes. "I'm going with you, then," she said.

Iain suppressed a smile. "Nay, ye canna. 'Tis too dangerous. Ye will remain here. Safe. I'll leave Will and Drake with ye, and at first light they'll take ye back to Braedûn Lodge. Stay there until I return for you."

"But, what will happen? The alliance— Will all the Chattan support you?" Her expression was tight with concern.

He pulled her into his embrace to comfort her. "I canna be certain of their aid. They will come, but I dinna know what they will do."

She knotted her fingers in the front of his plaid. "But without them Reynold's army will cut you down!"

Her voice caught and he pulled her closer, pressing her head to his chest. "Mayhap, but I must go all the same."

She choked back a sob, small fingers digging into his chest. He stroked her back and whispered words of love into her ear, trying to calm her.

Abruptly she pulled away from him and caught his hands in hers, her face alight, her eyes wide. "The dagger! The jeweled dirk! You have not told me how, but 'twill help you to gain their support, will it not?"

God's truth, in the flurry of the past two days, his only thought to save her from Reynold's treachery, he'd forgotten the weapon entirely. "Aye, it would. But I must do without it. There's no time." He squeezed her hands, then turned to leave.

She stopped him at the cottage door. "Iain, what will you do?" His back was to her and her voice was a whisper, almost chilling, sending a shiver up his spine.

He couldn't look at her. "Ye know full well what I must do—reclaim my lands, my castle, avenge my father's murder, or die in the trying." Her small hand gripped his elbow, and he fought the urge to turn and sweep her into his arms. "'Tis been my whole life—all I've lived for these long years."

Until now.

He tripped the door latch and stepped outside, bracing himself against the chill night air. He knew she followed, but he wouldn't allow himself to look back. His men were already assembled, his mount waiting.

She pushed past him and positioned herself between him and his steed. "For the actions of one man, you would wage war on an entire clan? *My* clan?"

The moon had set and in the dark he could barely make out her features, but her trembling voice betrayed her anger and her fear. He hardened his heart. "It canna be helped."

"It can be helped! You must not do it, Iain. Hundreds will die, and for what? One man's honor?"

"Nay! For the honor of a people—my clan—for those kinsmen who buried their dead on that day and were lucky enough to escape Reynold's bloodletting. No thanks to me," he added quietly.

"You were a boy, a lad of twelve. What could you have possibly done?"

He grasped her waist and strained to see her face in the blackness. "Perhaps nothing. But there's much I can now do. And do it I will."

"Then you will be no better than him."

"So be it," he whispered, and pushed her aside. He mounted the stallion but she grabbed the bridle, staying his departure. "I will avenge my father and my kinsmen. I canna rest 'til 'tis done."

He reached down and blindly felt for her, his hand coming to rest on the side of her face. "Ah, lass, I dinna wish to wage war against innocent men. Only too well do I know of the waste and misery it brings. But, Alena, ye must understand—I am no' a fit leader for my clan 'til Reynold Grant's blood runs hot from my sword."

He felt her hand light on his knee. She gripped it hard. "Promise me, Iain," she whispered. "Promise me you will not start this thing."

"I canna, love. 'Tis already begun—eleven years ago when Reynold killed my father whilst I stood by, helpless, and watched him do it."

Her hand dropped away. He grazed her cheek and brushed his fingers lightly over her lips. She didn't move and he perceived her coldness, her sense of his betrayal.

He felt as if his heart had been wrenched from his chest and smote in two, half of it cast before her feet and the other pitched headlong toward war.

"God keep ye, lass," he murmured in the dark, and reined his mount toward Findhorn.

Alena closed the cottage door behind her and collapsed against the rough timbers. That was it, then. 'Twas over, and all that had passed between them these last weeks—suspicion, doubt, rediscovery, their passion and their love—'twas all for naught.

She closed her eyes against the sting of tears and dug her nails into the splintered bark. What would she now do? Flee to Braedûn Lodge and wait for Iain's return? If he returned at all. What a homecoming that would be—his sword rank with the blood of her kinsmen, his eyes glazed with the frenzy of the kill. She'd seen men so before and shuddered to think of her beloved thus possessed. And what, then? He would ask her to wed him after he'd murdered her people?

Or, perhaps, 'twould be Reynold who would come for her with Iain's blood on his hands. Her cousin would hack them down like saplings beneath the battle-ax, and beat a trail of murder and carnage across the Highlands to her very door.

Jesu, was there no other solution?

She lifted the deerskin window cover and peered out into the darkness. All was quiet again, the only sounds the fidgeting of the three horses who remained and the rhythmic breathing of the two warriors Iain had left behind to escort her back to Braedûn Lodge. Will and Drake lay bundled in their plaids, huddled shapes in the blackness beside the cold campfire.

She dropped the deerskin cover back into place.

The parchment proclaiming her John Grant's daughter lay on the table where Iain had left it. She stuffed it into her pocket and moved silently to the door. Her hand on the latch, she paused, considering the rash move she was about to make. What else could she do? She cracked the door and slipped outside.

Moving slowly, she approached the three mounts tethered at the edge of the clearing, not twenty feet from where the warriors slept. Destiny was closest to her, set off from the other horses because of his ill temper.

She crept to the stallion's side, untied him from the laurel, then paused, glancing back at the bundled shapes by the fire ring. Stock-still, she stood there listening, straining her eyes to see in the darkness. Nothing stirred and the warriors slept on, oblivious to her.

Iain would have Will's head over this—Drake's, too—but it couldn't be helped. She must go.

She pulled herself onto Destiny's back and directed him into the wood. Fortunately the ground was damp, allowing them to move silently, deeper into the forest. When she was certain they were out of earshot of the cottage, she spurred Destiny into a trot.

'Twas pitch-dark and she could see little save the general shape of the land and the outlines of trees and large boulders. Destiny seemed unperturbed by the blackness and increased his pace. The air was cold and still. A few pinpoint stars peeked through the midnight canopy of larch and laurel. The predawn sky was a deep azure-black, the color of Iain's eyes in the moonlight. She leaned forward, pressed her face close to the stallion's neck, and whispered his name.

She knew where she was going and what she must do.

Northeast she reined the stallion, back toward Glenmore Castle. She was the best rider in the Highlands and Destiny the swiftest mount. If anyone could do it, she could. She urged Destiny into a gallop and they raced ahead toward dawn.

* * *

Hours later, perspiring and breathless, Alena reined the black to a halt beside a small brook. The dead-white light of morning lay on the wood like a cold shroud. Larks and wood finches warbled their new-day songs. While the black slaked his thirst she scanned the line of the brook as it snaked its way up a hillock. The trees grew thick near the top where a jumble of rocks gave rise to a small waterfall.

This was the place.

Leading Destiny, she climbed to the crest where the rushing cascade of water drowned out the melody of the birds. At the top she veered left and followed the edge of the thicket along the ridge line. It had been years since she'd come here, and the path that once had marked the entry to the copse had disappeared, buried under seasons of autumn leaves.

The trees had grown tall and thick. A tangle of heather and gorse lay at their feet, choking off entry. She narrowed her eyes, scanning the treeline. Aye, there they were.

Two gorse bushes, taller now and so thick they'd grown almost together, framed the entrance to the copse. Destiny would be fine here tied to a tree. She ducked under the tangle of bushes and, after pulling her hair free, stood upright and caught her breath.

'Twas the same! Every tree, every stone—but smaller, somehow. The hairs on the back of her neck prickled; she felt suddenly chilled. The sheen of perspiration that had warmed her during the ride now turned her skin clammy. She rubbed her arms through the woolen gown.

Eleven years.

She felt as if 'twas just yesterday she and Iain had played here. She took a step forward and her gaze slid sideways to a tall, stout larch. She laughed suddenly and her chill subsided, replaced by a warmth radiating from deep in her belly.

'Twas the very same tree Iain had used as an archery target when they were children. She walked up to it and stroked its rough surface. The smooth white bark was riddled with scars from the hundreds of arrows Iain had loosed into it.

She drew a deep breath, the air redolent with warm, green memories. Her heart soared momentarily with the love she had felt for the boy, now man, warrior and laird.

Her gaze came to rest, at last, on the wide spot near the brook where she'd discovered him sleeping that last morning. Her inner joy faded as she knelt and pressed her palms into the cool, damp earth.

The gurgling of the brook lulled her into a kind of peace. She let her thoughts wander, recalling that day. 'Twas here she'd crafted for Iain the lovers' knot, the circlet of child's hair, chestnut and gold. Tears stung her eyes and emotion, raw and powerful, welled inside her when she thought of him carrying it all those years.

'Twas more than a simple token of affection. She knew that now. Perhaps she'd always known it. 'Twas the symbol of their destiny, their love, their strength and unfailing loyalty. She closed her eyes against the tears and dug her nails into the earth.

'Twas here she'd tried to comfort him—the boy whose life had been shattered, whose soul had been destroyed by murder, carnage and a treachery she still did not understand.

'Twas here he'd spoken the words. *I will return—for you and for this. The Grants will pay. I willna rest until my father is avenged—until every last one of them is dead.*

She could help him, now, though it meant risking all.

She loved him, and now she must trust him to do what was right and honorable.

She pulled her dirk from its sheath and dug in the soft earth near the brook. Eleven years. Who knew if it was still here in the place where she'd buried it? Eleven winters of snow and ice, and the turbulent waters of spring.

She cast the dirk aside and dug with her hands, scooping earth from the unmarked grave. After a minute her fingers grazed something sharp and she paused, peering into the hole. Splinters of wood stood out against the black soil. Feeling her way, she found the edges of— Aye, the box!

"'Tis still here!"

She grasped it and, as she tried to lift it out, the wood shattered in her hands, rotten from long years in the wet ground. She brushed away the debris to reveal the tattered remnants of what was once a cloth—the Mackintosh tartan, now black with decay—a strip cut from Iain's own plaid.

The rotten wool disintegrated in her fingers as she carefully unwrapped the crude bundle. There it was. The dark and terrible treasure long hidden—the one thing that, for better or for worse, might turn the tide of war.

With trembling hands she lifted the jeweled dagger from its shallow grave. The blade was long and hideous, brilliant still but for the rusted evidence of blood, spilled that night at Findhorn Castle.

But whose blood was it?

Whose dirk?

Iain knew, and if this thing would somehow help him to withstand Reynold's might, then, by God, she would take it to him.

She held it high, turning it in her hands, marveling at the wealth of gemstones embedded in the finely crafted hilt of silver and gold. The first shaft of sunlight broke, radiant, through the trees and the gemstones exploded into a brilliant dance of color and light dazzling to the eye.

"Jesu," she breathed and lifted the weapon higher still, her gaze following the intricate pattern of sapphire, ruby and emerald.

So mesmerized was she, she ignored Destiny's snorts and the sound of hoofs tamping the soft earth, all muffled by the gurgling of the brook and the roaring in her own head.

The stallion's high-pitched cry of distress jolted her from her stupor. She whirled on her knees toward the entrance to the thicket, brandishing the jeweled dagger before her.

Her heart stopped.

A warrior loomed before her, broadsword drawn, dressed for battle in the colors of her own clan. She stumbled to her feet. A branch snapped behind her, and again she whirled. A dozen Grant soldiers, men she did not know, lined the creek behind her, blocking her escape.

She was surrounded.

Chapter Eighteen

She was dead, and Iain, too.

In her mind's eye she saw the graves, side by side atop the windswept ridge where first he kissed her, their pale stone markers reflecting the soft summer moonlight.

So be it. She lowered the dagger and braced herself for what would come. To her surprise, the warrior sheathed his weapon. He stepped to the side and she watched as another man ducked beneath the tangled gorse into the small thicket.

She nearly swooned when she saw his face. "Owen!"

"Lass! Good God, are ye hurt?" Owen rushed forward and clutched her shoulders as she began to sway.

"But…I thought you dead. Surely—"

"Nay. 'Tis a nasty wound, deep but not mortal." He nodded at his left shoulder, which was tightly wrapped in clean linen.

She reached out to touch him, afraid to believe he was really there. Her gaze darted to the circle of warriors who were now sheathing their weapons. "But—"

The warrior who'd preceded Owen cleared his throat, and with a start she realized who he was.

"Jesu," she breathed.

Owen drew her to her feet, careful to not let her go until she was steady. The man who stood before her was—

"George Grant."

She could do naught but stand there and stare at him. She'd seen him mere months ago, yet he seemed different somehow—older, commanding in his battle dress.

He did not much resemble Reynold, except for his height. He was broader at the shoulder, more muscled, and was a younger man—about Iain's age, she guessed. His hair was tawny and his eyes a warm blue, so different from Reynold's icy orbs.

George stepped forward and offered her a gauntleted hand. "Cousin," he said, and smiled.

She placed her hand in his. "You...you know, then, about me?"

"Aye, Lady, I do."

"I told him ye are John Grant's daughter," Owen said. "Show him the parchment."

She realized she still gripped the jeweled dirk in her right hand and tried to pull her left from George's grasp.

He held her fast. "Nay, 'tis no' necessary. I can see the resemblance. Ye have my uncle's eyes and his coloring." His gaze roamed over her face and waist-length hair. "And a strength about ye which confirms ye are his child."

Her pulse calmed and she finally found her voice. "Have you come to my aid, then—cousin?"

"Perhaps," George said. "My army waits out on the forest road."

She felt a surge of relief and gripped his hand more firmly. "Then, you do not serve my...laird?"

"Reynold? I swore an oath of fealty when first your father died and the council made him laird. But since, Reynold has broken his oath to serve and protect our clan." George's expression darkened. "I have heard of his atrocities and am only sorry I didna come sooner. My land lies nearly a day away to the east. I didna know until Owen came to fetch me. I have since spoken with the council and have seen with my own eyes Reynold's handiwork. Nay, all oaths of fealty are null and void. I willna support his deviltry.''

Her pulse quickened as she studied his tense, handsome features. Dare she trust him? She had no choice. She tightened her grip on the dagger and raised it high.

The muscle in George's jaw twitched almost imperceptibly.

''Know you what this is?'' she said.

He blinked a few times in astonishment. ''Aye. I do.'' He grazed his thumb over the jeweled hilt and narrowed his eyes at her. ''But where did ye get it?''

She hesitated, darting a glance at the shallow grave behind her, praying her trust in these men was well placed. ''From…from Iain Mackintosh. Eleven years ago.''

George's hand flew to her arm and gripped it so tightly she winced with pain. ''But—''

''It has something to do with the murders!'' she blurted, struggling against his grasp. ''But I know not what. Iain bade me keep it safe until he could return for it. And that I have done.''

She nodded at the hole behind her. George released his hold on her, and she exhaled in momentary relief, feeling the circulation return to her arm.

Owen knelt beside the disturbed earth and fingered the splinters of rotten wood, all that was left of the box. His gaze lit on the tattered remnants of Iain's plaid. Alena watched his expression closely as he retrieved the cloth and placed it into George's hands.

''The Mackintosh tartan,'' George said. The material

nearly disintegrated as he rubbed it between his fingers. "'Tis been in the earth a good long while.''

"Aye," she nodded. "Eleven years."

He placed his hand over the dagger's hilt, his gaze fixed on hers. She begrudgingly relinquished the weapon to him, her heart now racing. He weighed it in his hand, then held it high for all his men to see. They responded with appreciative murmurs and a few, low-pitched whistles. "And what had ye thought to do with this?''

"I must see it safe into Iain's hands. Even now, he rides for Findhorn Castle to join the Chattan clans." She lowered her voice. "Four hundred of Reynold's soldiers await them there."

George narrowed his eyes and again scrutinized the jeweled weapon.

She saw no point in hiding the truth. There wasn't time. She needed their help and she needed it now. "There's to be war. Iain would reclaim Findhorn Castle and his lands, which Reynold has held these long years."

George met her gaze and nodded. "I am familiar with this blood feud."

"But he has not the manpower to wage such a war, had he all the Chattan clans at his back."

"And the others? Davidson, MacBain, Macgillivray—they will support him?" Owen asked.

"They will be there, but not all have pledged support." She nodded at the dagger in George's hand. "I thought this might help his cause, somehow. Although I admit, I do not see how one dirk might compel an army to side with one man against another."

George studied her face. "Ye have strong feelings for this Mackintosh laird." 'Twas a statement, not a question.

"I do."

"And ye would aid him against your own clan?"

"Nay! 'Tis not my intention." She placed a hand on his forearm. "But I would preserve his life and those of his kinsmen. I would help him to recover what's rightly his." She paused, holding George's steely gaze. "And if that means bringing down Reynold and those who have aided him in persecuting our own people—well then, so be it."

Abruptly, George pulled away from her and paced the width of the small copse. His kinsmen widened their circle, allowing him more space. She watched as he hefted the dirk, studying it yet again. Her pulse raced and her forehead burned with a fine sheen of perspiration. Fear and desperation knotted her belly. Jesu, what could she do if he refused?

He stopped and looked at her.

She met his gaze. "Will you help me, then? Will you see me safe to Findhorn so I might deliver this weapon?"

George was silent, and for a moment she thought all was lost. He arched a brow. "Apparently, there is much of this tale I dinna know."

To her surprise he offered her the dagger. She took it and sheathed it in the empty scabbard at her waist.

"But ye shall enlighten me, cousin, on our journey to Findhorn Castle."

She blinked, his words not registering at first. Then a bracing relief coursed through her. "Aye. I will tell you all I know."

He directed her toward the gorse bushes marking the way out of the copse. "I canna promise I will aid this Mackintosh laird," he said. "But we will go to Findhorn, and then we shall see what is the right path."

"And you will tell me the significance of this dagger?" Her hand moved to the jeweled hilt.

"I will. There is much ye need know." George ducked

under the bushes and pulled her after him. "But later," he said, directing her to their mounts. "Now we must ride."

Moments later they were mounted and ready.

"Ye dinna use a saddle?" George asked.

"Nay."

His eyes raked her up and down in what she knew was not desire, but a cautious appreciation. "Fair strange for a woman, eh?" he said brightly.

"Not this woman, cousin." She shot him a pithy glance.

He laughed, blue eyes sparkling in the growing light. "Methinks there is much about ye that is more than fair strange. I would be happy to know ye better, cousin."

"And I you."

They spurred their mounts forward and made for the forest road. Once there, Alena knew they would turn west toward Findhorn Castle, as she had seen Iain do many times when they were children.

The sun was full up and blazed gloriously through the lush green trees. The air was warm and close, almost cloying, so thick was it with the scent of wild herbs. Alena urged Destiny faster in her excitement to break from the claustrophobic surroundings onto the cool, windswept moors that lay between them and Findhorn.

A ridge grew up before them, and at its crest a group of warriors loomed, mounted and battle-ready.

Alena turned to George. "They are yours?"

"Aye. Two hundred of them."

They scaled the hill and yet more warriors came into view. All natural sounds of the forest were obliterated by the thunder of hoofbeats, rocks and branches kicked up in their ascent, the creaking of leather and the shouts of warriors as they greeted each other. Never before had she seen so many warriors primed for battle. 'Twas frightening, though they were men of her own clan.

George raised a hand, halting their movements. The men fell silent and fixed their gazes upon their leader. "Take heed," he said in a deep, commanding voice. "This lady is my cousin." George nudged his mount to her side and placed a gauntleted hand on her shoulder. "Alena Grant, daughter of John of Glenmore Castle. Ye shall serve and protect her as ye would me."

Alena looked out into the sea of grim-faced clansmen.

As suddenly as he had halted them, George raised his hand again and the army sprang forward. Destiny was swept along with them and fell comfortably into the pace.

Moments later, a cry went up at the front of the procession. The clash of steel on steel rang from the wood. "Alena!"

She recognized the voice, and without thinking urged Destiny forward, snaking her way through the sea of warriors toward the sound. George quickly followed, calling out for her to stop. She ignored him and pushed through the crowd. His men were so consumed with the chaos at the front of the pack, no one thought to stop her.

She broke through to the front of the line and pulled Destiny up short. Her mouth dropped open as she surveyed the two intruders surrounded by Grant's men. Swords were drawn, bloodshed imminent.

"Will! Drake!" she cried, and drove the black forward.

George raced ahead and cut her off, positioning himself between her and the two men. "Nay!" He shot her a fierce look. His broadsword flashed silver in the morning light, and for a moment she feared he would slay them. "Who are ye?" he demanded.

Will drew himself up in the saddle, but Alena read fear in his eyes. "I am Will of Clan Mackintosh. And this is Drake, my kinsman." He nodded at the scout. "We are charged with protecting this Lady and have come to retrieve her.''

George cocked a brow and looked them up and down with distaste. ''Ye call this protection?'' He nudged his mount beside hers and, with his free hand, slipped his dirk from its sheath. ''I could slit her throat whilst ye sit there on your arses.''

Will's eyes blazed fury. He set his jaw, and his grip tightened around the hilt of his sword.

''Will, no!'' she cried.

The points of a dozen Grant swords flashed steel and held him at bay.

George moved toward him, shaking his head. ''Relax, man. This lady is my cousin. She is now under *my* protection.''

Will narrowed his eyes, looking from George to her. Drake's mouth dropped open.

'''Tis true,'' she said. ''This is George Grant, my cousin.''

Will studied the tawny-haired warrior. ''I have heard the name.''

''Aye, as ye should,'' George said, the arrogance in his voice unmistakable. ''Now, get ye gone before I change my mind about killing you.''

Will returned his even glare. ''Not without her.''

''Will, we ride to Findhorn Castle,'' she said. ''My cousin means to help us.''

''We go to find this Iain Mackintosh,'' George said. ''We have something that may aid his cause.''

Alena's hand moved unconsciously to the jeweled dirk sheathed at her waist. Will's eyes widened. He glanced at Drake, both brows raised in surprise. The scout shrugged.

''D'ye know this place?'' George asked. ''This Findhorn?''

"I was born there," Will said.

"Ye shall guide us to it, then."

Will scowled at him in silence. The air was thick and close, and perspiration beaded on both men's brows.

"You must trust him, Will," she said, feigning confidence.

George sheathed his broadsword, blue eyes riveted to Will's angry glower. "He doesna have a choice, now does he?"

Will's jaw relaxed. He settled into his saddle and reluctantly sheathed his sword. Drake followed suit, his wary eyes darting across the sea of Grant warriors.

Casting her a resigned grimace, Will turned to George. "Come, I know a shortcut."

Chapter Nineteen

Findhorn Castle loomed solemn and gray above the barren landscape. Iain shaded his eyes against the midday sun and let his gaze wash over the rough-hewn stone of its battlements. His grandfather had built the stronghold during Malcolm's reign, some fifty years ago. 'Twas once a bustling place full of life and laughter. Iain could barely remember those times. Mayhap they were but a dream, a child's fancy. He looked away suddenly, loathe to see the dark shell it had become.

Now when he thought on his childhood, 'twas not this place he recollected, nor was it the faces of his parents or his young brothers he saw. 'Twas the dirty face of a sprite, wheat-gold tresses tangled with sunshine and autumn leaves. A fairy forest, green and lush, a special place that was theirs, alone.

She had given him her love, her trust—precious gifts he would now cast aside to do what must be done. For family, for clan, for honor.

Iain threw his head back and inhaled sharply. The fresh scent of summer heather was choked by the pungent odor of lathered horses and unwashed men. He scanned the field below him where near five hundred Grant warriors, half of them mounted on seasoned warhorses, prepared for battle. Somewhere down there was Reynold Grant.

'Twas time.

He spurred his stallion forward to join Alistair and Gilchrist. His uncle and his brother both wore grave expressions. "Ye dinna have to be here, uncle. 'Tis no' your fight."

Alistair smiled. "Ah, but it is. Your father was my sister's husband, and while I am not a man who jumps headlong into war, 'tis far past time ye reclaim all that is yours."

Iain placed a hand on his uncle's shoulder. "Well, then, let's do it."

The Macgillivrays closed ranks with the Davidsons and the Mackintoshes, and the three clans spurred their mounts down the long grassy slope to Findhorn field. They were nearly three hundred. Not enough. Iain looked back and saw the MacBain laird and his hundred warriors, mounted but unmoving, at the top of the hill. MacBain would wait before he made up his mind whether or not to support them.

Hamish positioned himself on Iain's left. Gilchrist flanked Alistair and rode with the Davidsons. The Grants held their ground as the three clans approached and reined their mounts to a halt but fifty feet away.

Alena was right. 'Twould be a bloodbath. Thank God she was safe and not here to see it. Until this moment he hadn't considered what might happen to her should he die this day.

He surged forward, then turned and rode down the line to where his uncle and brother were positioned. He bade Hamish follow. Iain beckoned the three closer. "I would ask a favor of ye," he said quietly, and met each man's gaze in turn. "To keep Alena safe should I no' survive the battle."

The three men nodded, and Gilchrist said, "We will protect her with our lives, as you have us, brother."

He met Gilchrist's even gaze. Never had he loved his brother more than he did in this one moment.

A horse reared in the Grant line. Iain reached for the longbow slung across his shoulder. The Grant warriors fell back and opened a path in their midst.

One man, dressed for battle, rode toward them on a great warhorse. Iain's gut knotted as he recognized the face.

Reynold Grant.

The laird reined his steed to a halt just beyond the front line of his men. All eyes turned to Iain. His fingers twitched as he gripped the burnished yew bow. One shot, a few seconds and it could be over.

Reynold's gaze burned into him.

Nay, 'twould be far too easy to kill him like this. Reynold must die by the sword—Iain's father's sword. He threw down the longbow and cast his quiver of arrows to the ground beside it.

Reynold grinned and cocked a brow in mock surprise. "Mackintosh," he called out, "what brings ye here?"

He leveled his gaze at him—"Ye know why I have come"—and nodded at the castle in the distance. "To claim what's mine. And to settle an old score."

Reynold's gaze flit across Iain's small army. He chuckled as if some jest had been made. "What, with *this?*" With a sweeping gesture he indicated the Chattan clans.

Iain battled his rage. "Aye."

Reynold laughed in earnest, now—a high-pitched, near-mad cackle. "Ye are most amusing, Mackintosh. I see, now, why my lovely cousin was so taken with ye."

Blood pulsed hot in Iain's veins. He ground his teeth against the sharp reply poised on his tongue.

"Dinna let him bait ye, man," Hamish whispered at his side. "Choose your moves with care."

Out of the corner of his eye he caught Alistair's nearly imperceptible nod of assent.

Reynold drew himself up in his saddle and with a flourish stripped his sword from its sheath. Iain tensed. "Throw down, now, Mackintosh, and we willna rape your women or murder your children."

Cries of outrage went up among the Chattan. Their mounts stirred, snorting and stamping the ground. Iain watched, stunned, as Reynold's own warriors gaped at their laird.

"A man who would make war on women and children is no' fit to lead a clan!" Iain shouted over the din.

Reynold laughed and didn't notice how his own men dropped back.

MacBain studied Reynold. Iain could see the old laird wavered, withholding judgment, waiting to see what the Grants would do next.

"Ye seem to have had news of our little reception here," Reynold said. "'Twas not the surprise I had hoped it would be."

"'Twas no surprise," Iain said evenly.

"Ah...then, 'twould be my bonny cousin who gave away my plans. Perkins will be dealt a harsh punishment for allowing her to escape me yet again."

Now Iain smiled. "Ye are too late for that, Grant. He's already been punished. But 'twas no' nearly as harsh as I would have liked."

Reynold's grin faded. "And my cousin? Where is she?"

"Somewhere safe, where ye willna find her."

"Ah, but I shall, Mackintosh, and when I do...a man could lose his soul in that honeyed hair and those bonny green eyes, eh?"

Iain's sword flashed silver as he jerked it from its scabbard. "Ye touch one hair of her head, ye murdering cur, and I'll cut down every Grant from here to Inverness."

The Chattan warriors drew their weapons as Iain's mount surged forward. The Grants hesitated, their eyes darting from their laird to each other, unsure of what to do.

MacBain drew his sword and locked eyes with Iain. His kinsmen followed suit, falling into line behind their laird as he closed ranks with the Chattan. With MacBain's support they were still outnumbered, but it didn't matter.

Nothing would stop him now.

Hoofbeats thundered from across the moor. Iain pulled his mount up short, not twenty feet from Reynold, as the sea of Grant warriors parted before an oncoming army. The Chattan stilled their mounts and sat poised, weapons brandished. Even Reynold glanced back to see what was the commotion.

Iain narrowed his eyes, and his throat constricted when he made them out. "Bluidy hell."

Two hundred Grant warriors, battle-ready, approached the field. They drove through Reynold's pack like a mad dog splitting sheep. As they drew closer Iain's heart leaped to his throat. "Alena!"

"Good God!" Alistair cried.

"And Will and Drake, too," Hamish added, and drew his mount up beside Iain's.

As the army approached, the Chattan warriors fanned out, flanking their lairds. MacBain and Macgillivray joined Iain and Alistair at the center of the pack. The four men closed ranks, and Iain was barely aware of the lairds' solemn exchange of glances.

His eyes were riveted to Alena who rode atop Destiny like a queen, graceful and confident, as if she were used to leading an army of great warriors into battle. She was flanked by two Grants, their expressions grim, and was tightly surrounded by a half dozen others, Will and Drake among them.

The big, tawny-haired man who rode to her right shot her a quick, knowing glance as they reined their mounts to a halt before Reynold.

A cold fear gripped Iain as his gaze roamed over her, searching for signs she had been harmed. He was not afraid to die, but couldn't bear the thought of her in Reynold's hands.

Alena ignored Reynold's greeting and scanned the crowd. Iain willed her look in his direction. Finally her gaze met his and his heart soared as a radiant smile broke across her face.

"Iain!" she cried, and kicked Destiny forward. The tawny-haired warrior reached out and grabbed the bridle.

Iain raised his sword, but Alistair thrust a hand in front of his chest. "Nay! Wait and see what they mean to do."

Will caught his eye. Iain scowled back at him. By God, he'd not forgive him for allowing Alena to fall into Grant's hands. His friend shrugged his shoulders and cast his gaze to the ground.

Reynold tried to maneuver his mount nearer to Alena, but the Grant warriors who flanked her wouldn't allow his approach. Iain watched with interest as Reynold's face reddened with rage, his long, thin scar blazing crimson.

"Owen!" Reynold shrieked. "I will deal with ye and yours later." He turned next to the tawny-haired warrior. "Cousin, ye have come to watch your laird dispense with this minor irritation?" He glanced back at Iain and the other Chattan lairds.

"'Tis George Grant," Alistair whispered.

The tawny-haired warrior remained silent.

Reynold's murderous glare lit on Alena, and Iain's pulse

quickened. "I see ye have brought my bride." Lust gleamed in his eyes and it was all Iain could do to stop himself from surging forward and hacking off the bastard's head. "Excellent."

To Iain's surprise, George Grant goaded his mount forward. "Which one of you is Iain Mackintosh?"

"I am The Mackintosh," he shouted so all might hear.

They sized each other up. George drew himself tall in the saddle and said, "I have brought this lady, my cousin, to you at her request." He indicated Alena behind him.

Iain worked to hide his astonishment but knew George and Reynold both could see it in his face.

Reynold narrowed his eyes. "What do ye mean by this?"

"'Tis plain enough, cousin," George said. "This lady wishes to return something to the Mackintosh laird."

Iain held his breath as Alena threw back her cloak. Sunlight blazed a rainbow of colors at her waist. She withdrew the jeweled dirk from its sheath and held it aloft for all to see.

A hush fell over the hundreds assembled there.

Reynold's mouth dropped open and he recoiled, startling his mount. The frightened horse sidestepped into the open between the troops. Before he could react, the circle closed 'round him, George and his warriors on one side, the Chattan on the other.

The sight of the dagger after all these years and the unflagging bravery of the lass who bore it forced a swell of emotion to Iain's gut. Alena's eyes were only for him, and in her gaze he read not fear but trust, and a love so brilliant it outshone the fiery gemstones peeking between her fingers.

His eyes clouded. With the back of his hand he wiped

at the film of tears. He rode forward into the circle, his gaze now leveled on Reynold's ashen face.

George rode forward and nodded. "The lady says ye gave it her to safeguard for ye, some eleven years ago."

"I did," Iain said.

"And from where did ye get it?"

"'Tis the weapon my father drew from Henry Grant's back."

Hushed murmurs raced through the throng of warriors. Iain closed his eyes for a moment and recalled the hideous scene as if it had only just happened…

He pushed his way through the knot of clansmen and flung himself down on his father's body. Tears burned his eyes. He shook violently, his gut roiling with fear and pain. He fisted the rough fabric of his father's plaid, soaked black with blood, and touched his forehead to his da's. 'Twas cool and limpid, the life already gone out of him. His eyes stared unseeing, glazed with death. Iain blinked and his tears broke, bathing both their faces.

His da was gone. Dead. Murdered.

Something coiled inside him, then—a silent rage, dark and terrible, which seared his belly and blazed a white-hot impression on the backs of his eyelids.

He had no weapon and searched quickly around him for something, anything, to wield. Then he saw it, out of the corner of his eye, glinting gold and silver, ruby and emerald in the torchlight. 'Twas the dirk his father had pulled from Henry Grant's body, still firm in his death grip. Iain reached out and freed it, gently prying it from his da's stiff fingers. He held it aloft, marveling at its hilt—a shimmering field of precious gems set in hammered silver and gold.

The hairs on his nape prickled. He turned and looked up into the face of the young warrior, Reynold Grant, whose eyes bore into him—blue ice, startling against ghost-white skin and pale blond hair. He didn't seem at all a man, but rather some Nordic god looming over him, huge and terrible.

"You, boy. The dirk—give it to me," Reynold commanded with a chilling calmness, his broadsword dripping blood.

Iain scrambled to his feet and backed toward the last row of wine casks. "Nay, I willna."

"You will."

Reynold lunged at him but Iain moved quicker. He darted 'round the casks and raced toward the staircase. He gripped the jeweled dirk, still warm from his father's hand, and felt suddenly powerful.

He was The Mackintosh now. 'Twas up to him to avenge the horrors of this night.

Warriors poured into the cellar as Iain reached the staircase. As if invisible, he darted up the stone steps, through the kitchens, and out into the night.

George's clear voice jolted Iain into awareness. His eyes flew open. The warrior snatched the dirk from Alena's hands and held it high. "D'ye all know this weapon?" Cries went up from the Grants who were assembled behind him. "There were two made," he said, "by John Grant's order. One for his son, Henry, and the other for his nephew, Reynold."

The MacBain rode forward and cocked his head, studying the dirk in George's hand. "Aye, 'tis true. I remember them now. The two lads wore them that night at Findhorn Castle."

Reynold gritted his teeth. "Aye, the Mackintosh laird murdered my cousin Henry with his own weapon."

MacBain continued to nod. "'Tis true. I saw Colum

Mackintosh bent over the body, myself, that bloodied dagger in his hand.''

"That may be so," George said. "I wasna there, so I canna say. But I *was* at Henry's burial, and though I was but a lad, plain as day I saw Henry's jeweled dirk buried with him.''

MacBain drew a sharp breath and the crowd quieted. Iain glanced back at Alistair and the Macgillivray laird. Their expressions were grim, their gazes fixed on Reynold's back.

"So, cousin," George said, "whose dagger is this, then? There is only the one other and I dinna see it belted at your side."

Reynold's eyes flashed rage and he brandished his sword in front of him. The circle of warriors drew tighter and he drove his mount first left, then right, in a useless effort to protect his back. "What lies are these? Ye would all believe this upstart?" He spat at George then sought out the faces of his own warriors. Reynold's kinsmen wouldn't meet his eyes, and Iain saw the panic grow on his pallid face.

Macgillivray spurred his mount forward. "The truth of it is clear as a Highland stream, now that I see it for what it is," he said. "Ye murdered Henry."

"Your cousin," Iain said, his voice deadly calm. "So that ye might claim John Grant's affections and all that would have rightfully gone to his son."

The warriors drew back, leaving Reynold alone in the circle with Iain, George, and the Chattan lairds.

"Ye stabbed Henry in the back and laid the blame on my father," Iain said. "And then ye slew him, and a hundred of my kinsmen."

For a moment the only sounds were the wind whipping across the moor and the fidgeting of the horses who, like their riders, itched for battle.

"And ye are held accountable for more than the ruination

of my clan.'' Iain's gaze burned into the now-milky-blue of Reynold's eyes. ''MacBain's daughter was betrothed to Henry. Her young life was ruint, as well. But worst of all, ye split a great alliance—the Chattan clans my father worked his life to unite. 'Twas ruptured by one violent act of treachery, which pit clan against clan for all these years.''

''There is more,'' George said. ''John Grant is dead, and 'tis no longer a mystery to me by whose hand.'' He glared at Reynold.

Iain looked to the other lairds who sat silent on their mounts, each nodding. He drew himself up in his saddle and sought out Alena's face in the crowd. Her eyes brimmed with tears, and his heart nearly broke to see her so. He must get her out of here. Fast.

Will moved up to flank her, and with one look and a nod of his head Iain conveyed his wishes to his friend. Will grabbed Destiny's reins. With Drake at his side, he directed her away from the throng of warriors. George nodded at one of his kinsmen who moved quickly to accompany them.

Alena struggled to remain, but the clansmen guided her away and up a small hill overlooking the battlefield. Iain could hear her protests and spared her one last long look before turning his attention to his enemy.

The Chattan closed ranks, and George backed his mount into line with his own army.

Reynold spun in circles, seeking out those few kinsmen who would support him. He viciously kicked his mount and the horse reared, nearly unseating him. The leather thong securing his hair sprang loose and a shock of white-blond hair whipped around his face in the wind, giving him the visage of a madman. ''This changes nothing!'' He lofted his broadsword high.

''Oh, but it does, laddie,'' MacBain said.

Iain brandished his sword, and the screech of hardened steel cut the air as hundreds drew their weapons. Reynold screamed orders to his warriors. Those who were near the front of the crowd reluctantly rallied 'round him.

Positioning his men on Reynold's flank, George faced Iain, his expression grave, his eyes cool and deep as still waters. Iain's pulse raced as he realized George's intent. ''I dinna support him,'' the warrior called out. ''But I am a Grant and canna stand by and let ye slay my kinsmen.''

So this was how it would be.

He'd gotten what he wished for, after all. The Chattan, battle-ready and assembled behind him. The Grants awaiting his attack.

Iain wiped the sweat from his brow and tightened his grip on his father's sword. Aye, this was his destiny. His whole life culminated here, today, on the field of Findhorn. In the shadow of his ancestral home he would seize his honor, take his revenge, reclaim what was rightfully his.

He raised his sword and the cries of his warriors rang out across the barren landscape. He leveled his gaze at Reynold and could already taste the blood. All he need do was drive his sword into the soft earth, and four hundred Chattan warriors would spur their mounts forward into a sea of Grants.

Iain wavered, motionless, and the cries of his men died to a low murmur. He looked from Reynold to George, their swords also raised.

And all at once the folly of it struck him.

He scanned the field of men: Grant, Mackintosh, Davidson, Macgillivray, MacBain. Is this what his father would have wished? Is this what *he* truly wanted? Another generation of carnage and bloodshed, violence and spurious pride?

It sickened him.

But if not this vengeance, then what? Was his whole life for naught? What did he truly wish for—not only for his clan but for himself?

He turned his gaze to the small hillock flanking the battlefield. The gray stone of Findhorn Castle loomed up behind it, a silent power dwarfing the four who waited on the slope.

Alena stood before Destiny, hands fisted at her sides, wheat-gold tresses whipping in the wind. The summer sun illuminated her face, and Iain saw tears run in glistening rivulets down her fair cheeks.

He held her gaze and slowly lowered his sword.

He was aware of Hamish leaning down to whisper in his ear. "Now what will ye do?"

He tore his gaze from Alena and faced his enemy. Oh, he knew what needed doing, and he was far past ready. "Reynold Grant!" he called out. "My quarrel is with ye alone. 'Tis burdensome to involve these good men in our disagreement." He waved an arm at the throng on both sides of the field.

The corner of George's mouth twitched in what Iain could swear was a smile. The warrior lowered his sword and his army stilled behind him.

Alistair moved to Iain's side and shot him a wry glance. "Well done, lad."

Reynold narrowed his eyes and looked from Iain to George. His cousin ignored him. Reynold thrust his sword higher into the air. The few warriors who had rallied behind him dropped back, lowering their eyes. His face exploded with rage, and from twenty feet away Iain could see the cords of his neck stand out against the crimson pallor of his skin.

Aye, far past ready.

Iain swung his leg over the back of his mount and dropped lightly to the ground. He stripped off his shirt, strode to the center of the field, his eyes on Reynold, and drove his father's five-foot broadsword into the soft earth between them. Fists on hips, he stood back, awaiting his enemy's response.

A thousand warriors turned their gazes to Reynold Grant.

The cur dismounted and stripped himself to the waist. His eyes blazed murder, and Iain was glad. Brandishing his sword, Reynold stepped onto the field. "So be it," he said.

Iain smiled.

Chapter Twenty

"Iain!"

Before Will or Owen could stop her, Alena scrambled down the rocky hill toward the battlefield. She snaked her way through the throng of mounted warriors and burst into the open.

"Nay!" Iain cried. "'Tis no' safe!" He waved her back, but she ignored him.

She was nearly to him when George Grant slipped from his mount and caught her 'round the waist. He pulled her back from the opponents, her struggles useless against his iron grip.

Iain nodded to George, then met her gaze briefly before returning his attention to Reynold. 'Twas madness! She begged George to stop it, but he wasn't listening. Nearly all of the warriors dismounted, Grants and Chattan alike, and closed a tight-knit circle around the two lairds.

A flash of red hair caught her attention. Hamish. He elbowed his way 'round the crowd. She was startled when he stopped before her, his expression grim. Towering over her he resembled more Viking than Scot. For a moment he locked eyes with George Grant, and she felt her cousin tense. 'Twas a warning. After a moment both men relaxed and turned their gazes on the combatants.

To her surprise, George released his hold on her. She moved quickly between the two men and watched with them as her cousin wielded his sword against her lover, the husband of her heart. 'Twould be a battle to the death.

Scores of random thoughts raced through her mind as she grappled for a way to stop it. Nay, there was no stopping it. She read the bloodlust in Reynold's eyes and the determination in Iain's. A wave of fear and nausea gripped her.

They circled each other like two feral predators, eyes locked and broadswords hefted. The first blow came without warning, and she jumped as steel clashed against steel in a flash of light. The two men grunted and pushed off, one sword against the other.

"Is he good?" Hamish asked, his gaze fixed on the battle.

"The best I've seen," George said.

"Hell and damnation."

"And your laird—he is skilled with a sword?"

Hamish grunted. "Skilled, aye, but 'tis no' his strongest suit."

She recalled Iain's longbow and quiver lying in the trampled grass near his mount when first she arrived at the battlefield. Her love for him grew with her fear.

Reynold lunged and their swords clashed again as he drove Iain back against the wall of warriors. The circle widened to accommodate their movements and the clansmen urged them on with shouts that carried on the rising wind.

A sheen of sweat broke out on Iain's face and torso as he met her cousin's thrusts and lunges stroke for stroke. Reynold grinned as they both pushed back and circled once again. The shouts of the crowd died to a hush. All she could hear was Iain's labored breathing and the pounding of her own heart.

In a low, chill voice, Reynold baited him. "Your father died squealing like a stuck pig on the end of my sword."

Iain's eyes blazed fury. He raised his broadsword with both hands and let out a roar that shook her to her bones. He lunged and brought the weapon crashing down. Reynold deflected the blow, but with a dull thunk his blade was smote in two. He fell back on the trampled grass, his eyes wide with shock.

The Chattan warriors cheered Iain's name as he pinned Reynold to the ground, the point of his sword at Reynold's throat. Her cousin's face drained of all color save for the thin, red scar. She saw the lump in his throat as he tried to swallow.

Iain towered over him, his chest heaving, sweat streaming down his face and torso. He pressed the point of his sword enough to draw blood, and a crimson pool formed in the hollow of Reynold's throat.

Reynold frantically scanned the crowd, but no one met his eyes. His gaze lit on Alena and her throat constricted as his expression implored her to intervene.

Hot tears welled in her eyes. She fisted her clammy hands at her sides and willed herself hold his gaze. His face was drawn and tight, the near-mad, icy fire gone from his eyes. And with it her fear.

He was a man, but she saw only the boy whose mother had abandoned him to slake her lust for wealth and power. All she felt now was pity, and regret for the cousin she would never have.

With her eyes she sought Iain's pained face. His brow was furrowed, his jaw clenched tight. He stood, transfixed, his broadsword poised at Reynold's throat. He glanced quickly at George, who nodded his assent.

The shouts of the warriors died. The Chattan warily eyed the Grants, their hands moving to the hilts of their weapons.

Alena scanned the crowd and was surprised to see none of her kinsmen raised even a hand, nor did they seem distraught their laird was about to draw his last breath.

Without thinking, she took a step toward Iain, then froze. He held her glassy gaze for the barest second, but in that brief span a lifetime of emotion passed between them.

The moment passed and Iain hefted his sword with both hands. Reynold's body tensed. The two locked eyes. With a cry of rage and pain, Iain drove his father's sword into the soft earth not an inch from Reynold's head. "I am The Mackintosh! And Findhorn my demesne. Get ye gone from here and dinna return. Ever."

Iain jerked his sword from the ground, his whole body shaking. Not looking back, he strode toward his kinsmen. Alena started after him but George pulled her back.

Out of the corner of her eye something flashed silver. In the next instant Reynold was on his feet, dirk in hand, lunging at Iain's unprotected back.

She screamed and Iain turned, brandishing his sword. Hamish lurched forward, hefting his battle-ax, but froze as a brilliant flash of color cut the air.

Iain's sword found a home in Reynold's chest. After a moment he yanked it free. Reynold jerked hideously, then fell forward into the tall grass, the jeweled dagger embedded in his back. She was vaguely aware of George who had stumbled past her after releasing the weapon.

For a moment no one moved.

Then the world spun and she fell to her knees, her tears erupting in hot waves of relief. Suddenly Iain was there, his arms around her, whispering words of comfort and love, peppering her face with small, fervent kisses.

She clung to him and wept.

The lairds of each clan—Mackintosh, Davidson, Macgillivray and MacBain—gathered on the small hillock above the battlefield in the shadow of Findhorn Castle. Alena stood by Iain's side, grateful that he waved George Grant over to witness the proceedings.

"Clan Chattan!" Iain shouted, raising his wineskin.

Three hundred Highland warriors echoed the cry, their broadswords and battle-axes lofted high.

The Chattan lairds drank. Alena looked with pride and admiration on her beloved—the man who, against all odds, brought harmony to their clans and, more importantly to her, exorcised his demons and found his own peace.

George nodded. "All is as it once was. As it should be." He turned to her and offered his hand. "Come, cousin, there is much to sort out amongst our own clan."

She looked to Iain but did not speak. He held her gaze, blue eyes cool, and was also silent. They stood there for a moment, trying to read each other's thoughts.

She realized he was giving her the choice—to return to her clan or to remain here with him. She edged closer and suddenly felt his arm 'round her shoulder. The corners of his mouth turned up in a smile. Her heart soared.

They both looked to George and Iain said, "There is another alliance we have yet to discuss, Grant."

George raised a tawny brow and studied them. "I see. And you, cousin...do ye also wish this *alliance?*"

"I do," she said. Iain squeezed her shoulder. She looked up at him and smiled.

George stepped toward her and took her hand. She felt

Iain tense. His jaw tightened and his smile faded, leaving a barely disguised scowl in its place.

"With Reynold dead," George said, "and were I to lead our clan, the council is certain to bless us should you join with me. 'Twould be an excellent match. Politically, I mean."

She withdrew her hand from George's gentle grasp. But before she could speak Owen pushed forward and said, "And what of the Todds? The stable? D'ye wish to abandon all ye've built there?"

"Nay, I do not, but—" She looked to Iain, but his expression was unreadable.

There was a commotion behind her. She turned just as Duncan's son, Gavin, burst through the throng of clansmen. "Pardon, Laird," he said, nodding at Iain. "'Twould seem there will be much to occupy a stable mistress here in this place." Gavin waved an arm in the direction of the castle. "But I've always had a yearnin' to see the Clan Grant stable." He looked to George. "Me da had thought to foster me there with the Todds, before all of this. I am quite skilled and would gladly lend a hand there. If ye'd permit it."

Alena reached blindly for Iain's hand at the same time he grasped hers. She smiled at Gavin, nodding her assent, then looked to George, imploring him with her eyes to agree to this plan.

George looked the stableman up and down. He cocked a brow and said, "Aye. 'Tis settled then." He turned to his steed and pulled himself easily into the saddle. His warriors sat mounted and ready, awaiting his command. George turned to leave, then pulled his mount up short and shot Iain a stern look. "Mackintosh."

Iain stepped forward, and Alena moved to his side.

George narrowed his eyes at him. "Whilst in your care,

should so much as a hair on her head be harmed, I shall return—for *your* head.''

Iain matched her cousin's glower. ''Ye have naught to fear, Grant, for I love the lady more than my life and would protect her to my dying breath.''

The edges of George's lips curled and his eyes softened. ''I thought as much.'' He reined his steed east, and his warriors opened a path before him. ''Each year at Michaelmas we have a bit of a celebration. I should be pleased if ye would come, and bring my cousin along with ye.''

Iain smiled thinly. ''If my wife so desires it, we will come.''

George nodded, and in a thunder of hoofbeats the Grants departed, the vast army moving like insects over the green and golden fields.

Relief washed over her. She had so much to tell Iain, so many things to explain. But before she could even begin, he swept her off her feet. She clung to him as he strode to Destiny and lifted her onto the stallion's back. To her surprise he vaulted up behind her. The black immediately protested, but she soothed him with soft words and affectionate pats.

''He doesn't like you,'' she said.

Iain grinned. Securing one arm 'round her waist, he took the reins from her hand. ''Well, love, he'll just have to get used to me, now won't he?''

others ...

Epilogue

Six Months Later

A hundred beeswax tapers lit Findhorn Castle's great hall, the room a cacophony of sights and sounds and smells.

The bride glided down the curved, stone steps and into the arms of her new husband. He kissed her on the lips and the throng of revelers cheered, lifting their ale cups high. The musicians struck a merry tune and the couple began to dance.

Across the room, near the hearth, Alena and Iain smiled on the newlyweds. They watched as Will and Hetty spun faster and faster, red-faced and breathless, to the lively music.

"Is it as fine, do you think, as was our wedding?" Alena asked, tilting her head back to catch Iain's eye.

"Nay, wife," he said and smiled. "No' as fine as that." He pulled her back against his chest and she rested her head under the hollow of his chin.

"I suspect, husband, there will be another wedding here. And from the look of things, it could be very soon." She nodded to the alcove under the stairs where Gilchrist had again cornered Elizabeth Macgillivray and was madly kissing her.

Iain laughed. ''Nay. 'Tis only another of my brother's short-lived fancies. 'Twill no' last.''

''Mayhap not.''

The wonderful aromas of roasted pig and venison, wild greens and fresh-baked breads drifted from the tables next to them. She scanned the room and smiled, pleased with the decorations and the overall restoration they'd accomplished these last few months.

The stables were coming along, as well, but there was much yet to be done. She must remember to ask Iain about their next visit to Glenmore Castle. She wanted to see the Todds—the parents who loved her and had raised her as their own, the father who'd taught her all she knew of horses and breeding. Gavin wrote they had acquired some new mounts from Spain. Perhaps she could make some trades…

Hamish stumbled by, an ale cup in each hand, interrupting her thoughts. Both she and Iain laughed as the big, burly man crashed into one of the long tables laden with food. Young Conall rushed to help him but only succeeded in spilling ale over both of them.

Never had she dreamed of being so happy.

Iain drew his arms through hers and wrapped them 'round her swollen belly, cradling the babe within. His cheek grazed her hair, and she closed her eyes as he planted delicate kisses on her upturned face, his warm breath her gift of life.

''I love you, wife,'' he whispered into her hair.

''And I you, husband.''

He held her close, and in that moment she knew their future together, his love a herald of all the joys to come.

*   *   *   *   *

MONTANA MAVERICKS

MONTANA MAVERICKS HISTORICALS
Discover the origins
of Montana's most popular family...

On sale September 2001
THE GUNSLINGER'S BRIDE
by **Cheryl St.John**
Outlaw Brock Kincaid returns home to make peace with his brothers
and finds love in the arms of an old flame with a secret.

On sale October 2001
WHITEFEATHER'S WOMAN
by **Deborah Hale**
Kincaid Ranch foreman John Whitefeather breaks all the rules when
the Native American dares to fall in love with nanny Jane Harris.

On sale November 2001
A CONVENIENT WIFE
by **Carolyn Davidson**
Whitehorn doctor Winston Gray enters into a marriage of
convenience with a pregnant rancher's daughter, only to
discover he's found his heart's desire!

MONTANA MAVERICKS
RETURN TO WHITEHORN—WHERE LEGENDS ARE BEGUN
AND LOVE LASTS FOREVER BENEATH THE BIG SKY...

HHH Harlequin Historicals®
Historical Romantic Adventure!

COMING SOON...

AN EXCITING
OPPORTUNITY TO SAVE
ON THE PURCHASE OF
HARLEQUIN AND
SILHOUETTE BOOKS!

*DETAILS TO FOLLOW
IN OCTOBER 2001!*

YOU WON'T WANT TO MISS IT!

PHQ401

HARLEQUIN®
Makes any time special®

Silhouette®
Where love comes alive™

Harlequin invites you to walk down the aisle...

To honor our year long celebration of weddings, we are offering an exciting opportunity for you to own the Harlequin Bride Doll. Handcrafted in fine bisque porcelain, the wedding doll is dressed for her wedding day in a cream satin gown accented by lace trim. She carries an exquisite traditional bridal bouquet and wears a cathedral-length dotted Swiss veil. Embroidered flowers cascade down her lace overskirt to the scalloped hemline; underneath all is a multi-layered crinoline.

Join us in our celebration of weddings by sending away for your own Harlequin Bride Doll. This doll regularly retails for $74.95 U.S./approx. $108.68 CDN. One doll per household. Requests must be received no later than December 31, 2001. Offer good while quantities of gifts last. Please allow 6-8 weeks for delivery. Offer good in the U.S. and Canada only. Become part of this exciting offer!

Simply complete the order form and mail to:
"A Walk Down the Aisle"

IN U.S.A
P.O. Box 9057
3010 Walden Ave.
Buffalo, NY 14269-9057

IN CANADA
P.O. Box 622
Fort Erie, Ontario
L2A 5X3

Enclosed are eight (8) proofs of purchase found in the last pages of every specially marked Harlequin series book and $3.75 check or money order (for postage and handling). Please send my Harlequin Bride Doll to:

_____

Name (PLEASE PRINT)

_____

Address   Apt. #

_____

City   State/Prov.   Zip/Postal Code

_____

Account # (if applicable)   **097 KIK DAEW**

HARLEQUIN®
Makes any time special ®

Visit us at www.eHarlequin.com

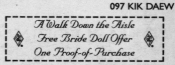

A Walk Down the Aisle
Free Bride Doll Offer
One Proof-of-Purchase

PHWDAPOPR2